PRAISE FOR THE G

"Mysterious and magical, *The Gri*
tales upside-down and then some. Fans of *Once Upon a Time* and anyone who likes their happily-ever-afters with a side of murder will love this fantasy thriller!"

—Rosiee Thor, author of *Tarnished Are the Stars*

"*The Grimrose Girls* takes the classic thriller story and fantastically twists it. For fans of classic murder mysteries, strong friendships, and shows like *Lost Girl* and *Grimm*, this is the series for you."

—Linsey Miller, author of *Mask of Shadows* and *What We Devour*

"Pohl weaves a suspenseful, thrilling tale full of all the dark magic, swoon-worthy romance, and courageous heroines we know and ... our teeth into this st... ."

... estselling ... *and Ruin*

"A twisty sapphic reimagining of all of your favorite fairy tales, *The Grimrose Girls* is darkly haunting and achingly romantic. In an exploration of grief and love, Pohl weaves a magical mystery of a murder most foul. These aren't the fairy tales you remember and certainly not ones you'll forget."

—Ashley Poston, national bestselling author of *Geekerella*

★ "Grief, identity, and friendship intersect in this enthralling mystery with dark magical undertones that ingeniously plays with fairy-tale tropes to tell a feminist story about empowerment and grappling with how to break away from the confines of societal expectations of girls... Fans of empowering feminist fairy-tale retellings will love this."

—*Kirkus Reviews*, Starred Review

ALSO BY LAURA POHL

The Last 8

The First 7

LAURA POHL

sourcebooks
fire

Content Warning

This book contains mention of suicide, parental physical and emotional abuse, and parental death. There are depictions of anxiety, OCD, and light gore.

Cover design by Ray Shappell
Cover images © VikiVector/Getty, konstantynov/Getty, R.Tsubin/Getty, Xvision/Getty, vectortatu/Getty, CoffeeAndMilk/Getty, paprikaa/Getty, Djomas/Shutterstock, kidstudio852/Shutterstock
Internal design by Ashley Holstrom/Sourcebooks

Published by Sourcebooks Fire, an imprint of Sourcebooks
P.O. Box 4410, Naperville, Illinois 60567-4410
(630) 961-3900
sourcebooks.com

Library of Congress Cataloging-in-Publication Data
Names: Pohl, Laura, author.
Title: The Grimrose girls / Laura Pohl.
Description: Naperville, Illinois : Sourcebooks Fire, [2021] | Series: The Grimrose girls ; 1 | Audience: Ages 14. | Audience: Grades 10-12. | Summary: While investigating the apparent suicide of their best friend, four students at an elite boarding school uncover a series of past murders connected to ancient fairy tale curses, and they fear that their own fates are tied to the stories, dooming them to gruesome deaths unless they can forge their own paths.
Identifiers: LCCN 2021028904 (print) | LCCN 2021028905 (ebook)
Subjects: CYAC: Blessing and cursing--Fiction. | Death--Fiction. | Fairy tales--Fiction. | Boarding schools--Fiction. | Schools--Fiction. | Magic--Fiction. | LCGFT: Novels.
Classification: LCC PZ7.1.P6413 Gr 2021 (print) | LCC PZ7.1.P6413 (ebook) | DDC [Fic]--dc23
LC record available at https://lccn.loc.gov/2021028904
LC ebook record available at https://lccn.loc.gov/2021028905

Printed and bound in the United States of America.
VP 10 9 8 7 6 5 4 3 2 1

To my sister, Clara, who kept adding princesses to every story we ever told.

Here's one with four of them.

PART I

ONCE UPON A TIME

CHAPTER ONE

ELLA

The first day of school started with a funeral.

This was not, of course, the usual for the Grimrose Académie for Elite Students, whose student body mostly went on to command corporate conglomerates or win Academy Awards, Nobel Prizes, and other such trifles and lived to their eighties. Therefore, everyone was shocked, and whispers were heard in every corner of the castle, from the library tower to the girls' bathroom on the fifth floor.

The whispers, especially, followed Eleanor Ashworth.

Ella gazed upward self-consciously, tightening her hand on the strap of her bag. "How long do you think this is going to last?"

Eleanor, known to her friends only as Ella, was a small girl of seventeen, with light blond hair cut to her chin and equally light brown eyes, reddened cheeks, freckles all over her face and arms, and clothes that had seen better days. The whispers had followed her before, but never with such commitment.

"A month, if we're lucky," answered Yuki, Ella's best friend, a crease appearing in her forehead.

"We won't be," Rory muttered, glaring at a group of younger girls who dared to dart eyes in their direction. "What the hell are you looking at?"

"You do realize that your attitude attracts even more attention, right?" Yuki said, raising an eyebrow.

"At least I'll get a reason to fight," Rory replied with a satisfied shrug.

The Grimrose Académie was exclusive not only in name, but also in reputation. Its location in Switzerland and the exorbitant price ensured that only the richest and most powerful were able to attend. It sat on one of the Alps' most beautiful hills and boasted a giant fairy-tale castle with four towers and white marble, gardens extending up to the mountains that surrounded them, and a crystalline lake to complete the view.

Studying at Grimrose was a guarantee of your future. When you studied at Grimrose, nothing could ever go wrong.

Except that on the eve of the first day of school, one of the Académie's most exceptional students had drowned in the school lake.

Alone.

For most students, it meant an uproar. For the Académie, it meant an open line for calling parents, reassuring them of the safety of their children, and keeping the death out of the papers.

But for Ella, Yuki, and Rory, it wasn't just another tragedy. Ariane Van Amstel had been their best friend.

Ella avoided the stares and the whispers, knowing all the students wanted to ask her the same questions. Had she been suicidal? Did she know how to swim? Did Ella know she was sad? And why hadn't Ella helped her?

The last question was the worst, the reminder a sting. How could she not know if one of her best friends had done the unthinkable? Ariane had been happy, daughter of a rich businessman from Holland, with a bright future ahead of her. Just like everyone in the Académie.

Well, everyone except Eleanor Ashworth.

The worst part about the stares was how they made her feel ashamed, because she ought to have done something. She should have acted. She should have saved her friend, because that's what friends did.

Ella stepped forward in the cafeteria line, looking at their lonely table in the corner. Everyone else in the cafeteria was lively, friends gathering for the first time in three months, groups coming together to murmur excitedly—maybe because they were missing their friends, or maybe to talk about the shocking news. But for them, the table was missing something. Stacie caught her looking wistfully, and she gave the smallest nod to her stepsister.

Stacie and Silla, her twin stepsisters, belonged to Grimrose in a way that Ella never had. They paid full tuition. Ella was the scholarship student.

In truth, Stacie and Silla owed their places at the school to Ella. The Académie had personally invited her, but her stepmother ruled that she would go only as long as there had been openings for her two daughters. That had been five years ago. Sharon said if Ella wanted to go to an expensive school, she had to *deserve* it.

Rory slammed her tray on their table as they settled down. The table felt too big for them now. There was a space where Ariane was supposed to be, at the table she had chosen herself. It felt like a part of her was missing, and Ella could not find anything big enough to mask its absence.

The three girls sat in silence. Ella finished her lunch and opened her bag, grabbing a pair of knitting needles.

"Knitting already?" Rory asked, chewing with her mouth open.

"This is just..." Ella started. "I promised Ari. Couldn't finish it because Sharon kept nagging me last week. So now I have to finish it before...before..."

She didn't finish her sentence, letting out a frustrated breath. Ella knew she was ranting. That she was stuck in a loop. She had to finish her goodbye present. If she didn't, then...

The good thing was that Ella's anxious brain could not imagine a consequence worse than what had already happened.

"The memorial is this afternoon," Ella said. "I promised it. I'm doing it. Ella Ashworth doesn't let her friends down."

Not even if they are dead, she thought to herself.

CHAPTER TWO

YUKI

Yuki Miyashiro waited for her friends in the garden.

She stood perfectly still as other students passed her, glancing at the tall, lonely figure with ivory white skin and dark hair like a raven's feathers that fell over her shoulders, turning their heads when they met the merciless black eyes.

The memorial was being held in the garden, the only place that could hold all the students, despite being inconveniently close to the lake where Ariane had drowned.

When Rory and Ella showed up, they walked in silence together. The gardens were lush and covered in flowers and bright tones of green, the last touches of summer.

"You all right?" Ella asked, and for a moment, Yuki's stomach twisted in guilt. She should be the one asking the question.

Ella had been her best friend since their first day of school, when Ella had declared Yuki's shoes were the most beautiful thing she'd ever seen, and therefore both of them had to be friends. Only later Ella confessed that she didn't like the shoes that much, but that she found complimenting people was always the best way to make friends.

Yuki wouldn't know. She didn't have a lot of friends.

"I'm all right," Yuki answered, even though it was a lie.

Ella pulled her knitting from her bag. Ella always needed something to do with her hands. Ella took a deep breath, and Rory glanced at them both.

"You've been taking the pills?" Rory asked.

"Yeah," Ella replied. "Wait, you think I haven't?"

"That's not what she said," Yuki interrupted.

"I've been taking them."

Rory looked at Yuki for reassurance, but Yuki could offer nothing. Ella had been diagnosed with severe OCD and anxiety over a year ago, and it was still an adjustment.

It was a short walk. Every student was wearing their uniform, liberty-blue skirts and pants, white shirts and silver ties and periwinkle blazers, a crowd of blue descending the path. The rain had stopped but the clouds had stayed, and the sky was gray like the mountaintops. Students started filing in, crowding forward, but Yuki preferred the back.

Ariane's parents were standing in the front row. There was no coffin—they would take the body home, sealed up so no one would ever see the bright red flaming head of hair, but there was a picture of her. Yuki avoided the picture and Ari's eyes and stared at the ground.

Ella sat down on a folding chair, and Yuki closed her eyes,

but there were the whispers, talking of the bloated body, talking of Ariane drowning, her body sinking into the lake, and how they had found her, faceup, barely recognizable. Accident. Suicide. It didn't matter. She was dead.

When Reyna Castilla stepped to the pulpit, Yuki was almost glad to hear her stepmother's voice.

"It's with great sorrow we are gathered here today," she started. "One of our most promising students has been taken from us abruptly. Ariane was a great student and beloved by all. It's difficult to describe how terrible her loss..."

Yuki tuned all of it out. Reyna didn't know Ariane enough to truly understand what it meant to lose her. Her loss was pure, untainted by knowing and loving Ariane.

Yuki's loss was not pure.

When she looked up, she saw another face in the crowd. Edric, Ariane's ex-boyfriend. Only one week after he and Ari had broken up, he'd been with someone else. All over each other in the halls.

Yuki wished she could watch him choke.

To calm herself down, she recited what she knew.

Ariane did not know how to swim. Ariane would not go near the lake at night. Ariane would not leave without saying goodbye. Still, there had been no foul play discovered.

Reyna's eulogy ended, and Ari's father took over the microphone, giving another speech thanking everyone. All the students in the school were courteous enough to pretend they cared, even though Ariane did not belong with them.

She belonged to us.

Yuki's heart beat faster, a rhythmic thumping she was sure others could hear.

The memorial dissolved a little after that. Ella got up before any of them could stop her and walked decidedly over to Ariane's parents. Yuki could almost hear what Ella was saying. She could imagine her words would be firm and kind. A flash of a smile from Ariane's mother, a hug, Ella handing them the sweater she'd finished.

Someone else approached Yuki, and she turned to see her stepmother.

Reyna rarely looked tired, but today, Yuki could glimpse something raw in her, as if she'd lowered a barrier that wouldn't be lowered again in the next hundred years.

Reyna didn't look like she was old enough to be Yuki's stepmother. Her medium-brown skin was flawless, and her rich chocolate brown hair fell in generous waves over her shoulders. She dressed the part of the headmistress at least, today a dark red dress that was both formal and elegant.

"Walk back with me?" Reyna asked, gesturing to the castle.

Yuki obeyed, as she always did. Perfect posture, walking calmly side by side. Their shoulders never touched. The silence stretched as they climbed.

"How are you doing?" Reyna asked at last, not unkindly.

Yuki didn't answer for a moment. She knew what was expected of her. She'd seen the answer in Ella's hands, in Ella's gestures, in Ella's words. She was supposed to be holding up, to accept her loss gracefully, to think of the others.

"Fine," she answered curtly. "Just fine."

Reyna paused as they climbed and Yuki was forced to stop her march.

"Yuki, one of your friends just died," Reyna said. "I'm asking because I know you can't be all right."

"Well, I am."

She spoke the words with such conviction that she almost felt like she could hear them ringing across the gardens, across the leaves and carried by the bird's wings. *I am. I am. I am.*

She wouldn't lose her composure. She was the headmistress's stepdaughter, after all. Her behavior would always be examined first.

"I'll ask the police to keep the questions to a minimum," Reyna said, and Yuki took a deep breath, because she did not lose her composure, because she was always, always, the image of perfect, no matter what happened, and she was not going to lose her cool today. Her stepmother gave her a look, then added, "It's all routine."

"It's fine."

"I'm just preparing you for what's to come," she said. "I don't want to make this worse for you. I know how hard it must be."

Except Reyna didn't know.

She had no idea.

She could never have any idea at all, because Ariane was dead, and it was Yuki's fault.

CHAPTER THREE

RORY

Out of all the notorious students in the castle, Rory Derosiers was probably the one most used to living in one. Not that she would ever admit to such a thing, because living in a castle was stupid, and the fact that she had lived not only in one, but three, seemed like something that counted less as a curious fact and more like boasting.

Rory Derosiers did not boast.

"Guess who's still in top form and ready to beat your ass!" she shouted as soon as she entered the training room in the first Friday of the semester.

No answer came from the emptiness beyond, and Rory frowned. She'd ditched class as soon as she could. The first week hadn't been as terrible as she imagined—well, if she didn't count the funeral. Rory refused to count the funeral.

She quickly changed in the dressing room, swapping her uniform for her usual oversized T-shirts and loose shorts, her long hair in a ponytail. But not even the outfit was capable of hiding her princess-like features. Round cheeks and heart-shaped face, big blue eyes, and glorious copper hair that fell in loose waves over her shoulders almost to her waist.

She started to run, her breath in a steady rhythm as she rounded the track, lungs expanding and heart racing, and when the pain started coming, she ignored it, as she'd always done. It was a lonely activity, where she only had herself to rely on. That was the downside of being on a team—they inevitably disappointed you.

Ariane had never let Rory down. Never.

She continued to run, pushing herself, thinking that she would have to get back to her room, where Ariane's bed would be empty, and Ariane would still be gone.

Her best friend, Ariane, who'd she seen only six days ago, lively and cheerful as ever, and now there was nothing left of her hurricane. Only the destroyed hearts she'd left behind.

Rory felt the tears prickle and she clasped her eyes shut. Rory Derosiers didn't cry.

She opened her eyes to see someone else in the room with her.

"You're late," Rory said.

"There's a first time for everything," Pippa replied, dropping her bag into a corner. "Enjoy your victory while you can."

"Over you? Always."

Pippa laughed, and Rory felt heat rise to her cheeks. Pippa pushed her braid aside, coiled black hair tied firmly back. There were muscles under her shirt, her dark brown skin showing, and Rory had caught herself admiring them more than once. Not that she would admit it.

Rory Derosiers was very much into not admitting anything.

"Arm yourself," Rory said instead, throwing Pippa a wooden sword. "We'll settle this the old-fashioned way."

Pippa cocked an eyebrow, catching the sword easily. Rory hated when she did that. Both the eyebrow and the catching things out of the air, like she was both strong and graceful. No one had the right to be both things at once.

"Careful there," Pippa warned. "You don't want to get beaten on the first day."

Rory did not reply. She attacked. Her sword was fast, but Pippa, somehow, was faster. She danced away from Rory's strike, parring it with her left hand. Her left hand! Rory was going to *end* her.

She recovered quickly, changing the blow to a feint, striking on Pippa's right. Pippa blocked it again, her brown eyes glinting as Rory attacked. She seemed to be in a good mood, and Rory wondered if she was trying to keep her spirits up for Rory's sake.

"You do know the element of surprise only works once, right?" Pippa mocked.

"Oh, shut up," Rory replied and went for another blow.

They fell into the usual dance. Rory had always known the rules of swordsmanship, fencing from a young age—the only dangerous thing her parents allowed because it had been under her uncle's supervision.

This, however, wasn't part of the team's training. This began for fun, with improvised wooden swords and real fights that ended in bruises and blood, brawls that left Rory thirsting for more than just the clash of weapons. Her blood rushed to her ears as she moved her weapon from one hand to another. Pippa blocked her blows or only stepped back from them as Rory advanced more and more until she felt her knees weaken and her body give out beneath her in a rush of pain.

Rory stumbled.

Pippa stopped immediately.

"You okay?"

"I can go again," Rory assured her.

"Shouldn't you—"

"Don't," Rory interrupted. "I know my limits."

Pippa said nothing. Rory found her footing and lunged forward again, twisting her wrist to block one of Pippa's blows, and parried to the left. It was another misstep, and as soon as her feet landed, she felt her body aching again, and she toppled over.

But not before Pippa could catch her. Pippa's hot skin and sweat stuck to Rory's neck, her arms holding her up, and Rory could feel as Pippa drew large breaths, her hands firmly around Rory's waist.

"You have to go back to your room eventually," Pippa said, her voice low.

She moved away from Pippa, fast.

Going down this road would end in pain and heartbreak and disappointment. Her love life—if she could call it that—was off-limits, even for herself. Her heart was locked behind silver gates and protected by a forest of thorns and possibly a dragon.

"I don't want to," Rory replied. "I could, if I wanted to."

Pippa looked at her, her sword pointing to the ground.

They never interacted outside of this, with their strict rules, only the two of them, their bodies and their swords. No words needed to be spoken, but Pippa always knew what was going on with her.

Rory hated it.

Pippa, over the course of three years, had gotten to know Rory more than she had allowed anyone else to. She knew how to get around Rory's defenses, and not only with a sword.

It felt like a breach, and Rory wanted to call her out on it. Challenge her to a duel, winner gets the silence. With Pippa, though, Rory wasn't sure if she even wanted to win in the first place.

"I hate her," Rory said, feeling her eyes prickle again, but she wouldn't let Pippa see her cry.

"No you don't," Pippa said simply. "You just miss her."

Rory dropped her weapon, clutching her hands into fists.

"She didn't kill herself," Rory said. "I know the whole school is saying it, but she didn't do it. She didn't leave a note." Rory felt her voice breaking, and she did her best not to give in to it. "What kind of person doesn't leave a note?"

Pippa had no answer to that, and she lowered to pick up the fallen weapon. She offered the sword Rory had dropped, wooden blade turned down. A gesture of peace. Rory took it, and for the briefest moment, their hands touched, and fire swept through her body, as bright as the flames of her hair.

"Sometimes losing people will hurt you," Pippa said, "and you'll have to let yourself feel it. I'll see you in practice."

Pippa touched her shoulder with a gentle hand before she went, and it lingered long after she was gone.

CHAPTER FOUR

ELLA

The first week hadn't been horrifying.

There were, of course, the whispers, and the fact that every time Ella turned around in one of her classes, she expected to see a familiar mass of dyed dark red hair, and every time she didn't, it was like Ariane had died all over again. Ella kept forgetting.

Ari was still gone, and the whispers kept following.

The police had asked some questions. Rory had gotten back the day Ari died. Yuki had seen her, but they hadn't talked. There was nothing further they could do but look at the death as an accident or rule it a suicide.

Ella didn't believe that. She *couldn't* believe that.

Hospitality had been a conscious choice as her elective class. Most schools didn't offer it in their curriculum anymore, but Grimrose was absurd in the same way most expensive boarding schools were. There were horseback riding classes, fencing, ballet, choirs, and anything a bored, rich child could think of to occupy their time. If it existed, Grimrose offered classes on it.

Rory had pointed out that taking a cooking class when Ella already knew how to cook was stupid, but she still found it relaxing that she could go and not have to really *learn* anything.

Each counter in the class sat two people, which meant she'd be working with a partner. Yuki and Rory had refused to take the class with her. Rory had her fencing practice; Yuki explicitly said she'd rather climb the tower on her knees than learn how to cook. Ella didn't blame them—and didn't blame the students who walked past the empty seat next to her.

Finally, the teacher walked in, and Ella was relieved to see Miss Bagley, one of the oldest teachers at the school, stout with an austere gray bun along with a sober blue dress.

"Hello, darlings," she said as a greeting, smiling, and Ella felt warmer, even though the seat beside her was still empty. "No need to introduce myself, I hope! This is the Hospitality class, and you'll be working in pairs. We're going to make pancakes today, start simple. Please don't tell the other students, or we'll have lines waiting out here when it's over!"

She chuckled to herself.

She picked up cookbooks and started handing them to the class. Ella tapped the table nervously, waiting for her turn, counting the stools, glad for the even number. When Miss Bagley finally turned around to her, she noticed the empty stool. "Oh dear. You don't have a partner."

"It's not a problem, Miss Bagley," Ella assured her.

"Well, we partner people for a reason." Miss Bagley looked at her pointedly, like Ella was trying to make a point by working by herself, and not just that the stool besides her was empty and it was likely to remain so. "It's not just because—"

She was interrupted when someone else walked into class. Stumbled in was the better way to describe it. A shock of bright red hair that, for a moment, sucked all the air out of Ella's lungs, was the first thing she noticed, but then he straightened up, and it was only a tall, lanky boy that Ella knew well.

"Sorry I'm late!" he announced loudly.

Ella resisted the urge to roll her eyes. Frederick Clement was an exemplary Académie student. That meant he was rich and probably owned half of a country. It also meant he was likely to ignore her as he'd done since they were twelve, even though they had been in most of the same classes growing up.

Not that Ella would point that out, because that would mean she had been paying attention to him. Which she definitely hadn't.

"Oh, good!" exclaimed Miss Bagley. "Come sit by Miss Ashworth over here."

Ella blinked. "What."

Frederick grinned, laying down his bag and perching himself on the stool next to her.

The teacher moved away, and Frederick started leafing through the recipe book that Ella had left untouched.

"Open up to page seven, and you can start picking up the ingredients. They're already packed in the back of the room.

And please remember your partner, because you'll be working together for the rest of the year."

Frederick looked up at her again and smiled, oblivious. It took Ella a moment to realize she wasn't returning it.

It didn't make a difference whether Frederick was there or not, and Ella picked up the ingredients from the back. She could cook pancakes with her eyes closed. She started cracking the eggs automatically.

"Aren't you going to let me do anything?"

"You don't need to," she answered without glancing at him. "If you're here just to fill up your schedule, I can do it."

Frederick frowned at her, his red eyebrows coming together. As Ella looked closer, she noticed that his nose and cheeks were lined with freckles, almost the same color as the bright orange of his ruffled hair.

"Why are you assuming I'm only here to fill up my schedule?"

"Why else would you be here?"

Frederick kept looking at her, brown eyes fixed on her hands. Ella cracked the eggs. Crack, bowl, trash.

Frederick was still staring, leaving her unnerved.

"I feel like you're being a little unfair," he finally said, leaning on the counter next to her.

Next egg. Crack, bowl, trash.

"You don't even know me."

"You're Frederick. We've gone to the same school since we were twelve."

"Maybe there's more to it."

"Is there?"

He gasped in mock horror, shaking his head and leaving his hair even more messed up, if that was possible. "Maybe. I know about you too."

"I bet," Ella muttered under her breath.

To her frustration, Frederick picked up the flour and started working it through the sieve. He worked slowly, but his hands were firm.

"Why don't you like me?" he suddenly asked as he poured the flour into a bowl through the sieve and handed it to her.

"I don't," she started, thinking through the words, her British accent more accentuated than ever, "*don't* like you."

"Which means you like me, in the most convoluted way possible," he replied. "Why?"

"Why do you feel like you're entitled to an explanation?"

"What? I'm not entitled," he said, sounding offended, stepping back from the counter. "I simply feel like I need to know."

"That's entitlement."

"No way," he protested. "Entitlement? In *this* school? Never."

Ella felt the corners of her mouth tugging up, and she resisted the urge to smile at him.

"We are going to be partners for the rest of the year," he continued. "I just want to be sure you won't turn around and stab me in the back."

"You really think I would stab you?"

"You look tough. For a five-foot-tall girl."

Ella wanted to shove him, and almost wanted to pick

up the knife. Frederick still had a smile on his face, the light shining on his freckles. It was kind of cute, Ella thought reluctantly, as if admitting that was giving in to him.

"I think the most dangerous weapons I've ever wielded are knitting needles."

"Yeah, I've seen those around. They look deadly enough."

Ella blinked. "You saw them?"

"Girl walks into class with a needle the size of her arm, furiously knitting a pink scarf, you'd notice too."

Finally, that got a laugh out of her. The sound escaped before she could stop it. She mixed in the flour, eggs, and milk, started working it into a batter, counting. Every five beats clockwise, one counterclockwise. If Frederick noticed this, he didn't comment.

"I'm not five feet," she said, even though that was exactly her height.

"And I'm not completely a jerk. Not most of the time anyway."

"Fine, you win."

Frederick smiled then. He didn't hold back.

"Since I win, do I get an explanation of why you don't like me?"

Ella didn't reply.

"I'll take a wild guess," Frederick ventured. "Because maybe I've hung out with Stacie."

"That wasn't wild at all."

"Well, Stacie is very clear on what she thinks of you."

"I bet," Ella muttered. Frederick didn't budge.

"If I believed her, I wouldn't have recognized you at all."

"No?"

"No, you'd be a blood-drinking and flesh-eating dragon."

"I'm so glad you didn't listen to her. A five-foot dragon would be very disappointing."

"And I'm assuming you don't drink blood."

"Not yet."

"You're young. There's still time."

The conversation was light and easy for the rest of the class, and Frederick was no burden. Ella didn't let him get near the pan, but he piled up the pancakes nicely, decorating theirs with fruit and sugar and syrup, and helped with cleaning. She didn't even need to ask.

The conversation was so easy that she almost forgot that when she talked too much, people got annoyed. She knew the distinct look of when to shut up, she'd learned to recognize it from everyone around her.

And Frederick hadn't given it to her once.

When the pancakes were all finally ready to be presented, she turned to him.

"I'm sorry about earlier," she said. "I was the jerk. I know what this school is like."

"Yeah, people can be awful. I get it."

Ella smiled. "At least you are honest about it."

"I am burdened by glorious self-awareness."

"I just wanted to say sorry. I didn't have to be that way."

"I understand, Eleanor," he said. "Really, I do. You don't need to explain it to me."

She liked the way he said her name, like he wasn't afraid.

"You can call me Ella."

Frederick dried his hands on the napkin at the table and offered them to her.

"Nice to meet you, Ella. I'm Freddie."

CHAPTER FIVE

NANI

The castle was... Well, it was a castle.

Nani Eszes didn't know how else to describe it. It had white polished stone, towers hidden among the mountaintops, big windows, a sprawling garden that extended from the outer walls to the castle itself and iron gates. When she thought of castles, she thought of places like this. She didn't think of castles often, though, and when she did, it wasn't because she wanted to live in them.

She waited with her bag, looking up at the enormous doors of the courtyard and the gigantic clock on the opposite wall above the stairs. She'd taken the train, almost got off in the wrong country—she didn't really understand how it took only twenty minutes and a wrong train stop to get off in an entirely different country—and now she stood looking up at the immense towers of what was likely to be her prison.

"Miss Eszes?" a voice called, and she turned around to

see a tall, older woman at the other side of the courtyard. "I'm sorry for my tardiness. I hadn't been informed you'd be arriving today."

Nani hadn't informed anyone she'd be arriving. She would show up to this...this school, in the middle of the mountains, in a forgotten place in Switzerland, and she would tell no one about it, because no one cared that she was here. Stuck in a castle full of people she didn't know and who she didn't care to meet.

The woman approached her, and she was the perfect image of a headmistress. Elderly, respectable, kind of looked like her grandmother, if her grandmother were white and had no lips.

"You're Headmistress Castilla?" Nani asked.

The woman laughed dryly. "Oh, no. I'm Mrs. Blumstein. I'm head of the teachers' council in the school."

"Oh," Nani said. "I'm here—"

"We know," Mrs. Blumstein cut her off, as if she didn't need any further explanations of what a seventeen-year-old girl was doing at the foot of the castle, wearing a short summer dress that violated school rules for uniform skirts, and looking completely out of place.

Mrs. Blumstein surveyed said dress. "I'm assuming you don't have a uniform yet."

Nani shook her head.

"We'll arrange that on the way." She gestured toward the front steps. "Why don't you follow me inside? I'll show you around. You should have been here for the first-day orientation."

There was a reprimand in her voice, a jab in Nani's direction.

Nani brushed it off.

Nani followed her inside the castle, and it was even more... castle-y than it was on the outside. There were carpets covering the stairs and the halls, paintings of patrons, and things that looked like they belonged in museums. The ceiling was domed, and the atrium opened up to a gigantic white marble staircase.

"I understand your father made the arrangements," Mrs. Blumstein continued.

Nani supposed she could say that. The letter had come in the mail. It had his signature, his words, all the papers she'd needed to come here. Tickets for her to find a way. She'd googled Grimrose Académie, but they didn't have a website. When they said exclusive school, they really meant it.

Nani thought she'd meet him there, but he'd never actually *said* he'd be here, and she had no way to reach his cell phone, since it was constantly turned off and going to voicemail.

"Yes," Nani said. "So, you know him?"

Mrs. Blumstein blinked. "Pardon?"

"My father," Nani repeated. "He works here."

Mrs. Blumstein frowned. "I'm not sure I know of him."

"He's a security guard," Nani insisted while she followed. "He sent me the papers for enrollment. I was supposed to meet him here."

Mrs. Blumstein turned around to offer her a smile that said nothing. "Well, if he works here, you'll have plenty of time to see him."

Mrs. Blumstein didn't say anything else, and Nani had to follow her up the stairs, even though all she wanted to do was go home.

Home. Back to Honolulu. Back to her grandmother's place, back to the house where she could smell the ocean, and the mountains that were really green, and not this piece of jagged land that people had the audacity to call "forest." Nani knew a forest when she saw one. This drab gray land with thin trees that spiked up and with few leaves was not it.

Home, she thought, embittered, where her father had walked away more than once.

Nani hadn't wanted to come here. She'd shut herself in her room, cried for three days, begged Tūtū to stay, but she wouldn't relent. After Nani's mother had died, Tūtū had lost her will to fight Nani's father's whims, even though most of them didn't make any sense, even though Nani was more family than her father. She was Hānai. Even though her father would come, stay with them, and then leave for his next posting, promising he'd take Nani next time.

After retiring from the Marines, he'd traveled all over the world and found a job as a security guard for the school. He promised Nani the pay was good, and that he'd see her soon.

Except he hadn't come back for her. His promise was empty. Again.

"Grimrose Académie is one of the best schools in the world," Mrs. Blumstein was saying, a monologue that Nani had completely tuned out. "We have already arranged a schedule, but there are few activities that you can choose for yourself. Friday afternoons are mostly free, and you can ask permission from your guardian to leave on weekends to visit the neighborhood."

That meant her father had to sign something.

That meant he'd have to reply to her letters, even though he hadn't answered a single one.

They crossed more corridors and passed some of the students on the way. Some barely glanced at Nani, looking like they were still half asleep. Others looked at her battered yellow dress, which she'd owned since she was fourteen, at her strong calves and round waist and her fat body, her dark brown skin, her rounded nose, and the wave of tight curly hair adding volume past her shoulders, the round frames of her beaten-up glasses.

Nani stared back at them and felt even more out of place.

"Do you have any questions, Nani?" Mrs. Blumstein asked.

Nani almost answered that she did. That she wanted to know why she was here, why she had been sent halfway across the world to a school she had never heard of, a school that her father could not afford, and why she hadn't seen him or gotten a reply to her letters or called her back. She had a lot of questions, none of which she could say out loud.

"Do I start classes today?"

Mrs. Blumstein nodded. "I can arrange for one of your roommates to take you around until you're used to navigating the castle. There's no reason for any time to be wasted."

Mrs. Blumstein sounded like someone whose very idea of

sin was wasted time, and Nani made a mental note to stay out of the teacher's path. She was not here for the studying; she was not here to make any friends.

"Here we are," Mrs. Blumstein said, stopping by a door. "This is going to be your new room."

Mrs. Blumstein knocked, and a voice from inside said, "Come in."

The teacher opened the door, and inside there was a spacious room with another door that Nani assumed was the bathroom, and three beds, each with a desk and a wardrobe side by side. One was not made, pink duvet thrown in the floor, a pile of things under the bed, the other neat and tidy, not a single thing out of place.

The third one was bare.

Two girls looked up when she came in. One had copper hair, blue eyes, an upturned nose. The other, one of the most beautiful girls Nani had ever seen, had pale skin, huge doe-like black eyes, and lips faintly tinted red.

"Good morning, girls," Mrs. Blumstein said. "Meet your new roommate, Nani Eszes."

CHAPTER SIX

RORY

Rory was not expecting a new girl so soon.

Truth be told, Rory was not expecting a new girl at all, ever.

Ariane's end of the bedroom had been stripped bare. There was no more sea-green duvet on her mattress, no more ridiculous shot glass collection on top of the shelves or empty perfume bottles, no more chair piled with glittery socks. Her side was a tomb as much as her casket, and Rory was fine with it that way.

Not fine, really, because she missed Ariane. But at least there wasn't someone ready to take her place.

"Hi," the new girl said, her tone decidedly unfriendly.

Rory didn't mind. That made things a lot easier.

Mrs. Blumstein looked between Rory and Yuki as if she expected an answer, and Rory realized she hadn't said a word since the girl was standing at the door.

"Hi," Rory said, her voice coming out croaky.

Mrs. Blumstein raised an eyebrow.

"Welcome to the Académie!" Rory said, way too loud and in a tone that was equal parts cheerful and threatening.

Rory was not good at meeting new people, a fact her parents had reminded her of whenever they remembered they had a daughter. Everything about Rory was the opposite of what was expected of her. She didn't own dresses, she hated pearls, and high-heeled shoes only made her fibromyalgia worse, her knees waking up sore, her neck hurting to the point where she wasn't sure she could even get up the next morning. For her part, she only shopped in the men's section, tearing off shirt sleeves so her arms could move freely, wearing layer over layer to cover herself. When it came to presenting herself to strangers, it had always ended in disaster.

"Nani has English with you first period," Mrs. Blumstein said. "I expect you to show her to class."

She waved off with one of her usual tight-lipped smiles that worked like a death threat, and then closed the door.

Rory was left with Yuki and the new girl who was still standing at the door, a single bag in hand, wearing a summer dress that had seen better days. Rory looked at Yuki, who looked back at her with a completely blank stare.

They kept looking at each other, wondering which one was going to budge first. It turned out that neither of them needed to do anything, since the girl walked up to her bed and dropped her bag.

There was only one empty bed in the room, so of course

that's where she went. But it was Ariane's. It belonged to her, not this standoffish girl who was already trying to take her place.

"They said I'd have a uniform," Nani said, looking at them over one shoulder.

"We weren't informed of your arrival," Yuki said tonelessly. Rory looked over at her in disbelief. She thought at least one of them was going to be nice. She didn't know why she expected it to be Yuki.

Actually, that wasn't true. Rory did know why she expected it. Yuki was like Ella. She was straightforward, yes, but she was always perfect. Perfect manners, perfect grades, perfect everything, and it was so damn annoying all the time. Yuki had never done anything wrong.

And Yuki had no right to be angry, to treat their new roommate like an unwelcome nuisance.

Rory did.

Mondays were always the worst, even in boarding school, when everything always stayed the same. Mondays were also vegetarian day in the cafeteria, which seemed doubly cruel.

"Your lunch is not going to run away," Ella said, looking at her over the table as Rory stabbed at a piece of eggplant lasagna in fury.

Ariane had chosen this table. It looked through the cafeteria window and out into the garden. It made you feel like you were in a fairy tale, and Ariane appreciated that—looking at it every day, making sure all of them were grateful for their blessings.

Now it had a nice view and an empty place where Ari was supposed to be, and at their backs, people who were still looking. Still talking.

Ariane Van Amstel had drowned in the lake by her own hand, and that was the end of it.

"Where's the new girl?" Ella asked. "Shouldn't she be with you?"

"She can look after herself," Rory said.

"Goodness' sake, Rory, she's *new*," Ella said, putting down her fork. "You can't simply abandon her. She's in your room."

Rory rolled her eyes. "She wasn't that interested in our help."

"Well, not with that attitude."

Rory looked at Yuki again, searching for some kind of backup, but Yuki was very carefully eating her lasagna without looking at them at all.

"I don't like her, that's all."

"You haven't even given her a chance!"

Rory glared at Ella, annoyance surging. She knew Ella wasn't doing it on purpose—it was just Ella, concerned with the well-being of new students, tending to them like they were the flowers back at her house, watching them with a careful eye, making sure they were taken care of. Ella had adopted Rory, even though Rory's mother had studied there, just like Ariane's mother had.

The story went like this.

Once upon a time, there was Yuki, the headmistress's

stepdaughter, who'd arrived at the tender age of eleven, for the first year of Sekundarschule. Ella arrived a year later, immediately picking Yuki as her best friend, and after that came Rory and Ari to share Yuki's room. They had been thirteen.

Ella welcomed both of Yuki's new roommates with open arms, lending Rory her German homework, discussing perfume scents with Ari. A week later, it seemed like it had always been that way—the four of them together.

Rory was the closest to Ari. They were both legacy, and it was something they complained about. And Ari always knew what to say when Rory was having another of her fights with her parents.

"If she doesn't come back to the room, we'll go after her," Rory promised, not wanting to linger in Ari's memory. "Besides, she can't get *that* lost."

"This castle has literally seventy-three different stairways, Rory."

"It does?"

"Yes, and the number annoys me. The architects who built this school, I say."

Just at that instant, Rory turned her head and saw someone else walk into the cafeteria. It was not the new girl, thankfully, or Ella would insist on her sitting at their table, and Rory didn't know what she was going to do if the girl took Ari's seat when she had already taken Ari's bed. It was Edric, Ari's annoying ex-boyfriend, hand in hand with his new girlfriend. It was one of Ari's few faults that she was straight, and with terrible taste in men to add injury to insult.

The three of them watched Edric with hawk eyes.

"His personality is the same as a piece of cheese that has been forgotten in the fridge for six months," Rory said.

"That's an extremely specific analogy, but you're absolutely right," said Yuki, glancing at Rory.

"You know what's worse? Ari was lactose intolerant."

Ella smiled, Yuki smiled, and suddenly, Rory was laughing out loud. It was ridiculous how easily they bad-mouthed him, and Edric was there, and Ari was just an ex-girlfriend, and not a real girl, their friend, someone who'd died and left them longing.

"Do you think he knows anything?" Ella asked, and suddenly, the mood in their table darkened.

They all looked over at the table where he was sitting.

"Don't go down this path," Yuki said, her voice low. "It won't do us any good."

"You know what they're saying," Ella replied, her voice a whisper, a furious blush creeping into her cheeks. "They're all thinking it, but you know it wasn't a suicide. You *know*."

"We don't," Yuki said.

"Unless we find something," Ella replied. "Unless we can prove it wasn't. No one else is going to do that."

"If you suggest talking to Edric, know that if I get within three feet of him, I'll punch his face," Rory told her.

"I said investigation, not punching."

"It's the Batman method of investigation."

"Never mind that," Ella said, "but I think we could uncover things, if we talk to the right people."

Rory knew what she was talking about. The name they hadn't really said out loud. They could resent Edric all they wanted, but he was just a stupid ex-boyfriend. He wasn't the real cause of things. He wasn't even the most important person in the room.

At once, all of them turned their heads toward the one girl who could give them answers.

Penelope Barone.

Penelope was sitting at a table by herself, blond hair falling in waves to her waist, green eyes sharp, her figure slender and lashes curled upward. Rory looked away immediately.

"One of us should talk to her," Rory said, and turned to Yuki.

Yuki shook her head. "Not me."

"Ella's too obvious. And you know, fussy to a point where she gets annoying. No offense."

"None taken," Ella replied good-humoredly.

"What about you?" Yuki asked.

"I'm Ariane's best friend," Rory said simply, and the words weighed heavy like a stone. Like it was a competition, and Rory had won, because in the end, she had. She did everything with Ari. Rory had attended every single one of Ari's singing concerts, and Ari had never missed a single of Rory's in-school fencing matches. They did everything together, and Ari had never demanded from Rory something she couldn't give. Yuki and Ella had each other, and they were a group, together, and it had always worked out.

But in the end, Rory was the one to lose her best friend.

"But you..." Rory finally found the words again. "You're... perfect."

Yuki's eyes flashed at the mention of the word, but finally, she nodded.

"Fine. I'll talk to her."

CHAPTER SEVEN

ELLA

Ella didn't like the idea of Yuki talking to Penelope, but then again, they weren't going to find out anything new about Ari's death if they didn't do some digging. There was a part of it that felt...unfinished.

She supposed all deaths felt like that. She remembered when her mother died, and she was too little to truly feel the loss. But with her father, almost six years ago now, she had truly felt that way. Unfinished. Unresolved. No matter how much time had passed, there was still this hole, this place where there should be something, and now there was nothing there to fill the emptiness where he should have been.

Ari's death could have been ruled as an accident, or even a suicide, and people would forget and move on.

But a girl had *died*. One of her best friends had *died*.

Ella felt like she needed to shake the entire world for it.

When she got to school Friday morning, she was surprised to see the new girl, Nani, standing in the hall, already wearing her new uniform—shirt a bit too tight over the chest, the skirt coming up short, because the uniforms had been designed by someone who did not understand that girls could come in different shapes and sizes—looking absolutely lost.

"Hi!" Ella said, reaching out and touching the girl's shoulder. "You're Nani, right?"

Nani jumped at that, her ears flushed.

"Sorry, didn't mean to scare you! I'm Ella. We didn't get to meet before, I'm friends with Rory and Yuki. I don't live here, though, I just come from Constanz each morning."

Ella realized she was already blabbering and shut up. Nani's brow furrowed.

"I—" she started saying, the moment another girl slammed into them.

Nani managed to drop all of her books at once.

"Watch where you're going!" a new voice said harshly.

Nani reached out for her glasses, which had fallen on the floor, but Ella got there first, rubbing them clean before handing them back. The round lenses had been so smudgy Ella wasn't sure how Nani saw through them at all.

"Oh, sorry," the other girl added, and Ella recognized Svenja, from their year. Ella knew almost everyone in school, matching easily faces to names, but Svenja was more recognizable than most. Not only because she was the only trans girl in their year, but because her cousin was almost identical to her. Svenja was the prettier and livelier, though, in Ella's opinion, and she was the pride and joy of the Grimrose ballet corps.

Ella offered a hand for her to get up, her brown hair having come undone, and she quickly pulled it once more into a ponytail.

"Thanks," she said in a small voice. Then she looked into Ella's eyes. "I didn't get a chance to say it, but I'm so sorry for your loss. I know how much you loved her."

A shadow passed over Ella's heart.

"Thank you," she answered. "It means a lot to me."

Ella smiled and saw that Nani was watching this exchange curiously. Probably no one had told her that she had taken a dead girl's bed. Svenja winked at Nani as she passed her by, and Nani clutched her books tighter, glaring.

"It's nice to see you're making friends," Ella said.

"If you think that's how you make friends, you need glasses more than I do."

Ella had no answer to that. Nani was still glowering in no particular direction.

"Okay," Ella said, hesitating a little. "But you're going to be here for a whole year. I'm sure you'll find plenty to like."

Nani turned to her. She was taller than Ella, but then again, pretty much everybody was. Yuki was the tallest among them, Rory a few inches shorter. Ari and Ella were the tiny ones, and Ari had always said it was best to be small, happily taking Ella's arm when they were together, going behind Rory and Yuki when they were in the corridors, letting them brave the way. Now Ella just felt alone when she walked to class.

"Come on," Ella said. "I'll get you to class."

It wasn't the best of starts, but she remembered when she'd met Rory for the first time, and Rory had challenged her to a duel.

Literally.

The rest of the day passed quickly, though Ella wasn't anxious to get back home. Sharon was going to spend the whole weekend with them. Sometimes though, if Ella was lucky, Sharon would take off with Stacie and Silla, go over to Milan, or even to France, and Ella could have the house to herself.

As she sat in Hospitality class, she made a list in her head of everything she had to do when she got home. Cooking dinner, then getting back to the castle for tonight's assembly. She'd also have to clean Carrot's stable. Making a list helped, but sometimes, all it did was feed her anxiety.

"You okay?" Freddie asked when class was over. His voice brought her back to reality.

Ella blinked, tapping her fingers three times on the counter. "Yes, sure."

"You look worried."

"Just got a lot of things to do."

"Want to run a list by me?" he asked. "It helps."

"Only if you have about twelve hours to hear all of it," Ella said jokingly, and Freddie's eyes widened.

"I take it back," he replied, his eyes wrinkling as he smiled, and they both walked together to the door. "Seriously, though, if you need any help..."

Ella looked at him. "I appreciate it."

"I never do anything on weekends." Freddie sighed as they headed toward the doors. "There was one weekend where I was so bored I just went around counting all the stairways in the castle. Do you know how many there are?"

"Seventy-three," they both said in unison, and Frederick's smile only grew.

It was infectious.

It was then that Yuki walked in and there was a change in the atmosphere. Yuki looked at Ella and Freddie, her eyes quickly assessing their smiles, their proximity, and her eyes looked even darker than before.

"Hey," Yuki said. "I was looking for you."

Ella cleared her throat, feeling her fingertips tingle. "Yuki, this is—"

"I know," Yuki interrupted abruptly, a strange tone in her voice. "I thought you couldn't be late."

Ella looked at her watch. She was one of the only students that still wore one, instead of looking at a cell phone. Not like her phone was more than barely functional. It scarcely had access to the internet because Sharon refused to let her use the Wi-Fi, claiming it was too distracting. Which was true, of course, but still, internet was practically a basic human right.

"I'm not late," Ella said. "Do you want to..." She didn't know how to finish the question.

"It's all right. I'll see you tonight," Yuki said instead, giving one last look at Freddie before turning to leave.

Ella hesitated for an instant, and then Freddie was by her side.

"You want me to walk you home?"

Ella bristled. "No, thanks, I got it."

"I can—"

"No. Thank you."

Freddie stopped in his tracks, and they both stood there awkwardly. Ella couldn't explain that she didn't want him near Constanz, didn't want him near a place that was not meant for such light things. Yuki and Rory had never been to her house. Only Ariane had sneaked in once or twice during her getaway strolls, the only company Ella had ever allowed. She kept her friends away for a reason.

A good reason.

"I'll see you next week, then," Freddie finally said, his voice even.

Ella smiled one last time at him while he waited patiently behind the door that kept him at Grimrose, a solid barrier between the school and her life outside the walls.

CHAPTER EIGHT

YUKI

Yuki had put off talking to Penelope Barone all week. She'd avoided the other girl in the corridors and in the few classes they took together. Trying to put off the inevitable.

She'd been chosen to do this because she was perfect.

That's what everyone who was close to her thought. Her father, with his strict rules at home, trying to fill the role of both parents, wanting so badly to do everything right that he insisted she'd be more accomplished than children three years older because Yuki's failure meant his own. Reyna hadn't enforced the same rules after her father died, but Reyna was the headmistress, and Yuki's behavior reflected on her stepmother. It went without saying that Yuki couldn't step a toe out of line. And in their way, Ella and Rory thought that too; they saw her as the person who could be everything she wanted without any effort.

It was all a lie.

Yuki was not perfect, and it took a *damned* lot of effort to pretend she was.

An effort that almost had come crumbling down when she saw Ella leave with Frederick, a secret smile playing on her lips, a secret she hadn't shared.

Ella always shared everything with Yuki, but she hadn't shared this.

Yuki couldn't let herself feel whatever this feeling was. Whatever revolting thought that churned at her stomach got crushed, and in its stead, she turned to steel and went to look for Penelope.

It was a beautiful Friday afternoon. The clouds rolled near the mountains and there was almost no breeze. The sun illuminated the gardens and the green grass where some of the students sat. She spotted Penelope sitting alone.

It was a shock, given that for the past few months of school she'd always been sitting with Ariane. The two had become close after Edric dumped Ari. Yuki remembered what Ari had told her, after Yuki asked why Ari wanted to spend so much time with the new girl after her breakup, and not with them.

It's not like you understand what it's like to love someone, do you?

The words hurt like Yuki had gotten slapped, a red mark across her cheeks, across her soul. A mark that no one else knew, because no one else heard Ari. Ari hadn't apologized, and neither had Yuki. She had nothing to apologize for.

Penelope looked up as Yuki approached, her golden hair in waves to her waist, green eyes sharp. She wore no jewelry except for a ring on her left hand that had the shape of the moon. Penelope had started Grimrose in their fourth year of Sekundarschule, gotten close to Ari, and then went away. She'd only come back again last year. No one had asked what happened, and if Ari knew, she didn't tell any of them.

It was only when she was standing right in front of Penelope that Yuki realized she didn't know what to say.

"Hi," Penelope said, looking up at Yuki, who was blocking the sun. "Can I help you?"

"Yes," Yuki said. "You've seen Ariane."

An awkward pause followed.

"When she was alive, yes," Penelope said slowly. "I have to say I haven't met her ghost yet."

There was a hint of an amusement in Penelope's voice, and Yuki realized she was an idiot, a realization that didn't come very often in her life.

"I'm sorry," the idiot announced loud and clear. "I shouldn't have come here to bother you. I—"

Yuki turned to go, but before she could move, Penelope grabbed her hand. Yuki almost jumped away, Penelope's cream-colored fingers holding her wrists. Instead, she froze, feeling the strange warmth of touch, trying to recall when she'd last let someone touch her.

She couldn't remember.

Penelope's grasp loosened. "You can sit down. It's a nice day."

Yuki licked her lips, tension in her shoulders. Forcing her body to obey her, she sat down mechanically, crossing her legs and adjusting the school uniform, doing it slowly so she could think of what to say next.

"So you want to talk about Ariane," Penelope said with a sigh, looking straight ahead. "Took you long enough."

Yuki blinked. "You knew we would want to talk to you?"

"She was your best friend, wasn't she?"

Another repetition of the same words. Another description of Ariane's loss, as if it could be whittled down to simply that. As if Ari could only be described as their best friend and nothing else.

"Well, I guess she was your friend too," Yuki managed. "Right at the end."

Penelope snorted. "Ariane wasn't my friend."

Yuki turned sharply, and Penelope opened her bag and got out a bar of chocolate. She snapped off a piece and handed it to Yuki.

"So what is it?" Penelope asked. "You want to accuse me of something? You better get to it fast, I have better stuff to do."

"Why would I accuse you of something?" Yuki asked, not eating her own piece of chocolate. The bar started melting, hot and sticky against her skin.

Penelope shrugged. "You wouldn't be the first."

Yuki frowned. "The first?"

"Eh," Penelope said. "Edric came to talk to me that week, asking if I knew anything, and then when I said that it was his own damn fault that Ari killed herself, surprisingly, he didn't take the idea very well."

Hearing someone else say it like that, so matter-of-factly, stirred something in Yuki, something she didn't know she needed. Rory and Ella were convinced Ari's death was no accident, that she wouldn't have put herself in danger like that. Ari never would have gone near the lake not knowing how to swim, and she sure wouldn't do it on purpose.

But they didn't know the truth.

They didn't know what Yuki had done.

It's not like you understand what it's like to love someone, do you?

"So you think she killed herself."

"Of course she killed herself," Penelope said, an edge in her voice. "She was miserable. She talked of nothing but Edric and her loss and how she wanted things to go different. I tried to help a couple months ago, you know, but she was mean."

If it were any of the other girls hearing this, they'd shut her down. Walk away. Accuse Penelope of lying, of distorting reality.

Yuki knew the truth of things. Ariane could be very mean, if she wanted to be. If she chose to be.

"Don't tell the others I said that," Penelope told her, eating her last piece of chocolate. "I know Ella and Rory are your best friends, but they can be intense sometimes."

"They can," Yuki agreed. Especially about this. "Sorry, I didn't want to bring this up."

"Why do you keep apologizing?" Penelope asked. "You don't need to say *sorry* every five seconds."

"Sorry."

They both laughed, and Yuki realized the chocolate was still melting. She ate it, licking what had melted from her fingertips.

Penelope got up, brushing grass from her skirt. "I don't care why you came here to talk, but I'm happy that you're at least being honest about it."

Penelope put her bag over her shoulder, walking away, and Yuki watched as she went. When she was a few steps away, Penelope turned around.

"I was hoping you'd be the one to find me," Penelope said, taking a few steps toward the castle, her words carried by the wind. "Not the others."

Yuki looked up, surprised. "Why is that?"

"You're the most interesting one," she said and left Yuki sitting alone in the grass.

CHAPTER NINE

NANI

Nani didn't unpack in that first week she was at Grimrose. And she hadn't seen her father, either.

She'd talked to some of the security guards, and yes, he *had* been the head of security, but that was before the school year started, and they hadn't seen Isaiah Eszes since.

Her father had told Nani he was working here for the past year, in this school, and now that he'd sent her tickets and she had to study here, he was nowhere to be found. She'd sent a letter to his last known address, but it came back unopened. If one thing could be said of the Swiss post, it would be that it's efficient.

It was the only reason she'd accepted the invitation. She thought he wanted to see her. Nani had flown halfway across the world to find her father, but now he wasn't even there.

To make things worse, she had to stay at Grimrose, and

she didn't know how she'd begin the search for her father. Maybe he didn't want her to find him.

So when Friday night arrived, Nani was almost thankful to attend the mandatory school assembly, just to distract her a little.

The students belonged to a very different world. There were the uniforms, of course, but also the shoes, bags, jewelry—everything spoke of a privilege and wealth that Nani had never seen before, meant only for the best of the best. The elite of the elite. That's who Grimrose was meant for, that's who the magic was built for, not some poor half-Black, half–Native Hawaiian girl like Nani.

Her father told her about places like this. It was the stuff of storybooks like the ones he'd brought her from his trips, so she could read and delight in the pages when he went away again. He'd promised to take her to the places he saw when he traveled, to show her the entire world. He'd promised, and now, here she was, and he wasn't there with her.

Nani sat down in the amphitheater next to her roommates and their friend Ella. She hadn't talked to them, but still, they were the only people she knew at the school, and it was better than sitting alone. Students crowded in different groups, some as young as eleven. She wondered what kind of parents would send such a young child to boarding school, to be seen only once or twice a year.

It didn't take long before the headmistress took the stage, climbing the stairs and standing in front of the microphone. She was younger than Nani expected, golden-brown skin, her dark chestnut hair swept aside, a ruby pendant gleaming at the base of her throat. Her dress was well cut, and she stood with her back so straight that Nani hadn't realized before that there were muscles capable of holding something so upright.

"This has been a turbulent start of the year," Reyna's voice rang out through the microphone. "The tragedy of the death of one our beloved students took us all by surprise." She paused for a breath. "You are safe here. Your safety is a priority to both the institution and me, and so is your education. To the old students and the new, I hope you all make the best of what the Académie has to offer. Lux vincere tenebras."

Nani didn't recognize the last words, but they were repeated back by the students, the Latin hanging clear in the echo of the room. She spotted Mrs. Blumstein, along with two other older teachers, side by side with Reyna as she left the stage. Nani recognized Ms. Lenz from chemistry, and she assumed they were all members of the teachers' council.

"That's Miss Bagley from cooking class," Ella whispered to Nani across the row of girls. "They're basically the three teachers you can go to when you're in trouble."

Nani had lived with Tūtū long enough to know not to trust all old women to be kind and generous just because they were old. Tūtū's sermons still rang in her ears weeks after she'd stopped talking.

Mrs. Blumstein took the stage to explain some of the curriculum, and after her, a white girl their age took the stage.

"That's Alethea," Ella explained. "She's the head of the student committee."

"Basically they just plan the events," Rory said. "Alethea's a snob, but at least she knows how to throw a party."

"She's not a snob," Ella said. "She's just a little touchy."

"Touchy?" Rory exclaimed with a snort. "Remember the pillow accident? That's what you call touchy? Could you not defend everyone at this school for once?"

"I don't defend everyone. I just think you're being unfair."

"Saint Ella the Just, patron of the bullied."

"Shut up."

Rory's teasing laugh was louder now, and a few heads turned. Yuki stared straight ahead, apparently pretending she didn't know them, something Nani found relatable.

Alethea cleared her throat in front of the stage, waiting for silence.

"We're following tradition this year," Alethea said with a smile that stretched across her whole face and looked wholly unnatural. "We'll have, of course, the big ball to celebrate the end of the school year in June, but we're also throwing another holiday party, to celebrate before winter break. This year, we'll do a masked ball."

Students started whispering excitedly, Ella murmuring something right away to her friends. Nani closed her eyes and ignored them. She couldn't care less about stupid parties. She never attended them back at her old school, and she wasn't about to try to dress herself in ridiculous clothes she didn't own to fit in with all these airheads.

After the assembly was done, Nani stood up.

"You aren't staying for the reception?" Ella asked. "They'll have food."

"I have a headache," Nani lied, making her way out to the door. She didn't have the stomach for receptions. She didn't know anyone, so she'd be stuck with her roommates, and besides, she had a plan to make.

She had to talk to Reyna. Surely she would know something about her father.

Just as she was leaving, someone seemed to appear out of the shadows, and Nani stumbled.

"Watch it." The tone was a spiteful warning, and Nani was taken aback as the girl turned.

"It's you," Nani replied, recognizing the girl who'd knocked all her books out of her hands that morning, but even as she said it, she knew something was wrong, like she was seeing the image through a distorted mirror.

It was the eyes she saw first, sunk deep into her face. They had the same skin tone of pale olive, and the hair, rather than a rich brown, was mousy. The girl glared at Nani as she disappeared into the corridor.

"I see you've met my cousin."

The voice came from behind Nani, and when she turned around, there she was—Svenja, Nani remembered suddenly. This time, the rich and colorful version of her.

"Your cousin?" Nani repeated.

Svenja shrugged. "That's Odilia. Not everyone in my family was lucky enough to be born with my stunning looks, so she does her best to copy."

Svenja flashed Nani a big smile. Nani stood in the corridor, uncomfortable, Svenja's smile making her turn away as she felt something stir in her heart.

She was the same height as Nani, her form lithe. Nani had always been big for her age, both in stature as well as shape, so it was strange to see someone who was as tall as her. The only girl taller was Yuki, who towered above them all.

"In a rush to leave the assembly?" Svenja asked, and Nani couldn't quite place her accent. Decidedly Eastern European, but she wasn't good enough with accents to place it.

"I have a headache," Nani lied again.

"I'll walk you to your room," Svenja said. "I don't feel like a party tonight either."

They walked side by side. Nani didn't need help navigating the school; she'd already learned where everything was. She always had a knack for learning directions, and this wasn't any different. Svenja followed in silence, and then, finally, they stood by her door.

"This is it," Svenja said. "Safe at home. What do I get in return?"

"I wasn't aware I needed to tip," said Nani.

"I'll accept other payments," Svenja said. "Perhaps a secret."

Svenja grinned at her, kind of wolfish—there was something untamed about that smile, something dangerous, something that spoke of the freedom to run wild in the woods, with no one to answer to.

"I don't have any secrets."

"No one is free of secrets, Nani the new girl. I'll find out yours."

"That sounds like a threat."

Svenja smiled again, nudging Nani slightly toward the door.

"I was going for welcoming, damn it. Let's try this again."

This time, Nani did laugh out loud. She couldn't help it. Svenja looked like she had just won a particularly difficult game of poker. Every part of her seemed both calculated and unbridled, both things at once. It surprised Nani, and her stomach fluttered with a feeling she had no name for.

"A girl with nothing to hide," Svenja said, enunciating the words, and it felt strange hearing her say it. Like Nani did have things to hide but couldn't hide them from her. "Tell me one thing then, Nani. Are you a fighter or a quitter?"

Nani inhaled sharply. She was not a quitter—she'd go after what she wanted. And she had no time for chats with girls who were nothing like her and who liked playing games.

"Thanks for walking with me," Nani said and then shut the door on Svenja's face.

With her back to the door, she breathed in relief. The room wasn't much, but it was nice to have it to herself for a moment.

Her bed contained only the bedsheets given to her by the school. Her bag was still sitting on top of the desk.

Nani didn't know how to feel about living in the space that belonged to a dead girl.

A dead friend. It made sense now, how Yuki and Rory

were treating her—why they weren't being overly friendly, like the other girl, Ella. She didn't want to replace their friend. She didn't want to replace anyone at all, because she wanted to find her father. She wanted him to take her away from here, to explain why he wasn't here when she'd thought they'd finally be in the same place, together.

She opened the wardrobe. Though it had been emptied out, there were a few clues that someone had lived here before. A ribbon, a sprawl of pink glitter at the bottom of the cabinet, a bag the color of aquamarine nearly hidden underneath the wardrobe, just an edge poking out. Nani ignored it all and unzipped her bag, finally putting her clothes away. The moment she did, Rory came in through the door, stopping short.

There was hurt in her eyes. As if Nani taking this space was a betrayal.

"There's a bag," Nani said, sliding it out and handing it over to Rory. "Here you go."

Rory frowned. "I thought we'd emptied it out."

For a moment, she held the bag in her hands, seemingly at a loss. She took a quick peek inside, but then shoved it under her own bed with such force that Nani wondered how she didn't break anything.

And as much as Nani hated to admit it, she understood Rory's hurt. Her taking over meant erasing a part of the past. Like Nani moving in meant she had to let go of her roommate. Tūtū had told Nani to let go of the past too, that her father would show up soon enough.

But letting go was a betrayal. To her father, to herself. Letting go meant forgetting. And forgetting was wrong.

Nani turned back, opened up another drawer, and slid in the few books she'd brought from her enormous collection at home, the scent of plumerias flowing from the pages. Her mother used to put the flowers between the pages of every book she was reading, so she wouldn't forget the scent of home. Nani let them go with a heavy thud. The heavy spine of *Les Misérables* cracked something in the wardrobe.

There was a fake bottom in the drawer.

She took the book out, peering curiously at the cracked wood. She found an edge and fought to pull it open. The inside revealed a book the size of a diary. Its cover was black, written in golden letters, with a tree and three crows printed in an ornate frame. A book of fairy tales.

"Here," Nani said, picking up the book and handing it to Rory, hoping it was the last thing. "I think this belonged to your friend."

CHAPTER TEN

ELLA

The first period of Monday morning was Latin, which added to the inherent torture of Mondays. She'd woken up at five thirty, made breakfast, took care of Carrots, and when it was six thirty, after she'd put on her layer of makeup, she left the house. Classes started at eight, and the bus was never reliable in the mornings, so she walked. Stacie and Silla were still asleep. Sharon usually took them by car, but Ella could never go with them; Sharon claimed she'd make them late because of her chores.

When she got to class, Rory was already sitting in her desk, and Ella frowned. She took her earbuds out, pausing her audiobook with only three minutes left to finish the chapter.

"What happened?" Ella asked.

Rory blinked. "What do you mean, what happened?"

"You're awake and in time for class. Couldn't you sleep?"

Rory scowled. "Of course I slept. I was just excited."

"For class?" Ella asked, putting a hand to Rory's forehead. Temperature was normal. "Is this a surprise test? You were possessed, and now I have to use Latin to exorcise you?"

"You're a born comedian," Rory deadpanned. "I wanted to talk to you. Nani was finally unpacking her things, and she found this."

Rory took out a book from her bag. Ella could not remember the last time Rory had carried a book anywhere of her own free will. She let go of it, and it landed with a soft thud on the desk.

Ella smoothed her hand over it and was surprised to feel soft leather under her fingertips.

"What is this?" Ella asked, tracing the delicate pattern on the cover—a gigantic tree, the leaves all painted in different shades of gold foil. Three crows soared above the tree, their wings open in flight.

"Good question," answered Rory. "It was in Ariane's wardrobe. I helped clean it out."

"You. Helped."

"Fine. I was present when Nani found it. She said it was hidden in a secret compartment or something. Also, Ariane's bag was there too."

Ella frowned. "Her bag?"

"Yeah. The one she was using the day she came back."

"How did we miss that?"

Rory shrugged.

Ella had helped clean the wardrobe, her and Yuki, and Rory had gone for a run, refusing to acknowledge the emptiness left behind. Ella hadn't minded. It wasn't the first time she'd put things into a box, never to be seen again.

"There's more," Rory said, opening the book with such carelessness it made Ella wince. The pages crinkled, brittle and yellowed with age. On the first page were handwritten notes, faint but distinct. "It's Ari's writing."

Ella frowned as she leafed through it, recognizing the titles of various fairy tales.

Why would Ari keep something like this hidden?

Ariane had always been dreamy—an artist's soul, as Ella's father would have put it. She spent days sketching outlandish landscapes and drawings, daydreaming about faraway places, but she was never the kind of girl who was fixated on fairy tales.

The book was full of notes—all of them in pencil, with quotes underlined, things written in the margins. Ella shook her head looking at it, the letters swimming on the page.

"It has to be a clue, right?"

Ella closed the book. "You know I don't have the time."

Rory's brow creased. "Ella, this could be important."

"Then *you* read it."

"You're assuming I know how," Rory said in a half-joking manner. Rory had never read a book in her entire life, and she was almost stupidly proud of it. "You'll figure it out sooner than I will."

"Yes, but I just don't have the time," Ella insisted. It wasn't as if Rory didn't know. Rory was acutely aware of how her life worked. Ella desperately missed sitting down and reading.

She wished she could, but Sharon thought reading was an idle activity.

So she'd sold all of Ella's father's books.

A library they'd built together while he lived, that had her mother's favorites and the old, expanded universe novels her father would read before she went to bed, editions that weren't worth anything to anyone but her own heart.

Sharon had gotten rid of them all.

Ella ran her fingers over the cover of the book again. It could be a clue. It could be nothing.

"Why didn't you talk to Yuki?" Ella asked instead.

"I didn't see her."

"You live in the same room, Rory."

"Yeah, but she spent the weekend at the library or with Reyna or something. Besides..."

Her voice trailed off, an uneasy silence filling them both. Ella hadn't tried to broach the subject before, thinking that she was just wrong. But if Rory had felt it, Ella knew she couldn't ignore it anymore.

"She thinks it was just an accident, doesn't she?" Ella asked, her voice quivering just slightly, pretending to brush it off.

Rory shook her head. "I don't think she wants to say it."

Ella felt tears coming to her eyes, tried blinking them away. She wasn't going to start crying over this. She wasn't about to break down here.

"But you think it's strange too."

"Of course I do," Rory said, her voice half anger, half

indignation. "She wouldn't have done this. She wouldn't have left us."

The words hung in the air. She wouldn't have left.

It hadn't been her choice.

It hadn't. It *couldn't*.

Ella picked up the book, stuffed it in her bag. "I'll try to see if I can convince Yuki to look at it. She's always been better at this stuff, anyway."

"Yuki, the perfect student."

Ella smiled, but her heart wasn't really in it.

"She really is."

CHAPTER ELEVEN

RORY

Handing the book off to Ella had been the right thing to do.

She didn't even know why Ari had it in the first place. It wasn't like her to have something like that. Same with the bag the new girl found, the bag Rory had seen the day they'd returned to school. Rory had spent the day sleeping instead of talking to her friend, not knowing Ari would be dead in a few hours. The only conversation they'd exchanged was about the return trip to Grimrose, and Ari saying she'd gotten the bag at the airport that very same day. The words were burned into her mind so Rory could recycle the same stupid conversation over and over again, a conversation that didn't even mean anything.

She wished she'd said something else. Anything else.

She wished she'd gotten more time.

And she didn't like that her best friend was keeping secrets.

At least, if Ella had the book, it meant something was being done about it. Even if Yuki didn't exactly believe them. Rory hadn't asked about Penelope, but she knew there was something going on there. Penelope had been just another girl in their year, then suddenly, she and Ariane had grown close. Shared secrets. Eaten lunch together. It's wasn't that Rory hated sharing her best friend (she did), and she didn't have to know everything about Ari's life (that too), but she just didn't understand what had brought them together.

She was so distracted thinking about it on her way to fencing practice that she didn't realize she was walking right behind Edric and his new girlfriend until she almost ran into them. The girl was one year younger, a perky girl who wore pigtails, a poor substitute for Ari on any day of the week. They were holding hands like someone had superglued them together. Rory scowled.

"Excuse me," Rory said, hoping they would make space for her to pass by and get to practice.

Edric's expression changed as soon as he saw Rory behind him.

Edric's girlfriend, Whatshername, only blinked, eyes wide like a doe's. Rory didn't change her expression. She wasn't as tall as Edric, but she could easily beat him up if she had to. She could beat up anyone at this school if she was determined enough. All it took was really believing in yourself, that's what Ella always said.

Rory wasn't sure giving everyone at the school a black eye was what she meant by it, but she could always hope.

"The hall's wide enough to go around," Edric replied in a haughty tone.

"Well, there's no need for you to walk side by side like the slowest turtles in the world, is there?" she snapped back.

"What is your problem?" Edric finally said. Rory had never found him handsome, but then again, to her, all boys looked pretty much all the same, and none of them interesting.

A vein popped in Rory's forehead, anger rushing her forward. "You either get out of the way, or I'm going to run you over."

Whatshername blinked rapidly this time, her face paling. It wasn't every day that Rory threatened people, but it was always a good day when she did. It was an especially good day when they looked at least a tiny bit scared.

"No," Edric said instead. "I know you're used to getting your way, but I know what this is about."

"Oh, you do? Because you're so smart?"

"Unlike you," he said, and the words were like a purposeful jab she couldn't parry. "Now that Ariane's gone, no one holding your leash?"

Her name in his mouth. Her name, in his mouth, like it was an afterthought, like it was something to throw away.

Rory didn't think.

To be fair, she rarely did.

She grabbed him by the shirt and slammed him up against the wall. Whatshername gave a little yelp, wide-eyed and idiotic, her mouth open in shock.

That finally got them to stop the hand-holding.

Edric, to his credit, barely seemed concerned.

"You don't get to say her name like that," Rory growled. "Not when you cheated on her." She looked in disdain at the other girl. "She was heartbroken, and now look what happened."

Edric's face went red. "You're saying it's my fault she did it?"

"If the shoe fits."

Edric tried shoving her away, but Rory's hold on him was strong, all her muscles working together to keep him there.

"You're insane," he told her. "You think I didn't mourn her too? She was a good person. I know I messed up, but that doesn't mean I didn't care about her. I apologized to her the weekend before school started."

Rory's grip faltered, and she blinked in surprise, but didn't let go. Giving your opponent an opening was one of the main reasons you could lose a duel. She tightened her grasp, trying to compensate, because Edric had been Ari's first love, first passion, first heartbreak, and if she'd moved past that... Didn't that say in the end that her death was no accident, that Ari truly didn't kill herself?

Shouldn't she be glad that she and Ella were right?

She felt her muscles rebelling, pain jolting through her from the sudden movement. *Not now,* she thought. *Please, not now.*

Her fists wanting began to uncurl against her will, the knuckles on her fingers shoot pain all way up through her neck, injecting it directly to her body, trying to make her falter. Trying to make her *weak*.

Rory Derosiers was not weak.

"Listen here," she hissed, as much to Edric as to her own body, trying to make it obey, trying to get it under control. "I—"

A gentle hand clasped her wrist. Rory looked up into the clear, steady eyes of Pippa Braxton, dressed in her fencing whites.

"Come on," she said calmly. "It's not worth it."

Pippa held her gaze, her hand still firmly over Rory's. She never touched her like this aside from practice, aside from the place they always talked. It was a violation of their rules. They both knew it.

Rory looked between her and Edric, her breath hissing out from between her lips.

"You don't want another change of schools," Pippa said, so quietly that Rory could barely hear her.

But she still heard it.

Rory had changed schools before, plenty of times. It was one of the few things Rory had shared with Pippa about her personal life. But she never liked to remember the experience. New school, new identity. Rory never wanted to change, but it wasn't her choice. Her overprotective parents, obsessed with her safety, moving her from school to school, so much so that she never even saw them. Like she wasn't even their daughter.

It's for your safety, were the first words Rory remembered hearing from her parents. She couldn't remember one single "I love you," and she tried, she tried *hard*, almost every day.

Rory felt her knuckles giving in to the pain, and she

schooled her face not to wince. She let Edric go, and he and Whatshername scurried away from her and down the hall.

Rory turned to Pippa, her jaw set.

"Next time you stop one of my fights, you're the one who's going to get beaten up."

Pippa looked down at Rory's hands, clenched at her sides now to hide their trembling, as if she knew what was happening. As if she knew Rory's body was trying to betray her in the worst way possible. The only thing Rory had, the only thing she could rely on, was her body, her strength, but right now it was turning her inside out with pain.

"Well," Pippa said with a grin, "I'd like to see you try."

CHAPTER TWELVE

YUKI

Yuki had been studying in the library her free period after lunch when Ella found her.

She'd been poring over one of the harder French essays, making sure her writing was legible. Her father had insisted she learned to speak English since she was a child, but writing was another matter. The letters were fine, but every word seemed to contain way too many syllables, the spelling waiting for her like a trap, a serpent in disguise, the sounds getting mixed, the meaning obscure. With French and Latin, it got even more complicated, but she'd learned it all the same.

Ella came into the room carrying Mephistopheles.

Mephistopheles was a monster in cat form—a huge black cat, weighing almost thirty pounds, his fur always rebellious and spiked up, making him seem bigger than he was. His ears were pointed as if he had horns, and his eyes were an abnormal shade of yellow. Sometimes Yuki would see him on top of the shelves at night, two yellow spheres watching in the darkness, lurking and preying on the weak. He'd shown up at the library a few years ago, and the librarian started waging a war—and Mephistopheles fought back, destroying pens and library books and half of the poor librarian's face. The librarian had ended up transferred to a hospital in Zurich with scratches, and that had been the end of it. Mephistopheles had won, and he was not going to move from the library, and no one could even come near him without fearing for their lives.

No one, of course, except Ella.

The cat hissed the moment he spotted Yuki, his mean yellow eyes narrowing.

"Oh, shush," Ella said, playfully slapping the cat's paws while she cradled him like a baby, with only one hand. "Yuki's a friend. Remember? Friend."

"That cat doesn't understand the meaning of anything besides pure evil."

"Mephistopheles is a very good boy, and I'll not hear you speak of him that way."

Mephistopheles did not look, even remotely, like a very good boy. Ella set him down on one of the tables, petting his head absentmindedly as she took something out of her school bag. A book.

"Nani found this in Ari's wardrobe on Friday," Ella said, extending it to Yuki. "Her bag was there too, but shoved under it. I think the book itself was in a secret compartment or something. At least that's what Rory told me."

Yuki took it gingerly. The book wasn't heavy in her hands,

but the moment she touched it, she felt something like a bolt of electricity run down her spine. The hairs on her arms raised, but there was nothing in that hidden corner of the library except for Ella and Yuki. Well, them, and the satanic cat.

"What's this?" Yuki asked, her fingertips tracing the cover. There was something about it that felt ancient. The bindings, the type of paper, the cover itself. "This looks old."

"Doesn't it?" Ella agreed. "Rory gave it to me, but I'm not going to have time to read it."

Yuki tore her gaze away from the book, registering the words. Rory had it during the weekend. Not that she'd seen much of Rory—she'd spent Saturday studying in the library, and Sundays were the days she usually spent with Reyna.

"Why didn't Rory say anything?" Yuki asked, her whole body tense.

"She probably forgot," Ella said, looking again at the cat, scratching his chin while he purred happily.

Ella was lying.

Well, not actually lying, Yuki knew, because Ella was incapable of lying. But she was covering something up. Maybe they knew. Maybe somehow, they had known all along. What she'd done, what she'd said, what had really happened. She stared at the book in her hands, Ariane's words like needles within her, then pushed it back toward Ella.

Ella turned her eyes to Yuki. In the summer light coming through the windows, they were hazel, the color of thick honey, dotted with hundreds of different shades of brown.

"You know Sharon won't let me read it," Ella said quietly.

"It's just a book."

"Ariane wrote in it," Ella insisted. "Look."

Ella flipped open the cover, and Yuki recognized Ari's handwriting, though she had to narrow her eyes to read some of them.

"Maybe you can figure something out," Ella said. "Why she was hiding it, and what she was doing with it."

Yuki flipped the pages, seeing familiar titles on the pages, names that she'd remembered seeing in childhood.

"They're just fairy tales."

Ella shrugged. "If anyone's going to figure out if this means anything, it'll be you."

She smiled again, and a small dimple appeared on her right cheek. She picked up the cat again like a loaf of bread.

She hovered for an instant more, and Yuki could feel that there was something Ella was holding back. Maybe a question about Ariane, maybe wanting to ask what Yuki thought. But in the end, she just waved goodbye, went down the library stairs, and headed back home.

Yuki stood in her little corner of the library, surrounded by old books. She looked at Ari's book once more, feeling the soft, leathery texture of the cover, the thickness of the pages, the familiar titles. Some of them she knew, some she did not. It was no use fixating on this. It didn't matter whether Ariane had hidden it or not, it didn't matter what she'd written. It didn't change a thing.

Yuki stuffed the book in her bag, and when she turned around, someone else was there with her.

"I was wondering if I'd find you here," Penelope said, her voice ringing clear through the library's atrium.

The library at Grimrose covered three different floors, with a main hall and four different staircases, and there were small nooks and rooms that seemed almost independent from the main library sections, cut off from the rest of the students. Yuki had claimed the uppermost room of the tower, which held only a few shelves of forgotten German literature, and a window that opened to a spectacular view of the mountains. If she wasn't in her room, she would be here, where rarely anyone bothered her.

"You're the only person I know who comes up here," Penelope said, confirming all of Yuki's theories. "I just saw Ella leave. She seemed...distracted."

Yuki's jaw set harder. "We found some of Ariane's things still in the room."

"Oh," Penelope responded. "I thought you cleared it all out."

Yuki hesitated, then said, "We missed a bag." She wasn't sure why she didn't tell her about the book, but Ella wasn't the only one who could hold things back.

Penelope gave her a small smile in solidarity. "Was Mephistopheles here? There are scratches all over the table." She tutted, and Yuki waited, watching. Penelope looked at her again. "You don't really waste any words, do you, Yuki Miyashiro?"

The use of her full name surprised Yuki. It's not as if the teachers didn't know it or called her by it, but she made sure to blend into the background and never call attention to herself more than she already did, being the headmistress's stepdaughter, and the tallest girl in school.

"Once you speak, you can't take it back," she finally said.

Penelope smiled. "Aren't you wise."

It didn't sound like a question.

Finally, Yuki's curiosity won out. "What are you doing here?"

Penelope tapped the table where Mephistopheles had left his mark. Thin lines marred the mahogany, as tiny as the scratches Yuki dug into her palms when she couldn't sleep at night, when she stared at the ceiling, unable to quiet her thoughts, sensing the breath of a hundred girls on the same floor slumbering soundly and sweetly all while she felt rooted to her bed, to this place, to what she'd built for herself.

Penelope licked her lips before speaking, looking up again.

"I liked talking to you," she said sincerely, her green marble-like eyes reflecting the sun. "No one came to talk to me about Ariane. You were the first. Even if your intentions were to find out if I'd pushed her into the lake or something." Yuki widened her eyes, and Penelope laughed. "I'm kidding."

"To be fair, it was kind of like that."

Penelope snorted, but her smile didn't waver.

"You're the first person I felt I could be honest about it," Penelope said. "You know how Ariane could be a piece of work."

Penelope hopped onto the table, crossed her legs elegantly, adjusting her shirt. She wasn't tall like Yuki, but there was a pliancy to her body, a grace that was not awarded to most girls their age. All of them were awkward, and most days, Yuki felt like her body couldn't contain her. That one day, she'd come spilling out of it, if she couldn't keep her mind quiet, hold everything back.

Penelope didn't look like she ever felt that way. Penelope looked in control.

"All people want to say is sorry," she continued, "and God, I'm tired of hearing it. Sorry about your loss, sorry, she was your friend, wasn't she, what a pity, I'm sorry, it must be so hard. They have no idea."

Yuki let herself approach the table where Penelope was sitting, her right foot swinging back and forth. Yuki noticed with a passing glance that her legs were shaved, smooth.

"I know," Yuki answered, her fingers on the table.

"It has to be worse when it's your own friends."

Yuki looked up sharply, her mass of dark hair covering half her face like a partially drawn curtain.

"I didn't need to talk to you more than once to know how you feel," Penelope said quietly. "They're looking for an explanation for what happened. You aren't."

Yuki felt her heart chilling until she couldn't feel it beat anymore, her whole body frozen like ice, like her cold, merciless heart. She tried to remember how to breathe. Her friends wanted to look for signs, for reasons, for explanations, but she knew the truth.

Penelope didn't try to reach out for her hand, and for that, Yuki was thankful.

"You don't need to feel guilty about it," she said gently.

"You don't have to explain yourself to me. I know how you feel, because I feel it too."

She gave Yuki a tight-lipped smile.

"They don't understand," Yuki found herself saying it, the truth spilling out like a river, like water that had been stuck inside a dam. Penelope had found the crack, and the dam was going to break. "They think they knew what Ariane was like. They didn't."

"That sometimes she was mean and selfish," Penelope completed, her blond ponytail swinging slightly as she turned her head. "It's okay to speak ill of the dead. They're dead. They can't hurt you anymore."

Yuki's hands curled into fists, her nails turning to claws, digging deep into her palm until she could feel her own heartbeat. She knew to bite it all down, to keep all of this in, this struggle, this anger. It wasn't meant to be hers. It had no right to be hers.

She was good, perfect Yuki.

She would not allow herself to crack.

"I'll tell you the truth," Penelope said. "Ari and I had a big fight before she left for the summer. She'd invited me to stay over with her parents, I said no."

"Didn't you go home?"

Penelope hesitated. "I don't talk to my parents anymore. Not after they sent me back here."

Yuki looked up, letting her curiosity show.

"I never wanted to come to Grimrose in the first place," Penelope said. "I went home after that first year, tried another school, but my parents wouldn't have it. So, they sent me back here. It didn't matter what I wanted."

"I'm sorry."

"I thought we were over the whole saying sorry thing," Penelope said, her eyes sharp.

"All right," Yuki agreed, struggling again not to repeat herself. The words echoed within her almost automatically, the apologies on her tongue, even when she didn't mean them. She'd learned to use the words as a shield, mostly for herself, and now they were the only words she knew. The only words she was allowed. "So she invited you?"

"She took it back," Penelope said. "Ari was fickle like that, and she thought I'd offended her somehow by saying no, like she was being magnanimous offering me a home when I didn't have any. As if I needed it."

"Didn't you?"

Penelope turned to her. "What did you do for your summer break?"

Yuki stayed in Grimrose, because that's what Reyna did. They'd traveled around for a week, but Europe in summer was buzzing with tourists, and neither Yuki nor Reyna felt like facing the crowds.

"I stayed here," Yuki answered.

Penelope gave her a quick nod of understanding. "Seems like you don't get a real home either."

It wasn't mean. It was a recognition. Yuki wanted to contradict her, but it was the truth. She did not get a home either, nothing outside of the walls of these castle, and she'd learned to live with it. To live with the expectations it brought, to live with the choices she hadn't really made, and to never, ever listen to any other voice within her, because Reyna had brought them here, and Yuki should be thankful. When her father died, Reyna had been there for her. Yuki couldn't disappoint her.

She curled her fingers within her palms. "Well, it is. Reyna is here," she managed, and that had to be enough.

"If you say so," Penelope said in a tone that didn't believe what she said for a second. "I came here to tell you the truth, because I thought you were the one who would want to listen to it. The person who would understand."

Yuki knew the others weren't going to accept an easy answer, one that involved Ari going to that lake willingly, knowing what she was doing. They would never understand.

But Penelope did.

"If you ever need to talk about it," Penelope said, and her offer dangled in the air like a dangerous prize, "you know where to find me."

CHAPTER THIRTEEN

ELLA

After leaving Mephistopheles at his favorite sunbathing spot in the library, Ella rushed to the bus stop, praying she was on time. It had only taken a few extra minutes with Yuki. She climbed down the path from the mountain to the gates, saying her goodbyes to the security team that always greeted her outside the main entrance.

At the base of the mountain in which stood the imposing Grimrose Académie, there was a road that eventually would lead to Constanz.

Constanz was small, and its population was no bigger than fifteen thousand people, between the German- and French-speaking territory. The Académie taught the two, plus Italian, though all classes were administered in English. It was a small town, split into two very distinct parts. There was the rich neighborhood where the students of the Académie would spend their weekends, buying clothes and shoes and eating gelatos on the sidewalk. And then there was the less ostentatious part of town, where the gardeners, security guards, cooks, and shop attendants lived.

It wasn't as big as Cambridge, and their house here wasn't as cozy as before, but she liked Constanz all the same.

The bus came quickly. She counted the trees on the way home. Eighty-eight, a number that felt good, a number that fit the way her mind perceived the world.

It hadn't always been that way. As a child, she would count things, but it was for fun, and not like her life depended on it. Now, there was an order to things. And no matter what, her hands never really kept still, her body trying to keep her alive in the only way it knew how.

Her house was located in the better part of town. It was a traditional construction, with three stores and chimneys and the traditional German design with the brown wood windows and squared-eaves roof. It was too big, something Ella thought unnecessary when Sharon bought it with some of the money Ella's father left when he died. It was only the four of them, but the house had two living rooms, a huge staircase, and even a small stable—where they kept a single horse Sharon had given Silla when she'd decided to compete in horseback riding tournaments, though that hadn't lasted long.

She opened the iron gates silently. Noticing the garden was in full bloom, she felt proud of her work. She took the pail and watered the plants quickly, checking in on Carrots and filling the stall with hay. Carrots whined, knocking his hooves on the floor. She opened his stable door so he could roam more freely until it was time for bed.

Finally, she went to the back door to the kitchen, and it opened with a creak. She winced, hoping it had gone unnoticed.

It was no use.

Ella glared at the door, while her stepmother's voice rang clear through the house.

"Eleanor? Is that you?"

"Yes, Sharon. I'm here."

A few seconds later, her stepmother appeared in the threshold. She was wrapped in a dark robe, hair wet from showering. Her gray eyes glowered cold.

"What took you so long?"

Ella looked at her watch. She was seven minutes later than usual, had taken longer to walk than predicted. Seven was one of the good numbers.

"The bus was late," she lied, trying to keep her tone light, trying to convince Sharon it wasn't her fault. She started taking the pans out of the cabinets, moving over to the fridge.

"You expect me to believe that in Switzerland?" Her look was pointed, but Ella knew better than to try and make up an excuse. "The girls and I are taking a quick trip on the weekend. You're all right taking care of the house by yourself?"

"Yes, Sharon."

Ella kept her head down. She expected more insults, but today, it seemed like her stepmother was too tired for any further comment on her incompetence. And she'd have the weekend off. She could go into town, start thinking about what they would wear for the winter ball in December. Ella had a vague idea of the design. She'd sketch it later, maybe even get fabric for her and Yuki and Rory too. The winter ball was one of the very few things she was looking forward to this year, and the idea of designing dresses added a little bounce to her step.

Ella set out to make dinner, putting her hands to use. She loved doing housework, really, as long as they left her alone. That was all she asked. If she took it care of it by herself, then Sharon would have one less reason to bother her. If Ella did everything, there would be no complaints.

Ella was tired of living like this, but she had nowhere else to go.

She knew she sounded pathetic. She wondered if people saw her that way, but they were outsiders, and they knew nothing about her life. Ella had no money, and if she left, she'd be on her own. No money, no house, no school. Where would she go? She wouldn't last a week.

Ella wasn't stupid. She weighed her best options, and she waited. When she turned eighteen, she'd inherit her father's money and her mother's house, and then she would leave everything behind. She'd finally be free.

Five years were nothing compared to a whole life of freedom. Besides, it wasn't all that horrible—she had a roof over her head, an excellent education, work with which she could make money from time to time, and best of all, her friends. They kept her together, so she wouldn't crumble to pieces.

And so Ella endured.

She slid in her earbuds, playing an audiobook she'd found on fairy tales. She hadn't done much research while in class—the only place where she could access the Wi-Fi was school, so she'd only done it during lunch break, and Ari's book had no title, no other clues. She remembered reading fairy tales with her mother at home, her voice one of the last things that lingered in Ella's memory. The voice in her ear was soft but unlike her mother's, and it was a pang in her heart. She wished she had more time for reading, but she could barely sit still. She learned to watch movies while doing crochet or sewing, and she listened to books and podcasts while she cooked and cleaned. Every bit of pleasure, every bit of rest, was still laced with work.

When she turned back to the fridge to get the salad, Stacie was leaning against the door, arms crossed. She hadn't inherited Sharon's gray eyes. Stacie and Silla had nothing extraordinary, but were still pretty, with dark hair and brown eyes.

"What is this I hear about you hanging out with Frederick?" Stacie demanded.

Ella took her earphones off. "What?"

"You heard me," Stacie said, but her voice was low. She didn't want Sharon to hear either. It was one of the things the three of them shared, reluctantly. Sharon would torment Ella, but she didn't entirely leave the twins alone, demanding they get perfect scores, not eat too much, not be failures. After Silla quit horseback riding, there had been war for a month after Sharon had thrown the medals she'd won into the fire, because if Silla was quitting, it was best not to have any reminder of her failure.

"I know you're partners with him in that stupid cooking class," Stacie continued.

Had Freddie complained to Stacie about having to partner with her? Ella's face burned, imagining them talking about her. "You should tell your friends to arrive early if they don't want to get stuck with other people."

Stacie's eyes didn't leave Ella's face. "He's not really my friend," she said. "Silla likes him."

Now Ella understood. She turned back to the fridge. "Why would you think that particularly interests me?"

"I'm only looking out for you," Stacie said. "I don't want you to get hurt. It's not like he could possibly like you that way, anyway?"

The words stopped Ella dead, and she breathed deep, trying to find anything to look at besides Stacie. Twelve fridge magnets. Three knives on the kitchen counter. Ten plates on the drying rack.

She thought about answering, but said nothing, not rising to the bait.

It was how it worked, a game she played with herself. She was allowed many things, as long as she kept her head down, as long as she didn't fight back. She appeared defeated, cowed, wearing ugly shoes and secondhand clothes. This was her cover. Her cover knew how to stitch clothes together but not make dresses, her cover knew how to survive without drawing attention to make her life even worse. Her cover was barely alive, barely enough.

Ella had played this game for so long that she wasn't sure it was even a game anymore.

"He's just feeling sorry for the girl whose friend died," Stacie said. "What else could it be? The most interesting thing in your life is that the people you love die."

Ella opened her mouth, feeling the tears come, but when she'd found her voice, Stacie had already run back up the stairs to her room.

CHAPTER FOURTEEN

NANI

It'd been three weeks, and Nani still had no answers about her father. She'd tried approaching Mrs. Blumstein again, but it was fruitless. She'd come to a dead end, and all she wanted was to go home.

She didn't like her classes. She didn't like the other students. They were all snobs, looking down on her. She didn't care about making friends, not when she was sure they'd do what people had done all her life—turn and laugh behind her back. Nani knew that attitude too well, and it wasn't going to be different here.

So she cut it off at the first opportunity, before she got really hurt. It was easier that way. She didn't approach anyone, and didn't let anyone approach her.

There was only one thing she was interested in.

The whereabouts of her father, and why he'd sent her to Grimrose.

The last time he'd left, it was with the same words as always. *Next time, ku'uipo.*

He always called her that, like he'd called her mother before, because it was one of the few words in Hawaiian he knew because of the stupid Elvis song, and even then, he didn't use it correctly. Nani's mother always laughed at the pronunciation, too much of the continent, no matter how hard he'd tried. It was one of the few things Nani remembered from her mother. He called her mother that, and then, after she passed, the word befell on Nani, a painful reminder of what was gone.

There was only one way she was getting her answers at Grimrose. Nani knew by now that her father couldn't afford to send her there, and that meant he had done something, offered something to someone. And that someone had to be the headmistress.

She'd already become familiar with Grimrose's architecture, and when Saturday came, she knew exactly where she needed to go. She climbed the stairs of the administrative tower, finding her way across the teachers' wing and stopping at the end of the corridor in front of a closed door. She knocked, waiting.

"Come in." Reyna's voice sounded muffled.

Nani opened the door swiftly.

The room itself wasn't different from any other part of the castle, but the furniture was. The room was austere, albeit comfortable—simple black wood chairs, a dark table. Behind her was a glass window, opening the view to the mountains to the west of the castle. Glass and brassy metal in decorations.

The only thing that could be considered personal was a picture of Reyna and a much younger girl who Nani easily recognized as Yuki. Yuki was beautiful even as a child, her eyes large with long lashes, her mouth so red it seemed unnatural. The picture had to be taken at least ten years ago, but Reyna didn't look like she'd aged a day.

"Miss Eszes, I assume?" Reyna asked.

Nani blinked, surprised that the headmistress knew who she was. "Er. Yes. How did you know?"

"You have your father's eyes," Reyna said, and Nani faltered. She'd always felt like she was right in the middle between her father and her mother, belonging to neither.

But a complete stranger had still recognized her.

"I wasn't expecting you," Reyna said, gesturing to the chair in front of her. "Sit, please."

Nani wondered if this was some type of power game. Honestly, she didn't care if it was. She just wanted answers.

"That's what I'm here to talk about," Nani said. "About my father."

Reyna's eyebrows raised in surprise. "I'm not sure how I can help you, Miss Eszes. We do have a telephone you can use, if you'd like to talk to him."

"That isn't—" Nani stopped herself, calming her nerves. She wouldn't back down. "I came here thinking I'd find him. I got a letter, tickets to come here. I thought I was coming to meet him here."

Reyna blinked in surprise, her hands clasped together over the table. Her nails were long and sharp, a smooth, glossy red.

"I can't offer any more explanations than what your father has already given you," she replied. "You have a place here, in one of the best schools in the entire world, an opportunity not many have."

Reyna said opportunity, but Nani knew what the word really meant. Privilege.

She'd been handed the privilege of a lifetime, and she was supposed to be grateful.

"I'd like to know why," Nani said. "Why am I here?"

"You're here because you got a spot in the school. You have an excellent school record, good grades. There's every reason you should be here, you understand."

"No, I don't," Nani said, more vehemently. How was she supposed to understand? "Our family has no money. I could never come to this school. I don't belong here, and I want to know what happened to my father."

She finished her sentence without knowing where the outburst was going, without even being sure she had breath enough to finish the sentence. She adjusted her glasses, trying to give her hands something to do.

"Then I'm afraid I can't help you," said Reyna. "Your father left our service after the school year was done."

Nani's heart stilled, her fingers digging into the wooden armrests which offered no comfort.

Reyna sighed, glancing at the photograph of her and Yuki for a moment.

"This is a confidential conversation," Reyna told her, finally, turning her intense brown eyes back at Nani. "I'm not sure I should be telling you this, but I thought your father would have explained the delicate situation. When he applied to the school to work here, he wasn't interested in making a salary. He was interested in a place for you at the school. He worked for us for a year. We offer scholarships to our employees so their children can attend the school, and we make no distinction between them and those who pay full tuition."

Nani let that sink in, but Reyna's voice was distant, like it was coming across a roaring ocean that was taking over Nani's heart.

Her father was gone.

"So where is he?" Nani finally said, finding her voice again.

"I don't know," Reyna answered. "When his contract was up, he left our services. I only knew you'd be arriving. That's all he told me before he left."

If Reyna didn't know, if no one knew, then her father was gone. Again. And not only gone, but missing. No one knew where he was, and he wasn't coming back for her.

He'd left her at Grimrose, and she had nowhere else to go.

Nani's breakdown was interrupted by a sudden knock at the door. Mrs. Blumstein put her head in the door, peeking into the room.

"May I come in?"

Reyna primmed herself on her seat, sitting straight. "You may."

Mrs. Blumstein came in, wearing one of her usual red dresses, ones that Nani was already getting used to seeing. She offered Nani a smile.

"I need to talk to you in private," Mrs. Blumstein said. "Was it something urgent that Miss Eszes wanted?"

"No," Reyna said, locking her eyes with the girl.

Nani looked between them both for one moment. She saw Reyna's tense shoulders, Mrs. Blumstein's amiable demeanor.

"Come now," Mrs. Blumstein gestured to her. "A girl like you shouldn't spend so much time stuffed indoors. There's so many things to explore."

Nani looked at the open door and got up. "Thanks for the help."

She could feel Reyna's eyes following her to the door, and Nani heard muttered words behind it, though she couldn't distinguish any of them. But it didn't matter what else was going on inside this school, or that Nani had taken the place of a dead girl, or she was stuck inside this castle by a bargain her father had made. That wasn't important anymore.

Her father was gone.

CHAPTER FIFTEEN

RORY

Rory tossed and turned all night and woke up in a foul mood. She'd gotten a bad night's sleep, which was the usual for her, her bones unable to settle within her body like they didn't belong there. She rose with bags under her eyes and an unbearable pain in her back that stretched the entirety of her spine in a way that made it hard to breathe.

She got out of bed and swallowed two of the pills she kept hidden, glad Yuki and Nani weren't awake to witness her sweating, to see her shaky fingers as she screwed the cap back on. She usually took her medicine in the dark, where nobody could see, where no one could know what she needed. But the pain was too much this morning.

Weak, she thought to herself. *Weak*.

She sat on the edge of her bed, breathing hard, until her body became numb under the painkiller's guidance. When she finally managed to get up, she took one step then another, trying to teach her body how to function again, trying to show the way, like she'd had to learn how to walk every day since the day she was born as if it was the first time. She took a hot shower that almost boiled her skin, but it helped.

When she got out, she was Rory again, and not some dark, crawling creature inhabiting a girl's body.

Of course, she immediately regretted getting up after she remembered they were going to Constanz to meet Ella and do some shopping.

Six hours later, she was still regretting it.

"Hm, no, not this one," Ella muttered, testing a brighter tone of pink against Rory's skin. "I hate organza. I need more rose gold, I think, less pink."

Ella tutted at the fabric in a very English manner, which Rory found amusing in usual circumstances, but not when they'd been stuck in the same fabric shop for the last two hours.

Rory avoided most activities that weren't running or sports, but to Ella and Ari, shopping *was* a sport. Rory couldn't tell the difference between anything, but Ella was the expert. The shop always had the best things—and it was, after all, the only trip the students were allowed to make by themselves on the weekend.

It felt strange, being here without Ari. Ari would be next to Ella, offering her opinion on everything, matching fabrics with accessories and perfumes. Ari had shopped with Rory too, but mostly so Rory wouldn't feel alone browsing the men's section for her comfortable clothes, shirts that fit her better, that made her feel like she was in control of who she was. Completely different than she was at home—but then, Grimrose was her real home. The only place where she could be even a sliver of herself.

A place where she didn't have to hide.

Rory almost wanted to laugh at the irony of it all.

And now they were here, the three of them, and it felt good, but every time Rory looked around, she wanted to scream. It was like she could never be just with Yuki or Ella, because with just the three of them, Ari would always be missing.

"This one arrived last week." The shop attendant took one of the pieces to show Ella. She examined for a moment, then shook her head. The saleswoman did her best to hide the exasperation in her face at the capriciousness of this particular client.

"I am *not* being unreasonable," said Ella to no one in particular. "What about a silver voile? Nothing shimmery, though, just for the base of the dress."

"Won't the dressmaker have some trouble sewing that together?" asked the woman, looking doubtful.

"Nonsense," Ella replied, dismissing the comment with a wave of her hand.

The change in Ella's attitude was impressive. In the shop, it was like another person overcame her—she was imposing and critical, and she scoffed at half of the pieces shown to her. Rory watched, entertained as the saleswoman ran around, trying to find what Ella wanted.

Finally, after Ella had found the last of the missing pieces for the dress, they were ready to go.

"I can't wait to get to work on these," Ella whispered confidentially. "You'll love it."

Rory suspected that Ella wouldn't care if they hated the dresses—if she thought they were glorious, then so they were. Rory had to admit it, though, that when it came to stuff like sewing and cooking, Ella was the unbeatable champion. She *loved* it.

"Are we done then?" Rory asked.

"Yes, we just have to pay," Ella said, turning to the saleswoman. "These are theirs, and this one—"

Both Rory and Yuki cut her off at the same time, putting their hands in front of Ella in a synchronized move.

"I'm paying for them all," Rory said, glaring at Ella, daring her to protest. Ella's eyebrows knit together, but she didn't say anything. "Just wrap them all up together, I'll take it."

Her credit card had to be of use for something. Ella got the fabrics, holding the bags close to her chest. For someone who refused to take part in any sports, Ella was strong. Rory knew where that came from, and just thinking about it made her stomach turn.

Rory paid for everything, barely looking at the receipt, and they all walked back into the sunny afternoon on the last weekend of September. The breeze was starting to change, the wind blowing through the mountains, and in a week or two, the leaves would start turning yellow and red. It was Rory's favorite time of the year, that last stretch of warmth, right before the cold took over.

Except that right now, it felt like something was missing.

Rory's seventeenth birthday was coming up next week, and she didn't even want to celebrate. Couldn't celebrate it, because Ari was not here.

"So what now?" Rory turned around. She yearned to go for a run around the lake, to feel the wind sweep through her hair. But that wouldn't feel right either. Rory knew that there was something else they needed to do before they could truly find peace. "We could take a look at the book."

Yuki gave her a blank look.

"Did you read it?" Ella asked Yuki.

Rory waited, and at the same time, she dreaded the answer that was surely coming.

"No, I'll look at it later."

"It's been a week," Rory said.

"So?" Yuki raised an eyebrow. "If you're so worried, maybe you should have read it."

A flush crept over Rory's cheeks.

"I'm sorry," muttered Yuki. "It's not a big deal."

"It is a big deal," Rory insisted. "It could be a clue about what happened to Ariane."

"We all know what happened to Ariane!" Yuki barked. "She *died*!"

The words echoed around the cobbled street. Birds flew from the trees, but thankfully, the rest of the street was empty.

"There's no need..." Ella started muttering under her breath, trying to get between them both. Rory hated fighting her friends, but this wasn't just a disagreement. This was important.

This was about Ari.

"I get Edric saying there's nothing more to it," Rory breathed, her voice throaty and low. "I get Penelope. I get everyone in that fucking school saying it, but I don't know why you're so eager to just leave it behind. We might have found something that could help us understand what really happened, and we need your help. Ari needs your help."

Rory met Yuki's eyes and didn't back away. But there was nothing behind the coldness, that black color of void.

For the first time, Rory didn't recognize her friend.

"I'll do it later—"

"Forget it," Rory interrupted, her voice coming out more strangled than she would have liked. "You know what's the worst part? I always thought she was your friend too. Maybe I was wrong."

Rory was just in time to see Yuki's shocked face before she turned around and left them both.

CHAPTER SIXTEEN

ELLA

Rory marched down the street before Ella could stop her. It wasn't unlike Rory to do that—she'd explode, go on a rampage, crawl back later meekly. She'd go for a run, return dripping with sweat, honing her body into something bigger, into something better, into a weapon and a shield to protect her from the hurt. It was just how she was; Ella knew it the day she met her.

What she didn't know was how Yuki would respond, standing next to her, still as the mountains on the horizon.

Ella wanted to reach out, but thought better of it, keeping her hands on the bags, heavy with fabrics. She couldn't wait to get home and get started.

Ella tried not to think that she'd be making one less gown than she ought.

The morning had been fine. They hung out together, talked about class and the dresses and Alethea's plan for the ball, and all of it had been normal. All of it was as it was supposed to be.

Except it wasn't.

There was no Ari to make them hang back because she was tired of walking, no Ari to roar her loud laugh in their ears and make everyone in restaurants look at her, no Ari to tell them elaborate stories about each of their classmates, no Ari to hum to herself while they walked. There was no Ari with her bright hair, with her big green eyes, her soothing and beautiful voice.

There was no Ari, and it was all wrong.

Ella tried not to focus on it, because she still had Yuki, she still had Rory. They were all still friends. But she'd had Ari too, and to be here without her felt like a betrayal. To enjoy something where Ari should be but never would be again felt like something she shouldn't enjoy it at all.

"We should go get ice cream," Ella said lightly, watching Yuki's face.

Yuki nodded, her eyes still fixed somewhere in the distance.

"You know how Rory is," Ella said, venturing her thoughts. "She'll get over this."

"You told me to read the book too."

Ella turned to her. "Because you're good at figuring things out. Because maybe you'll find something."

Yuki still didn't look at her. Her hair was tied into a knot on the top of her head, tucked with a red band. She looked calm, and overwhelmingly beautiful. Sometimes, Ella would look at her best friend and feel her breath catch, even after all these years.

"How are you so sure?" she asked. Her voice was softer than usual, a whisper afraid to be let out.

Ella didn't know what to make of that. Yuki was never afraid.

"What do you mean?" Ella asked, frowning.

"How are you so sure there's even something to find?" Yuki repeated. "How can you know?"

Ella blinked, feeling the loss of Ariane between them. Now all that was left was the three of them, each trying to find the way they fit, even when a part of the puzzle had gone missing. Struggling to keep themselves together.

"What's the alternative?" Ella finally asked. "That we failed her?"

Yuki shuddered, and Ella felt it as if it were her own.

"You didn't fail her," Yuki said.

"And neither did you."

Yuki finally turned to face her, and Ella recognized her best friend again. Still seeing a part of that fear, but Ella understood where it came from. Where it was going to lead them if they didn't acknowledge it.

Because Yuki was also right. Ariane *was* dead.

There was nothing they could do to change the fact. They couldn't bring her back, and they couldn't act like she wasn't gone. Leaving it at that, though, meant forgetting. It meant that Ariane had died and the had world swallowed her up, and that one day they'd wake up as if nothing had happened.

Except it had. The only way to honor Ari was to find out what truly happened.

"Maybe the book won't offer us anything," Ella said. "But maybe it will. Maybe we'll find something we didn't know."

"And maybe we won't."

"Right," Ella agreed. "But we'll have tried."

Yuki nodded, finally, her eyes distant once again.

"Come on." Ella nudged her slightly with one of the bags. "We can still get some ice cream. It cures everything."

They walked side by side, and Ella watched her friend carefully, afraid that she was looking at something made of glass that was about to break if she touched it the wrong way.

CHAPTER SEVENTEEN

YUKI

Yuki lay awake in bed for a long time.

Rory was already snoring, her soft breaths echoing through the room, her face half smashed into a pillow, her right arm out of the bed, the sheets rumpled. Nani's breath was slow and shallow, like she was about to wake at any moment. Yuki turned again, trying to get comfortable, still thinking about the conversation they had that afternoon. Ella's words echoing within her bones.

What's the alternative? That we failed her?

Yuki buried her nails within her palms until there were holes in the shape of half-crescent moons in her skin. She switched on her lamp, holding her breath, waiting to see if it woke the others. It didn't, and slowly, Yuki picked up Ari's book of fairy tales.

She opened the book to a random page. Ariane's scribblings were hard to read. They looked half in a hurry, purposefully illegible, making it almost impossible to make out the letters. She flipped back to the beginning, but there was nothing inside the front cover to mark it as belonging to somebody. The book did not even have a title page or an author.

Some of the fairy tales, as she thumbed through the thick pages, were familiar—not only because she'd watched most of the Disney movies, but because she'd seen them a dozen times, told again and again, different by a little margin in each version until they were all smoky, nebulous renditions of the original, until there was not such a thing as an original in the first place.

They came in threes. Three tasks, three bears, three daughters. Three friends. Three little princesses stuck in three towers. Sometimes there was an apple, or a shoe, or a spinning wheel, or a flower. Sometimes summer, spring, autumn, or winter. Sometimes earth, water, air, or fire. In most stories, there was a curse. The curses varied too—sometimes they danced until the soles of their feet were raw, sometimes they had to kiss frogs or turn into swans, and sometimes, in the worst of them, they slept forever. Until true love's kiss. Until there was proof that love could beat even death.

They repeated themselves from country to country, over and over again, Cinderellas turning to Vasilisas, Snow Queens into Father Frost, Beauties transforming into Rose Reds and into Briar Roses. Wicked stepmothers, evil fairies, dancing princesses. A curse and a kiss.

Rinse and repeat.

The list was long, and the book had volume, the type small like a bible, covering almost five hundred pages. Right at the beginning were the tales each child had read at least a dozen different times: "Snow White," "Cinderella," "Sleeping Beauty," "Beauty and the Beast." They greeted her with a warm familiarity. Her eyes skimmed the pages, and she found other titles she knew: "Little Red Riding Hood," "Hansel & Gretel," "The Twelve Dancing Princess," "The Goose Girl," "The Princess and the Frog." Two she'd heard from her own father, "The Mirror of Matsuyama" and "Kaguya-hime," and she remembered her father telling them with his solemn voice, after they'd had dinner together, a tradition passed down by his mother, and her mother before her, and since Yuki had no mother, it became her father's duty. There were more she'd never heard before, but seemed like they were still all same part of the story. "The Silent Princess," "Rose of Evening," "The Woman with Two Skins," "How Night Came."

Even though she didn't know them, they the same familiar themes, though a slight difference in the words used: a king's daughter who became the daughter of a chief, a horse who became a camel, a forest that became an ocean, a castle that became an island.

Ariane's scribblings lined some of them, but not all, sometimes a single word, mostly just underlining specific sentences that didn't seem to be special. Yuki turned the pages, but it was repetitive—almost half an hour later, her head was swimming, bogged down by so many tales.

Yuki had no idea why Ariane was so interested in the book at all, or why she felt the need to hide it.

Her notes bore no clues. Some of her words seemed like names. The passages she'd underlined were about dead mothers, or dead fathers, or children being abandoned. Some of the fairy tales, though, seemed off, but it was too late for Yuki to understand what was bothering her.

She didn't make it to the end of any of the stories, since she lost her patience at the fourth paragraph at most. They always ended the same anyway, in happily ever after.

She yawned, trying not to think of Ariane. Ariane, on the day she'd gotten back to school, on the day of her death.

Yuki wasn't going to find anything in the book that could shed new light on Ari's death. She already knew what had happened.

Yuki closed the book with such force on her lap that a stray piece of paper flew out.

The paper was one she recognized, a welcome note they all received on the day they returned to school, the one waiting on their pillows when they got there.

Yuki picked it up, turning the note around to find something had been written in it.

I'LL TELL YOU THE TRUTH.

BRING THE BOOK.

CHAPTER EIGHTEEN

RORY

"Rory," Yuki's voice called to her, and for a moment, she thought she was still dreaming, but then her arm was being shaken through the bedsheets "Rory, wake up. You've got to look at this."

Rory groaned in response and opened her eyes, but everything around her was still dark. For a moment, she wondered if she'd really woken up or if it was just one of the lucid dreams she used to have. She would not even be sure if she was awake or sleeping, petrified and unmoving, terrified that she wouldn't fully wake up, her heart so still it was as if she were dead.

But then the image of Yuki blinked into view above her head.

"What time is it?" Rory said, rubbing sleep out of her eyes.

"It's one in the morning."

"*One in the morning*?" Rory exclaimed so loudly that Yuki clasped a hand against her mouth. Rory blinked, seeing Nani's sleeping form with her back to them. Completely still. Yuki lowered a hand quickly, avoiding the touch, her eyes still full of warning. "You've got to be kidding me."

Rory groaned, sorely tempted to turn around and go back to sleep. For the first time that week, her back muscles seemed fine, didn't seem like they were trying to protest their way out of her body or demand a raise. Something about Yuki stopped her. Those cold, hard black eyes like a raven's.

"What is it?" Rory sat up, suddenly tense, her hair falling in waves around her.

"I was reading the book," Yuki said, her tone careful. "You were right."

"You can say that again," Rory muttered.

"I found this," Yuki said, ignoring the last comment, slipping a note into Rory's hand.

There was only Yuki's lamp to cast a light over their shadowy room. Nani's breathing was quiet, too quiet, and Rory narrowed her eyes at her back before turning her attention to the note. It wasn't in Ari's handwriting, that was for sure. Rory knew because half of her notebooks were covered in it, since Ari often took notes for her when Rory couldn't be bothered.

I'll tell you the truth. Bring the book.

"Book?" Rory asked. "What book?"

"It has to be this one," Yuki said, slamming her hand against the cover. "I found it in here. But Ari didn't take it with her, whoever she was meeting."

"How can you be so..." She turned the note around, seeing the welcoming card. Rory's had been put to the trash immediately the morning she got here. "It was someone at the school."

Yuki nodded. "Probably another student."

Rory blinked again, trying to wrap her head around it. She'd spent so much time since Ari's death not believing it had happened. Not believing it was real. That it couldn't be real, that it couldn't be an accident or suicide, and now this.

Not proof, but a clue.

"Who do you think she was meeting?" Rory asked, the card still in her hands. "And why the book? You didn't find anything in it, did you?"

Yuki shook her head. "There are Ari's notes, but I don't get why she marked them the way she did."

"Maybe it's a code."

"Ari would leave a coded message?" Yuki asked, her eyebrow raised like she knew Rory was bullshitting her.

"All right, she probably wouldn't. But it's gotta be something else, or it's just a stupid book. People don't get themselves killed over books."

I'll tell you the truth.

What truth? And how were the two things connected?

Rory picked up the book in her hands, brushing her hands against the pages. She'd barely looked at it when Nani handed it to her, putting it in her desk to hand it to Ella later so she wouldn't have to deal with it.

Now it seemed heavier, as if it held a secret truth. It knew what happened. Rory brushed the pages quickly, seeing words and words until the lines of text were blurred in her mind.

"There's nothing more," Yuki said, but Rory kept going until she got to the end.

And wedged between the pages of one of the very last tales was a page from a notebook. Rory recognized it immediately—it was one of Ariane's, her notebook pages full of doodles of hearts and smiley faces in a green gel pen across the corners.

"What's that?" Yuki frowned.

Rory unfolded the paper. "It's a list," she said, frowning. "It has...names on it?"

Yuki got closer to peer over Rory's shoulder, her cold skin brushing against Rory's warmth. It wasn't cold in the castle, or even outside yet—the autumn was just turning now, the flowers starting to wilt and vanish, but Yuki, as always, was as cold as marble, like she was permanently made to be that way.

Yuki frowned. "We're on the list." They were among the first names, in fact. Yuki, Eleanor, Aurore.

The use of her real name startled her. Ariane never used it. Never wrote it anywhere, not even in the letters she gave with her birthday gifts. Only Rory's parents ever used it.

They weren't the only ones in the list.

It kept going, a list of twenty, thirty names, mostly girls. First names only. The names sounded somewhat familiar.

"There are so many," Yuki muttered. "Why was Ariane making a list?"

"I don't know," Rory said, once again taken aback by how

much she didn't know. How much Ariane was hiding. How much she hadn't told them.

Rory hadn't pushed her away when Edric had broken up with her, but Ari still had taken herself out of their group, in a way, mourning something that the others didn't understand. Rory had felt guilty over it, but she hadn't pushed Ari on it, especially since Rory couldn't muster sympathy over Edric's loss. Rory knew she was a lesbian from the day she met another girl her age, and dating boys seemed like something incomprehensible.

At the very bottom was another of Ari's notes, but not a name this time.

I'm one of them.

"I'm one of them?" Rory read out, louder than she intended. "What the hell does that mean?"

Nani stirred in the bed, and they both stopped dead, suddenly aware of how loud their whispering was.

"We'll talk to Ella in the morning," Rory said, her eyes fixed on Nani's back. The girl who'd found the book, who'd put it in their hands.

The girl who was in Ari's place.

"Yes," Yuki agreed quietly. "We're going to find out what this means."

Rory nodded, closing the book and handing it to Yuki again. When she closed her eyes to go back to sleep, she could still see the list of names in her mind, infinite, unending, stuck on a loop.

CHAPTER NINETEEN

ELLA

It didn't matter how many times Ella had been to the library, it was always like seeing it for the first time.

All the shelves were filled with books settled in mahogany shelves, thick carpets covered the floors, with plenty of tables to study, and the occasional cushy chair waited in the wings for impromptu naps. It was Ella's favorite part of the castle, with its gigantic glass windows that filtered the light through the room. In spring, the flowers on the ivy stands that covered some of the garden walls would blossom, covering the balcony in a beautiful wall of red and yellow roses.

When Ella saw the Grimrose castle the first time, she thought it was so beautiful she couldn't hold back her tears. She felt silly standing in the hall, among the paintings, her eyes pooling with water in awe.

She found Yuki and Rory on the third floor. Mephistopheles was nowhere to be seen, likely tormenting some of the first-year students who were giggling downstairs. Rory lay with her head on the table, drool coming out of her mouth.

"You're here!" Yuki exclaimed when Ella came in.

"All right!" Rory shouted, lifting her head from the table, eyes still slightly unfocused. "I'm awake! It was only a nap!"

"You were drooling over the mahogany."

"Lies!"

Ella pointed to the tiny pool where her head had been resting.

"Fight me," Rory demanded.

Ella sighed, sitting down on the table while Rory cleaned it using the sleeve of the school uniform blazer.

"I don't have much time," Ella said. "What happened?"

Rory and Yuki exchanged looks, neither of them saying anything.

"You say it," Rory said, grinning.

"I found a note inside the book," Yuki said.

"And?" Rory asked, her voice teasing.

"It was written on the welcoming note."

"Aaand?" Rory said, eyebrows cocking incessantly.

Yuki sighed. "Rory was right. The book is important."

"Thank *you*," Rory said. "With that said, yeah, I think Ariane might have been murdered."

The word dropped like a stone, the mood changing considerably. Yuki handed her the note and Ella frowned at the words.

"It sounds like blackmail," Ella said.

Rory frowned. "That's a bit of a jump in the logic."

"If someone's promising her the truth," Ella replied, "then Ari must have talked to them before. This isn't a way to start a conversation."

"It's a way to end it," Yuki said, catching on to Ella's meaning.

Wasn't that what Ella had been trying to prove? That Ari hadn't simply left, that her death hadn't been an unhappy accident or purposefully done by her own hand?

"There's more," Rory said, taking out a sheet of paper and handing it to Ella.

Ella read it over. There were a few names she knew and others she didn't recognize.

I'm one of them.

One of who? One of what? And what did the list mean? Ella knew their names, but wasn't sure about the rest. Were they all students?

"We don't get it," Rory continued. "The list, the note. There's something here, obviously, but what was Ariane trying to say?"

Ella furrowed her brows. "Can I see the book?"

Yuki nodded, pushing it across the table.

Ella turned the pages, seeing Ariane's notes, though they were so tiny and almost illegible, purposefully hard to read. She tapped the table with her left hand, almost unconsciously, as she examined the book. The book didn't fit with the rest of Ari, didn't fit with the rest of the school.

If the book was somehow related to Ariane's death, Ella wouldn't be giving up. Not until she had figured out what exactly had happened.

Ella went back to the beginning. She knew all of these tales too well—but she liked them, or the happy versions of them. Eleanor was a sucker for a happy ending.

"No need to be judgmental," she muttered.

"What?" Rory asked across the table.

"Nothing," Ella replied. "Talking to myself. I know most of these already."

She started on "Cinderella." There wasn't a lot of Ariane's notes on it. In fact, the only parts that were underlined were simple facts of life—Cinderella worked hard. Cinderella had a cruel stepmother and two nasty stepsisters. She worked all day in the house, people wouldn't let her out. She wanted to go to the ball.

She went on. "Sleeping Beauty." Neglectful parents, gave up their daughter to be raised by someone else. Daughter did not know who she really was. Sleeps forever. "Snow White." Father died, stepmother stepped in to take care of the child, grew resentful of the child's success.

All these were meant to be something. They had to be clues. Like some kind of safe—tap in the right combination, and it gives up all its secrets. Ella had to just find the password.

"Beauty and the Beast" was completely devoid of any annotation, as well as some of the others. But when Ella got to "The Little Mermaid," she realized there was a note from Ari in the margins. Ari's own name.

A shiver ran up Ella's spine, making her whole body tremble. She wanted to close the book and pretend it never existed.

There was a strange vibration coming from it. A warning for them to not pick it up, because it would contain secrets they couldn't bear.

"Can I see the list again?" Ella asked, trying to get her voice under control, trying not to make it seem like she knew something.

She didn't know. She couldn't know.

Ella had an excellent memory for details. Sometimes, her anxiety made anything impossible to forget. And this time, she was glad for it as it worked in her favor. She went back to the other tales, picking up Ari's list.

And at last, when she got to the tale of "The Little Mermaid," Ella stopped once again.

I'm one of them.

She knew how the original tale ended.

Ella remembered it, because it was tragic. "The Little Mermaid" was told she had to kill the prince to get her legs permanently, if not, every step was like walking on broken glass, pins and needles puncturing her skin. She couldn't do it, so she turned back into sea foam.

"The Little Mermaid" drowned herself so she would spare pain to her beloved.

Ella's heart started beating faster, and she skipped back to the tales she'd known since she was a child. She was looking for happy endings. Stories where Cinderella got her prince and Sleeping Beauty woke up.

But they weren't in this book. Every single one of these tales ended in death or tragedy.

She shook her head, pushing the book aside, fingers trembling. She dropped the list she was holding.

"Ella?" Yuki asked, frowning. "Are you all right?"

Ella shook her head, ever so slightly. She didn't know if she could say more. She didn't know if she wanted to.

And yet, Ariane had known it too.

"What is it?" Rory asked, concern in her voice.

"You're going to think I'm crazy," Ella whispered.

Yuki narrowed her eyes.

"If you have a theory..."

Ella took a breath.

"Ariane made the list because the book is..." Ella couldn't finish the sentence that way, so she tried something else. "I think the book predicted her death."

PART II

A HEDGE OF THORNS

CHAPTER TWENTY

NANI

Nani overheard the whispers, but she wasn't sure what to make of them.

Yuki had woken Rory during the night, and the two of them had left, bringing the book Nani had found in Ariane's closet. Nani made sure her breathing was quiet, still, asleep so she could listen closely to the mutterings.

People don't get themselves killed over books. That's what Rory had said. Did that mean what it sounded like?

Did it mean Ariane hadn't just died? Somebody had killed her? Someone at Grimrose? What other secrets was the school hiding?

To discover what happened to her father, maybe Nani would have to start unveiling the secrets of Grimrose itself.

She didn't have to be anyone's friend for that. She only had to learn what they knew.

The girls had left in a hurry, and Nani enjoyed the time

she had to herself. She opened the window, feeling the wind shift outside, the leaves carried by the air, and once again, Nani missed home. She missed the summer, the real summer she knew in Hawai'i, where the days were sweltering, and the ocean breeze was always singing in tune with the sun.

Nani had only brought a few of her dresses. She had no clothes for winter, no idea of what it would look or feel like. She only knew the feel of the cotton against her skin, her skirt always short because of the way her body curved. She loved her clothes, even if they were old and the fit was tighter because they belonged to her mother—but every time Nani wore one of her dresses, she felt closer to her.

Nani looked out the window and called Tūtū. It rang several times before she picked up, and Nani waited to hear her grandmother's thin, croaky voice.

"Nani, mo'o, shouldn't you be in class?" was the first thing that came through. Tūtū always used the shorter word for grandchild, her mouth rounded in a circle as she stretched the vowels. "It's late."

There was an eleven-hour difference between them now, all the way across the world. Nani had never gone so far before, never been farther than the ocean that surrounded them.

"It starts in about half an hour," Nani said. She could hear the noise of evening on the other side of the speaker, the neighbor's music, the far-off sound of a motorboat near the beach. Sounds that made her think of home.

"Good, good," Tūtū replied. "We miss you here, mo'o. You're studying hard?"

We miss you here. Nani heard the words, but then she wanted to forget them. Who was *we*, but her own grandmother, who hadn't even stopped her from leaving.

Nani's mistake was thinking she belonged there too.

"Yes, Tūtū," Nani said, feeling the heartache of a world away.

"Made any new friends?" Tūtū asked, half hopeful, half trying to hide it.

"No," Nani said, though in her mind's eye, the image of the girls flashed. Rory and Yuki in the room, Ella offering for her to copy the homework. Svenja, asking for her secrets. "You know I'm only here to study."

"Making friends never hurt. You were so lonely here, with all the books, all day at home."

"Did you get anything from my father? Any news?"

Tūtū's voice went silent over the phone. "Nothing yet. But there could be something soon. You know how he is, Nani."

"He promised me. And he isn't here."

"Don't you think you're worried over nothing?" Tūtū asked, her voice gentle, careful. Trying to work her way around Nani's stubbornness, the trait she'd inherited from her father, same as his eyes and nose. "The school was a gift. You should enjoy it, not be worried about him. He's going to come home."

"His phone goes straight to voicemail, he left no address. How can you not be worried?" Nani's voice came out strangled at the end, her anger finally showing. Tūtū always made excuses for Nani's father. Tūtū, whose daughter had married a man from the continent who left the following day and spent weeks away while three women waited for him to return. Tūtū, who lost her only daughter to this fate and never made a point of fighting back.

Nani didn't want to be like Tūtū. She didn't want to be like her mother.

She refused to spend her life waiting for things that would never come.

"I have to go," Nani said to her grandmother.

"Take care. Do your homework. My heart is always with you," Tūtū said, as if Nani needed to be reminded. "Aloha wau iā ʻoe, moʻo."

"Love you too, Tūtū," she muttered to the phone, but the line was already dead.

With Reyna out of the equation, and none of the teachers cooperating, Nani didn't know where to go, except the one place where she always found her answers: the library. She had already seen it once, a place so ostentatious she'd lost her breath the first time she saw it. A place woven out of dreams that everyone in the school treated as if it was ordinary, something that made her hate them even more.

Nani wanted to start with the basics. The library itself didn't offer much on the history of Grimrose, only the history of the building and the school mission, which were deeply uninteresting, not to mention uninspired.

Someone sat down next to her at the table, and Nani turned around to tell them to go away before she realized it was Svenja. She wore her chestnut hair down this time, her eyes lined in black.

"Hey," Svenja said, crossing her legs elegantly in the chair.

"Hi."

"Haven't seen you around that much since the assembly."

"Looks like we don't have the same schedule."

Svenja gave her an amused smile, her tongue clicking. "You do know we're in six classes together, right?"

Nani blinked, opening her mouth to answer and realizing she had none to give.

"It had me wondering whether you were really clueless, or if you were just ignoring me because you were angry about something I did."

Svenja's posture was erect, her shoulders straight. Nani didn't think she could make her body do that even if she tried.

"So are you?" Svenja asked, raising a single eyebrow.

"Am I what?"

"Angry?"

"Why would I be? I barely remember even talking to you," Nani lied.

"I think you remember just fine," Svenja said in an easy tone, leaning back on the chair. "I didn't want to scare you off so fast."

"Why do you care?"

"Because I like you," Svenja said, winking. "But if I did scare you, I'm hoping it was a good scare. Butterflies in your stomach, that sort of thing."

Nani felt them now, as if summoned by Svenja's words. A sense of her knees turning wobbly as Svenja got up, moving gracefully, every step like she was moving on air.

"You really should pay more attention in class," Svenja said, one finger resting against Nani's shoulder, deliberate, pressing against her shirt. "Would be a shame if you have to get stuck here one more year. Maybe then you'd actually have to talk to people."

"You assume a lot for someone who doesn't know me."

"But I do kind of know you. You're a girl with no secrets. There isn't a lot to tell."

Svenja smirked, then took out her hand off Nani's shoulder, the last trace of her spicy perfume lingering as she walked away. Nani swallowed her anger, feeling it bob on her throat like a ball of fire, trying to ignore the lingering feeling Svenja's presence left on her.

She closed the book in front of her. Grimrose's history was going to be useless if she didn't know what was happening in the school now. Her father had gone missing before the beginning of the year, not a hundred years ago.

Just at that moment, Nani saw Ella climbing the stairs in a hurry. Letting her curiosity get the better of her, Nani followed her up into one of the smaller hidden rooms at the library. Ella closed the door behind her, and Nani put an ear against the wall. Yuki and Rory were there too, their voices rising.

They were still talking about that damned book they'd found. Nani didn't know why it was so important. She listened to the conversation as it got more tense, overhearing only a couple of words that were louder, as Ella said something too low for her to hear.

Something brushed against Nani's leg, and Nani looked down as a black shadow crossed her path. When it turned, Nani saw his yellow eyes, and the cat opened his mouth in a hiss, showing his sharp fangs. The cat slammed his paw against Nani's leg, cutting three identical lines across her calf.

Nani yelped, slamming against the door hard enough it pushed open. She fell in, right in the middle of the room—and the girls—she'd just been eavesdropping on. The cat sauntered into the doorway, hissing in a way that Nani could only describe as self-satisfied.

"Oh my God," Rory said.

"What *is* that?" Nani asked, clutching her leg in pain as the scratches started turning red with blood.

Ella walked toward the cat, picking him up easily, ignoring his hissing menace.

"This is Mephistopheles," she said simply. "He can be a bit overprotective if anyone's listening in."

The three girls turned to Nani, and Nani didn't even know how to begin explaining herself.

CHAPTER TWENTY-ONE

YUKI

The four girls sat around the library table, the book laid open with Ari's list, and the evil cat curled magnanimously in Ella's lap, purring like a happy kitten while his victim still clutched a bandage to her leg to stop the bleeding.

"Bad cat!" Ella murmured while she scratched his ears.

"What even is that monstrosity?" Nani said, glowering at him from the other side of the table, the blood still welling from the scratches.

"The scourge of God," Rory replied. "The spawn of Satan. The devil incarnate. The father of all lies, the enemy, the beast, the Evil One reborn."

"He's just a cat," Ella said protectively, putting her hands over Mephistopheles' ears.

"That's not a cat, that's a whole-ass panther," Nani deadpanned.

"You are all ridiculous. He's mostly harmless."

"Ella, he scratched the librarian's face off."

"She deserved it," Ella said, the meanest comment Yuki had ever heard her make. "Mephistopheles has never done anything wrong in his life, and I love him."

"His name is literally Satan."

"That's because the librarian hated him," Ella said. "My suggestion was Fluffington, but no one would hear of it."

The three other girls looked at the evil cat, whose unbound fury let them know that their resentment was mutual.

Finally, it was Rory who turned back to the matter at hand. "You were snooping."

Nani felt her ears grow hot. "You were the one shouting."

"I wasn't shouting," protested Rory.

"I heard you talking last night," said Nani. "I know you think your friend was murdered."

The heavy silence that followed left Yuki unnerved. It had been one thing when they'd entertained the possibility, but hearing it out loud from a virtual stranger seemed to make it real.

"Because of this book?" Nani asked, eying it open with curiosity. "Isn't it just a fairy-tale book?"

Yuki met Ella's bright eyes across the table, willing her to say something because Yuki still couldn't quite wrap her head around everything yet.

"I think the book and what happened to Ari are connected," Ella said carefully, still eyeing Yuki. "Ari definitely thought there was something...*strange* about the book, and someone claims to know the truth about it, whether that means the truth about the book itself or the list she made. If we find what it all means, maybe we can find out why Ari died."

Nani looked between the three of them. Yuki couldn't assess the girl. She'd brought only a few things, a collection of dresses and old books that she had piled on her desk that smelled like plumerias, and nothing else. Nothing to show who she really was.

"What do you mean?" Nani asked.

"Why do you want to know?" Rory asked suddenly, the challenge clear.

Nani met her gaze across the table. "I'm one of the students here."

"And so are six hundred other people. Why should we talk to you and not them?"

"Because I wasn't here when your friend died," Nani said. "Because I can help."

The offer fell heavily between them, and Yuki finally found her voice again to speak. "Help us how?"

"Someone wants the book, right?" Nani said, picking up the note. "That person is not going to stop because your friend died. They might think you have it, so they will come after you, but they don't know that *I* know. I can ask questions because I'm new."

"And how do we know we can trust you?" asked Rory, her voice still on edge. "You just got here. Why are you offering us this?"

Nani set her jaw and adjusted her round glasses, her curls falling over her shoulders. "I have my own reasons."

Yuki eyed her, evaluating her answer. Nani's answer was evasive, but she couldn't possibly be hiding a secret worse than her own.

"You have to give us more than that," Rory said, saying what they were probably all thinking.

Nani took a long time, and Ella reached out for her hand. The brush of skin made Nani jump, and Ella offered her a sympathetic smile.

"It's okay," Ella said. "You can talk to us."

It was the wrong thing to say, and Yuki knew it. Not because Ella was wrong to offer her sympathy, but because Nani didn't want to talk, she didn't want to share. Yuki knew the feeling.

"My father sent me to study here without telling me anything," Nani said, taking her hand away, her voice hard. "I want to know why. I want to know what is happening in this school as much as you do."

Yuki looked at Ella and Rory. Rory was still fuming, her arms crossed over her chest. Her dislike of Nani wasn't new. Ella, though, was doing what she always did. Reaching out.

"If you decide to help, you have to be honest with us," Yuki said, her tongue heavy as she said it, her mind calling her a hypocrite. "About everything."

Nani's brown eyes met Yuki's, and she didn't flinch. Yuki couldn't remember the last time someone had looked at her and not looked away. Sometimes, Yuki thought that the others could see the darkness that lurked there even when she tried to hide it, and that's why they always broke away first, turned away so they didn't have to acknowledge it.

Sometimes, she was afraid they would look and see right through everything.

"Tell me what you know," Nani said simply.

Ella shoved the list in Nani's direction, with Mephistopheles still in her lap, fast asleep, looking considerably less demonic, with the exception of ears that still looked very much like horns.

"Ari made notes," she said. "She made a list of names, but I don't know who most of these people are. Except for us, of course."

Nani frowned deeply, brows creasing as she looked at the list, then back at the book. Yuki wondered if she could feel it too—feel that something was off with the book. She thought back to the first time she picked it up, to the shock wave that rippled through her body. Like there was something she should remember, hid deep within the marrow of her bones, deep within her, even deeper than the darkness she felt, just out of reach.

"Besides, she put her own name to it," Ella continued.

Nani flipped through the book, carefully turning the pages. "The list could mean anything."

"It could," Ella admitted. "But the thing is... She wrote her name down in 'The Little Mermaid' story. And she drowned."

Yuki couldn't help herself. "It could be just a coincidence."

"It could," Ella agreed. "But the rest of the book is wrong."

"What do you mean, wrong?" Nani asked, looking up again through her smudged glasses.

"All of the tales end badly, not just 'The Little Mermaid,'"

Ella replied, and she looked at Yuki, as if willing her to understand.

Nani skipped to the tale and read it in a blink, her eyes skimming the page so fast that Yuki almost didn't believe she'd truly read it. "Oh."

"Exactly," Ella said.

Rory sighed, exasperated. "Look, you'll have to be clearer than this. My only fairy-tale knowledge comes from *Shrek*, the greatest fairy tale of all time. Don't they all end the same, happily whatever after?"

"The Disney versions all get happy endings," Yuki cut her off. "But that's not how all of the original tales go."

"No?"

"Little Mermaid needs to kill her prince if she wants to keep her legs," Nani said nonchalantly. "Sea Witch gives her a dagger, mermaid backs off the deal, throws herself into the sea."

Rory looked up sharply, a horrified look in her face. "What? She *dies*?"

"That's how a lot of them go," Yuki said, something turning in her stomach. "Sleeping Beauty is raped when she's asleep and only wakes up when the baby is born and sucks the splinter out of her thumb."

"Red Riding Hood is eaten by the wolf," Nani added. "Cinderella's sister's eyes get pecked out by birds, and they cut their feet off. Hansel and Gretel both get devoured by the witch. Snow White's heart gets eaten by her stepmother. They're fun."

Rory kept looking at Nani. "That's your definition of fun?"

Nani shrugged, going back to the book like she wasn't listing terrifying things that gave any child nightmares. "They are an allegory of what happens in real life. Girls get beaten up and die. It's a warning, to live chastely. That if you're a good girl, you get to live."

"Like how 'The Little Mermaid' is mostly about how the author couldn't live with the one he loved because he was gay and it was illegal," Ella said, sighing.

"Really?" Rory asked.

"I thought everyone knew."

"Well, nothing like some good old gay pining."

"Why?" Ella said, looking pointedly at Rory, leaning into the table. "Sounds familiar?"

"Shut up."

Yuki shook her head again. She felt a headache coming. Her arms rested in a weird position in the chair, like she was a puppet tied up by strings. Though that was exactly what Ella was saying, wasn't it? They were all puppets, their strings being pulled in a play they didn't know the ending to.

"These stories are allegories. We have no idea what Ari was thinking," Yuki said, massaging her temples. "We need proof something actually happened to her. And then we need to see if this book had anything to do with it."

"You wanna google secret magic fairy-tale book?" Rory asked. "That's your suggestion?"

"No, I want to know why somebody would be after it,"

Yuki said. "Where did she even find this? Who are the names on the list?"

To Yuki's surprise, it was Rory who had the answers.

"Last year's history assignment," Rory said.

Yuki blinked, unsure how an assignment had anything to do with it.

"It was an essay or something," Rory said. "I can't remember what. We'd partnered up, but, you know. She pretty much did all the research, and I signed my name. But that was what she was researching. Grimrose's history. Maybe that's how she found the book. Maybe that's how she came up with the list."

"Even then, we can't take this for truth," Yuki insisted. "Maybe this book had nothing to do with what happened to her."

"It can't be just a coincidence," Ella said quietly. "We have to know where the book came from, see if we find any more connections between the names and the stories. And find out if anyone knows more about Ari than they're saying."

"I can do that," Nani offered. "No one is going to wonder why the new girl is asking questions."

"Good," Ella nodded. "I think I can take the list of names. Maybe I'll look to see if they were other students, I can ask around..."

Yuki's eyes met hers across the table, and something wrapped around her heart. A clenching she didn't want to give way to. Something that beckoned her. Something lurking. Ella would talk to more people. She'd talk to everyone in the school, and that included...

"Is this just an excuse to talk to Frederick?" Yuki deflected. "If so, someone else could take the list."

Ella frowned, a crease in her blond eyebrows. It didn't matter that Ella was hanging out with Frederick, but Yuki couldn't help herself.

"Frederick?" Rory asked. "Who's that?"

"He's in our year," Yuki said. Rory never knew who anyone was. "Freddie. Tall. Very red-haired."

Rory frowned again, her face full of confusion. "I don't know anyone—oh wait. Ella, no! No, you can't!"

"Why?" Ella asked, genuinely surprised, forgetting Yuki's jab of a moment before.

"He's French!" Rory protested.

"You're half French," Ella pointed out.

"So I should know!" Rory exclaimed. "It's okay to be French in like, fiction, but not in real life. I know you're a sucker for redemption arcs, Ella, but this is going too far."

"I'm not—" Ella said.

"It's a fatal flaw," Rory continued. "Sometimes people are evil or French and can't be redeemed. They just have to be put down, like a mad dog. Does he shower? Please tell me he showers."

"Can we get back to the matter at hand?" Ella asked, her face blushing furiously. "And of course he showers. Good God."

"All right," Nani interrupted, clearly losing her patience. "So each of us gets a different task. I'll ask around about Ariane's death. Ella goes after the list, see if she can make anything out of it. Rory and Yuki try to find out where the book came from, and if anyone else knew about it."

"*Without* telling anyone about the book," Ella said.

"That one was for me, wasn't it?" Rory sighed. "I can be discreet."

Three pairs of eyes blinked in her direction.

"Fine!" Rory said, throwing her arms in the air. "Fine, I get it. I'm not going to screw up. I'll be completely normal."

Yuki sighed, picking up the book again, the leather beneath her hands warm, almost alive. She felt a jolt of energy, and she buried it again, trying to avoid any more sinister thoughts. She knew the truth. This was all make-believe.

CHAPTER TWENTY-TWO

ELLA

Ella knew the fairy tales that were in the book now, she'd copied their titles, trying to remember what she knew of each. Made a list in alphabetical order and tried to remember what was important for each one.

There were stories she couldn't place even though so many of the tales were the same, interwoven across cultures from all over the world to make the same pattern. It's what Nani had said. Fairy tales were warnings, things that happened to girls if they're not careful.

She was sure of where to put Ariane. It wasn't a coincidence that she'd drowned in a lake, that she always wanted to leave her family behind and go somewhere else, reach for worlds other than her own. That left the others.

She was so focused on poring over the list she barely noticed the approach of Frederick.

"What are you doing?"

Ella jumped as he sat down next to her. She folded the list and put it inside her notebook. "Nothing."

Frederick narrowed his eyes. "Doesn't seem like nothing. What are you hiding?"

"What, you think I hide things now?"

"Well, you *are* mysterious," he said. "With not letting anyone see your house, vanishing as soon as class ends. I'm starting to think Stacie was at least kind of right about you being some sort of entity, you know."

Ella pressed her lips together, trying to keep herself calm even when her heart seemed to beat faster in her chest.

"I'm just organizing some things for the winter ball," she said.

"Isn't it too early to do that? It's hardly October."

"You think a whole dress is made overnight?"

"Wait," Frederick said. "You're making the dress?"

"Shh. Don't tell anyone."

"Making. An entire dress. An actual ball gown."

Ella felt her entire being blush to the core, something she did not appreciate, her whole body heated from how closely Frederick was watching her. She couldn't hide her joy at having impressed him.

Ella sighed through her nose. "It isn't that hard," Ella said quietly, trying to play it off. When people asked how she knew how to do those things, she'd never been able to give them a real answer. Or why she loved it so much.

She'd never been a painter, never been a writer, nor a musician. Those things she could appreciate, but they were always regarded in a more elevated position. They were art, they meant something.

Ella's cooking wasn't art, nor her sewing dresses, nor her cleaning. They were things women were expected to do since forever, since they couldn't be allowed to do anything else. Now they were allowed, and they made beautiful, amazing, world-changing things, and Ella did her things quietly, because when people were out making the world more beautiful, they had to have a safe place to be themselves in. A good home to thrive in.

Ella's art was making everyone comfortable, so they could be free to go and make the best thing possible with their own special skills.

"I think you're underestimating yourself," Frederick says. "So, what are you going as? It's a masked ball, right?"

"It's a secret."

"Ah, so it is," Frederick said, suddenly serious, then leaning over conspiratorially. Ella could smell the scent of his cologne. It was a bright, almost flowery smell, and Ella wanted to be close to it forever. "So I'll have to find you, then."

He smiled at her, Ella's eyes meeting his. Her heart skipped a beat, and then she realized.

Was he...*flirting* with her?

Ella had no idea what to say, opening her mouth and then closing it again like an idiot. "I'm sorry, I..." Well, she tried, but words still eluded her, apparently.

"Speechless in my presence, eh? I have that effect on people. It's usually because I say incredibly stupid things, but I'll take what I can get."

God. He *was* flirting. With her.

She was almost seventy-five percent sure.

"I won't tell you mine either then," Frederick said. "It's only fair."

"Well, I'm a great finder," answered Ella, and then immediately regretted saying it in the most stupid way possible.

"So whoever finds each other first," Frederick replied. "Winner gets a dance."

Ella stared at him.

"Did you just... Did you just invite me to the ball?" she asked.

He threw his hands in the air, exasperated. "Was it too subtle? Should I have knelt?"

"I can't believe this," Ella said.

"Was that a no?"

"No!" Ella exclaimed, loud enough for some classmates to turn their heads.

"No? No, you aren't going with me? Or no, you are going?"

"No, I accept. Wait. Yes. That was a yes."

"I'm so confused," Frederick said.

Ella started laughing, and Freddie did too. She never noticed the way the light seemed to find every single one of his freckles. It was adorable. He was adorable.

Their laughter faded, leaving them just staring at each other. Ella felt the blush creeping back in.

Someone else walked into the classroom.

"Who died?" Micaeli asked, coming in and seeing them both dead quiet. "Oh. Shit. Sorry, Ella."

Ella took a moment to realize that Micaeli was talking about Ari, and then it hit her. For a moment there, she'd forgotten. Ari was dead, and here she was, giddy and at a loss for words because a boy had invited her to a dance.

"It's all right," Ella said automatically, guilt draining her happiness.

Micaeli was the last girl Ella wanted to speak to right then, but she was also the person who might have answers. It's not that she wasn't nice. She was. She was lively and fun and would never stop talking about period dramas.

She was also the biggest gossip in the entire school.

"You guys okay? You both look out of breath," she said uncertainly, eyes narrowing, searching for anything that might give her a good story. She flipped her short brown hair back, her pale face glowing with highlighter.

"We're fine," said Frederick, catching up fast. "I was just having a..."

"An allergy," Ella completed for him helpfully.

Micaeli did not look sympathetic at all, or that she even believed it.

"Well, we've had enough deaths for some time," Micaeli said. "You better not choke on anything else."

"He's fine," Ella promised, looking at Frederick for support.

"I am absolutely fine," he replied, which made him go even redder, almost matching the shade of his hair.

But Ella wasn't focused on him anymore. She blinked, realization dawning. "Deaths, plural." She couldn't believe she didn't think of it before. "Ari's wasn't the first."

Micaeli looked at her like she was wondering if stupidity was contagious. "Excuse me?"

"There were more people who died," Ella repeated, trying to remember.

"Ella, you surprise me. I always thought you were too nice to be interested in something so gruesome."

"I'd forgotten," Ella said, feeling her heart sink, because those were things she was supposed to remember. Grimrose was an elite boarding school. Deaths weren't supposed to happen. "Who was the last one?"

Micaeli tilted her head, as if, she, too, was trying to remember something more specific now, struggling with details.

Ella's stomach sank. What if that happened to Ari too? What if they all simply let go and forgot?

"It's at the tip of my tongue," Micaeli said. "She was a couple of years ahead of us, I think. Wore that awful red headband as if it was 2007. Like, hello."

Micaeli snapped her fingers, completely entertained by the idea of gossip, like always, and Ella was suddenly glad to be making at least some sort of progress.

"Wait, I know who's going to know. Hey, Molly!" Micaeli called, gesturing to a smaller girl on a bench at the back of the room. "Molly, what the hell was that girl's name? The dead one, whose grandmother owned that cake baking shop?"

Molly blinked, her round brown eyes narrowing as she tried to place it, oblivious to Micaeli's insensitive tone. "Flannery?"

"Yes!" Micaeli exclaimed excitedly. "Thank you! I knew you'd remember it. God, Ella, it was all over the papers. They found her and the grandmother with blood smeared all over the walls. Looked like an animal attack, but it wasn't. Might have been the boyfriend."

And then suddenly, Ella remembered all of it. The news all over Constanz. Flannery O'Brian, who lived with her grandmother, who always brought sweets from her grandma's cake shop to school. Flannery, who never took off her red headband. It couldn't have been more than two years ago.

Ella didn't need to slip out the list to know that "Little Red Riding Hood" was also on the list of tales.

If she looked, if she really looked, how many girls in the list would be dead?

And if she didn't remember this one, how many others had been cast to the shadows?

"There were more deaths," Ella said again, Ari's list running in her mind.

Micaeli tilted her head. "Of course there were. There's like, a whole list. Grimrose is a haunted castle."

They weren't just girls in the list. They weren't just students.

All of them were *dead* students.

CHAPTER TWENTY-THREE

RORY

There were few things Rory hated more than her birthday; one of those things was picture day. This year, through sheer bad luck, both were on the same date.

She got out of bed groaning. She put on her uniform, brushed her teeth, did not brush her hair, adjusted the earrings she wore in her right ear, and marched downstairs to the garden, where there was already a line of students.

Rory's head had been swimming since the talk in the library. She didn't want to believe that it could be something as wild as this. She knew it had been no accident or suicide, but this? This felt too unreal.

Still, she didn't doubt that whoever contacted Ari was also after the book and what it contained. It just showed someone else was also willing and eager to believe in this kind of wild theory. The names on the list blinked in the back of her brain, like it did not want her to forget.

When she got to the grass, the first person she saw was Ella. Ella ran to her, tackling her in a hug, making Rory stagger back.

"Happy birthday!" Ella shouted. "I brought you cupcakes."

"Thank God, I'm starving."

Ella gave her the package, and the chocolate cupcakes had pink frosting spelling her nickname in dramatic letters. Rory picked the first R and shoved it in her mouth, crumbles falling down her shirt.

"Where's Yuki?" she asked, mouth full.

"She came earlier," Ella explained. "She's way ahead in the line."

Rory looked at the long line of students ahead of her and muttered a curse. This would take hours, and then they'd have to get a picture of the whole class, and Rory never got the point. At least it wasn't raining.

"How are you feeling?"

Rory shrugged. "Seventeen is not a big deal."

"Not a big deal? You're almost an adult!" Ella said, and something sunk in the bottom of Rory's stomach, as she realized that each year that passed was one year closer to going home, to her parents, to everything that had been set out for her from the day she was born.

Thankfully, other people arrived a second later, and Rory could change the subject.

Not so thankfully, the people in line after them were none other than Penelope Barone and her roommate, Micaeli Newman. Rory didn't want to talk to Penelope. She still held a grudge against her, because she'd stolen Ari away from her, away from all of them. If Penelope hadn't existed, Rory could have spent more time with her best friend.

"Looks like we're not the last," Rory said.

"You can thank Micaeli," Penelope said, hiding a yawn behind her hand. "She tried a hundred different hairstyles."

"It's picture day," Micaeli said, as if that explained it all, confirming Rory's theory that she was most certainly a psychopath. "I love it."

Rory didn't like to listen to gossip, but she knew Micaeli had been sent to study abroad as punishment after breaking and entering about five other rich people's houses. She'd stolen shoes, clothes, bags, taken selfies in Timothée Chalamet's closet.

"Yes, my parents love seeing how happy I am in school," Rory muttered, ironically.

"I don't talk to my parents," said Penelope dryly. "Not after they sent me back here."

Rory could relate to that, unfortunately. Not that she had stopped speaking to her parents, because that would imply she talked to them in the first place. It was hard talking to people who were so overcome with the idea of her fragility that they pushed their only daughter away as not to endanger her, to the point where they'd seemed to have forgotten her very existence.

Ella blinked. "You've been here for two years."

"The point being?" Penelope said.

"Let's change subjects," Rory suggested, trying to keep the peace. She would love a fight, especially with Penelope, but she knew it wasn't going to be satisfactory. "Talk about some other daddy issues for a change, and God help me, Ella, if you mention *Star Wars*, you're gonna show up in your picture with a black eye."

Ella rolled her eyes. Rory noticed Ella was fidgeting, more than usual. Moving her fingers too quickly over the strap of her back, tucking her hair behind her ear, tugging it again.

It didn't help that Penelope seemed to be as aware of them as they were of her, a thick tension rising in the air. Micaeli seemed to be aware of it too.

Rory decided she had to do something, quick.

"Yuki said you guys talked about Ari."

Not the smartest thing to say. Penelope looked up, her shoulders tense. "Yeah, we did. Why?"

"We were just trying to figure out things, that's all," Ella said smoothly.

Micaeli blinked. "Is that why you were talking about the deaths in school?"

"Deaths?" Rory asked. "What deaths?"

"We remembered Flannery's the year before last," Micaeli said, and Penelope's eyes narrowed toward her roommate. "But you know, Ari's is different. Wait. You guys don't believe that she killed herself?"

Rory felt her hands curling into fists all on their own. "She didn't leave a note."

"Well, I wasn't even at the school when she died, if that's what you're asking," Penelope said, her voice harsh. She threw her shoulders back and stood taller. "I got here on Sunday morning, ask anyone."

"We're not accusing you," Rory replied, annoyed Penelope was taking it so personally, adjusting her own posture so that they stood level.

"It sure seems like it," Penelope said, meeting Rory's blue eyes with her own green stare.

"No need to be so tense," Micaeli said, giggling nervously. "It's only part of the grief process. Trying to figure out what's happening."

Rory didn't want her prying anything else, but she couldn't help herself. "She was going to come back."

"She took stuff with her?" Micaeli asked, ears perking up.

"Well, no," Rory replied, annoyed. "She didn't take anything."

"That just goes to show," said Penelope.

"Show what?" Rory demanded.

"Do I need to be clearer?" Penelope asked. "If she was just going for a merry walk, do you really think that she wouldn't have packed that garish little aquamarine bag, put her perfume bottle and red lipstick in it?"

"Yeah," Micaeli said. "When you put it like that."

It's what the police had said. Ariane had been found with nothing, which just corroborated the suicide theory. Rory's rage grew, desperation clawing at her throat, because Ari had started keeping secrets from her, and now Rory didn't know why she was defending her.

"You didn't know her."

"I knew her pretty well," Penelope said. "Maybe you're the one who refuses to see that your *best friend* didn't want to hang out with you anymore."

"Take it back," Rory said, and Ella put a hand automatically in front of Rory.

"No," Penelope replied. "I lost her too. I have as much claim to her as you do. You're not the only ones who get to be angry."

Rory stared daggers at Penelope, who stared back, unrelenting.

Ella seemed desperate to grasp at anything else as a subject.

"That's a beautiful ring you're wearing," Ella said, looking sideways at Rory, imploring for her not to pick another fight.

Penelope looked down at her finger, her ring catching the light. "Yeah. One of a kind. My parents had it made for me on my fifteenth."

Micaeli then launched into an overcomplicated story about a ring she had as a child, name-dropping at least three different celebrities. Rory ate another of Ella's cupcakes, trying to calm down, while Ella politely managed the conversation.

When they finally got to the pictures, Rory was glad to have it done. At least it wasn't in the ranking of her top five worst birthday experiences. At her first birthday, there had been a security breach in the castle, and they all had to flee the threat. Rory didn't remember it, of course, but stories had been told. It's why her parents had grown more paranoid over the years. It's why they decided to send her away, rather than have her close. Because she needed *protection.*

Rory spotted Yuki then, sitting on a bench in the gardens,

reading a book. She waved them over. Yuki was barefaced for her pictures too, and Rory was glad for it, though Yuki's no-makeup face was still eerily beautiful. Rory stuffed a third cupcake in her mouth.

"Real piece of work, your new friend," Rory said as way of greeting.

Yuki frowned. "Who are we talking about?"

"Penelope," Rory replied. "She's charming."

"Oh, you're one to talk. Happy birthday, by the way."

"Fuck you."

"Guys!" Ella snapped. "I found something about the list."

Rory and Yuki immediately snapped their attention back to Ella.

"There's a connection?" Rory asked.

"I think we've been looking at it wrong."

Rory cocked an eyebrow.

"I think Ari saw the same patterns I saw," Ella said. "There's more than one death. It's how Ari knew. She wasn't the first."

"The first?" Rory asked, confused. "The first what?"

"The first to die," Ella said. "Ari is not the first death to happen here at Grimrose."

Yuki's frown deepened. "You're saying?"

"Remember Flannery O'Brian? She was two years ahead of us. She was killed. Give me your phone."

Rory did as she was asked, handing it over, and Ella typed with quick fingers. Seconds later, she turned the phone to show it to them.

GIRL AND GRANDMOTHER BUTCHERED IN SMALL TOWN

Rory took the phone in her hand, Yuki peering over her shoulder.

Flannery O'Brian was a student at Grimrose. Rory remembered flashes now, her dark hair in a ponytail, always wearing a red headband. She had a boyfriend—an outsider, someone who nobody trusted. Flannery didn't care. Rory kept reading the newspaper. One day the boyfriend asked her to take him to her grandmother's house in town.

The boyfriend had slashed both Flannery and her grandmother into little pieces, their blood splattered on the walls, their flesh torn.

Rory's stomach turned.

"Flannery is Red Riding Hood. It was in the book. They're connected. And if we dig deeper, if we find the other names, we'll see that all of the names match. All of the girls are dead, exactly like the book."

"Ella, I don't think..." Yuki started.

Ella turned to Yuki. "You don't think this is a little more than a coincidence now?"

Ella's face was red as Rory looked. Yuki was calm, impassive, and for once, Rory wished she didn't have to pick a side. She was always the first to have an opinion, the first to know which side was right, but this time, she wanted no part in it.

"No," Yuki finally said. "You're jumping to conclusions

ever since you found the book, and your mind has been running wild with it."

"Oh, yes," Ella laughed, a scornful sound that made Rory flinch. "Me and my wild imagination. Maybe I've been too idle this week, and it's why I'm so full of ideas."

"That's not what I said," Yuki replied. "I'm saying that if we want to find out what happened to Ari, we can't rely on fairy-tale magic. We have to keep our minds on what is real."

"This *is* real," Ella said. "Ari died because she believed in it. Someone wanted the book."

"Then maybe the person who killed Ari believed in these stories, wanted to turn fairy tales into real-world deaths," Rory cut in, finally weighing in on the argument. "Look, I know nothing makes sense right now, but the only thing we know is that Ari's killer wants the book. Nothing more."

Ella's eyes fixed on Rory, and her lower lip trembled slightly, like she was going to cry.

"If we don't believe in Ari, we've failed her," Ella said, looking at Rory. "We can't find the truth if you're not willing to believe in it."

Rory's stomach twisted again, and Ella marched her way back to the castle.

It still didn't rank as one of her five worst birthdays ever, but it came close.

CHAPTER TWENTY-FOUR

NANI

Nani knew there was more to the world than she understood—and hadn't she been waiting for this part all her life? For a moment when things would change, when the world would turn upside down, when it would show a path where there was none, where the things that made her different could magically not matter anymore?

Nani belonged between the covers of the books she read, hugging their worlds, trying to be swallowed into their oblivion. Books rarely disappointed, even when they had terrible endings, because she could just move on from it and find another she liked. Books had been safe.

She still felt some guilt at hiding her true motives from the rest of the girls, but they wouldn't understand. They were so focused on Ariane's death. They didn't care about Nani or Nani's father. They wanted the truth, and so did Nani. They had a common goal. As soon as she uncovered Grimrose's real secret and found out where her father was, she would leave and never look back. Not even once.

When the week started, she decided she'd pay more attention in class, and as soon as she walked into first-period English, she realized Svenja was there, with an empty chair next to her. Nani squared her shoulders.

"Is this seat taken?" she asked.

Svenja narrowed her eyes, looking up from her phone.

"I don't know," she drawled, and then she looked down at Nani's bandaged leg. "Oh my God, what happened to you?"

"Got attacked by a demon," Nani answered, putting her bag on the desk and sitting down. The scratches were better now, but they still hurt like hell when she showered that morning. Her hair was still damp, curls twisting in different directions.

"Oh. Mephistopheles, I see." Svenja nodded knowingly. "Now you have completed the full ritual of being a Grimrose student."

"You couldn't have warned me about the satanic cat in the library?"

Svenja gave an expression of mock horror. "I thought you already knew everything you needed to know about school."

Nani's mouth hung open.

"I'm joking," Svenja clarified.

"Anything else in school I need to be warned about?" Nani asked.

Svenja paused, and her expression became a little more serious. She scrutinized Nani, and Nani kept her eyes fixed on her face and the strange, eerie feeling Nani always had when looking at her. Like she was taking in something not meant for her eyes, something that was too powerful for her to deal with.

"Not really," Svenja said. "I'm sure you've heard all the rumors by now. Especially since..."

"I took over the dead girl's bed?"

"I would have put it more delicately, but yes, pretty much."

Nani sighed, but she was steering the conversation where she wanted. She couldn't trust Svenja, but their connection was better than nothing. Svenja could be the person Nani was looking for, for all she knew.

"I think we got off to a rough start," Svenja said. "Mom always said Odilia had the best personality of us two."

"Odilia? Your psycho cousin?"

"Can you believe it?"

"Your mom doesn't know anything," Nani replied, frowning, and then realized she might have put her foot in her mouth. "Sorry, I didn't mean that."

"Oh, no, you meant every word," Svenja said. "I don't have the best relationship with my mother, especially since I began transitioning. She thought it was a phase, you know, and then when she realized it wasn't, she mourned. But she didn't lose a child. I'm still here."

Nani didn't know what to say to that, because she'd never gone through something similar, but she adjusted what she knew about Svenja—which was next to nothing, since she hadn't been paying close attention, absorbed in her own thoughts. Ella hadn't mentioned anything, but then again, why would she?

"Must be hard having someone mourn you as if you died when you finally feel like your life is beginning," Nani finally said, conjuring up the feeling of her own mother. She'd never even got to have a real, solid beginning with her. "My mother died when I was young."

"I didn't realize we were comparing sob stories," Svenja said, and Nani appreciated that she didn't apologize. Didn't offer condolences, like she somehow knew Nani didn't want anyone's pity. "I'll go next, let me think. It's very hard to complain when you're living in a castle. It puts things in perspective."

Nani laughed at that, and the dark moment passed like the sun coming out from behind a cloud. Like Svenja, with her smile, had brushed it all away.

"I was kind of rude at the library, provoking you," Svenja said. "I'm not going to apologize, but you don't have to face this whole castle on your own. You just moved halfway across the world, for God's sake."

"I like doing things on my own," Nani said, even though she didn't know if that was true anymore.

"I'm going to start on the right foot this time," Svenja said. "How were your first couple of weeks here?"

Nani hesitated before answering.

She *wanted* Svenja's help. She needed someone who belonged in the school. Someone who knew the castle inside out, someone who knew the students, someone who noticed things.

Svenja was going to get her where she wanted.

"It's been...complicated," Nani said. "I thought it was weird that I was put into a room where the previous girl had died and no one wants to talk about it."

"A lot of people seem to think it was suicide," Svenja told her, neutrally. "Besides, the school doesn't want us to talk about that. It gives us a bad rep."

"And what if it wasn't an accident?"

Svenja blinked, assessing Nani.

"I don't know what you're hoping to find," Svenja replied. "Grimrose is more than a hundred years old. It has as many secrets as it has sets of stairs. And Ariane's death was strange, but it wasn't unheard of."

"What do you mean?"

Svenja sighed. "There was this history assignment some of us got last year. It was for extra credit. We had to do a report on an aspect of Grimrose's past. Most people just focused on architecture or the gardens. I did mine on the students."

Just like Ariane's essay, the same thing Rory had mentioned. It was strange that both of them went for the same topic. Strange that they both had noticed the same thing when none of the others had.

"And?" Nani asked, trying not to let her curiosity show.

"There were others," Svenja said simply.

"And it doesn't make you wonder?"

"Ariane was well liked. She had friends. She had everything a girl could want here." Svenja gestured vaguely, indicating Grimrose in general. "So, sure, it was strange. But it happens—though I can tell you're not going to rest until you get to whatever the truth is, are you?"

Nani adjusted her glasses. "How do you know that?"

"You sound like the curious type," Svenja mused. "You want answers? I'll get you to the student archives."

"You're going to help me?" Nani asked.

"Why wouldn't I help you?" Svenja asked.

"No one has before."

"Well," Svenja said, unleashing one of those flashing, cunning smiles, "I'm not like everyone else."

CHAPTER TWENTY-FIVE

ELLA

Ella was walking by herself when Nani found her.

"Svenja said she'll get me into the archives," she said as a way of greeting, walking faster to catch up to Ella in the hall. "That way we can match the remaining names on the list."

Ella raised an eyebrow, surprised. She'd memorized the list and could recite it backward. Instead of counting numbers, she now recited the names, like a prayer inside her head. She hadn't found a lot about the other girls, even though she'd spent her lunch time in the library, typing every possible combination of the Grimrose, Constanz, and names that she could find. The search had yielded a couple of results, but didn't provide the details she needed.

"Do you think they're all students?" Ella asked.

"It's likely," Nani said. Ella was so used to walking behind Yuki and Rory that it was strange walking beside Nani, who was taller, broader, and who never dodged out of anyone's path. It was kind of impressive, the way everyone made sure to get out of Nani's way. Nani didn't seem to notice it. "They have to be connected to the school if Ariane found them through her report."

"Probably," Ella agreed, something digging at her. "You know students aren't supposed to enter the school archives without permission, right?"

Nani looked down at Ella through her glasses, her jaw tight. "I thought you wanted to investigate this."

"I want you to be careful," Ella said. "I don't know who we can trust. Svenja is nice, but we don't know if she was involved in this somehow."

Ella hated this. She was always willing to extend a hand to anyone who needed it. She was always willing to try, because that was what she knew she could do when others couldn't. She could be kind and trusting, but now with Ari dead, it was like the school was trying to take that from her too.

"I don't need you to look after me," said Nani irritably. "I know what I'm doing. I offered to help."

Ella looked up at Nani; her eyes were fixed ahead. Ella could see her blazing, wanting answers as much as they did. Ella just didn't understand why. She'd accept Nani's help, take her in, but it was harder when Nani shut herself off as if the walls of Grimrose itself were raised around her.

There was something Ella saw there, though: Nani's curiosity. Nani's willingness to go further. Her ability to brush things off. There was something that reminded her of Yuki in the beginning, and Ella wanted to offer a place where Nani could feel comfortable being who she was.

"What about the others?" Nani asked.

Ella blinked. "What about them?"

"Did you talk to them about the list?"

"I did," Ella replied, trying not to feel the growing lump in her throat. "They're not exactly convinced about the book."

Regardless of Yuki's dismissal and Rory's skepticism, Ella knew there was something strange going on at Grimrose, and it hadn't started with Ari's death.

"It *is* a little weird," Nani admitted when they got to their class. "You don't expect people to just believe in magic, do you?"

"Who believes in magic?" Rhiannon asked from the front row, turning as they both entered the room.

Ella stopped in the doorway as a circle of classmates turned around to look at her. Ella knew them all. Her memory was terrifyingly good for that sort of thing, which was the reason Flannery's death bothered her in the first place. Ella never forgot a face.

Nani crossed her arms defensively by her side, apparently disliking the attention. Rhiannon was one of the stars of the swimming team. Micaeli was sitting on Rhiannon's desk, facing Molly. The rest of the circle was composed of two other girls, Alethea, the president of the student council, who Rory hated, and Annmarie, a quiet girl who Ella had never really talked to.

"It was just a bet," Ella said, wilting under their stares. "About things at Grimrose."

"Oh, you believe in the haunted school now, do you?" Micaeli said, raising her eyebrows, which had been bleached to contrast with her dark hair. "I told you."

"I've seen a ghost once," Molly said.

"You didn't," snapped Micaeli. "That was Sabina in a bath towel. She's white as a sheet."

The other girls started laughing, and Nani walked past them to sit at her desk. Ella took the desk behind Rhiannon's, and the girls turned around to face her.

"Don't tell me you've seen Ari's ghost," Rhiannon said conspiratorially. "Micaeli said you were talking about her the other day. And Flannery."

Micaeli jabbed Rhiannon with her elbow, but this time, Ella didn't care.

"It was just strange," Ella said. "I mean, we've never even talked about it. And people were friends with Flannery, right?"

"I bought her grandma's cakes, like, every other week," said Molly.

"And you didn't miss her when she was gone?" Ella asked.

Molly chewed on her bottom lip. Ella could see the concern in her eyes, but it was hazy. There was that feeling of wrongness, of something unexplained. Something they all should know but kept forgetting.

"Well, kinda," said Molly finally. "But I don't know, Ian and I focused on other things. After she was gone, she was just gone."

"Bingo," said Micaeli.

Ella didn't like any of it. She turned to Nani, who was pretending to read a book, except Ella hadn't seen her turn a single page since they'd sat down.

The problem wasn't Flannery.

The problem was that Ella was afraid she was going to forget Ari.

She didn't want to forget. Ari was someone who had made her laugh, someone who never made her feel silly when she talked about the way she handled things. Ari never made her feel guilty for not being strong enough, for not fighting back enough. Ari never made her feel wrong for who she was.

First Flannery, and now Ari, and it could be any of these girls next. Girls Ella had known since she was twelve. She didn't want any of them to follow the same fate.

"We're not forgetting Ari," Rhiannon said, as if reading Ella's thoughts. She squeezed her hand. "She's not gone."

"Cheer up," said Alethea, trying to come out on the practical side. "You can believe whatever you want to believe. I do."

"Oh, here we go again," Micaeli muttered under her breath. "Alethea, no one wants to hear about your trip to the town psychic. One palm reading and now you think you're the reincarnation of Cleopatra or something."

"Excuse me," Alethea said, offended, "that's not what she said at all."

"Who are we talking about?" Annmarie asked, lost in the conversation.

"It was just a fun weekend trip," Alethea said, dismissively. "I didn't believe *all* of it."

"But you believed enough." Rhiannon laughed.

"As if you need the encouragement," said Micaeli with a sneer. "This castle may be haunted, but the true horrifying thing about it is your unstoppable ego."

"Shut up," said Alethea. "You're so mean. I'm not inviting you to the annual Halloween party."

"You wouldn't dream of leaving me out of it," said Micaeli. "You love me, you hate me. Anyway, wasn't Annmarie with you the day you went?"

The other girls all turned to Annmarie, who was doodling on her notebook. She looked up with her dark eyes. "That wasn't me. I don't really believe in all the hippie stuff."

Micaeli roared with laughter.

"Actually," Alethea said with a frown, turning to Ella. "It was Ariane. She's the one who suggested we go see Mrs. Vãduva."

"What did Ariane want with a psychic?" Micaeli snorted. "What use was it if she didn't even dump Edric's ass?"

"I don't know," Ella said, just as the teacher was coming in. "Ari kept her own secrets."

CHAPTER TWENTY-SIX

YUKI

Yuki hadn't talked to Ella since their disagreement on picture day. She'd seen Ella only in classes, and sometimes she'd seen her with Frederick in the halls, both of them laughing happily.

Yuki hated it, but she didn't let anyone else see it.

Anyone but Penelope. Somehow, Penelope knew what was bothering Yuki all the time, and there was no judgment. Of all the girls in the castle, Penelope was the one who knew what she was going through. What Ari's death meant.

And Yuki wanted to believe. Wanted to believe Ari had died because of a stupid book, and not because of her. It was so much easier that way, so much better. Nothing was supposed to change.

Except she was changed, and Yuki could feel herself breaking into a hundred pieces every time a new conversation came up, every time she was forced to try and be understanding. Ella did it so easily. Ella talked to all the other girls, saw their losses, acknowledged their pain. Yuki tried, and she kept failing, again and again.

It's not like you know what love is.

She kept pushing Ari's words further back, each time burying them deeper. They were down at her core, down to her very self, and now she couldn't get rid of them, no matter how hard she tried.

She knocked on Reyna's door on Saturday, happy for a distraction. Reyna lived in one of the farthest towers of the castle, her personal suites separate from the headmistress's office. When Reyna didn't open up right away, Yuki let herself in.

Her stepmother liked clean lines and had minimalistic tastes—almost everything in her living quarters was made of either metal or glass. There were no patterned vases, no portraits, no feeling of overcrowding, and the only decoration on the wall was a huge mirror, its metal frame imitating the likeness of branches intertwining. Yuki looked at her reflection for a moment, wondering if anyone who looked would see more than her ivory skin, the smooth black hair, the lips that were always tinted red.

The only personal object in the whole room was a single photograph that sat on a glass shelf—a picture of Reyna with Yuki when she was eight years old. They weren't touching in that picture, but Reyna was as close as she could get. She and Reyna looked nothing alike, which came up constantly in airport security, and Yuki always felt a pang of disconnection when Reyna explained that Yuki was her daughter. As if Yuki had no right to be called that, because they were so different.

"You're here," Reyna said, coming into the living room and finding Yuki looking at the picture. Her dark hair was wet from showering, and Yuki was always amazed to see how young she still looked. "Good. I think I might have burned our lunch."

The smell coming from the kitchen was divine, and Yuki had her doubts. Reyna was constantly worried about her cooking, and she always thought everything was going wrong right up until the food was served.

"You should lock your door."

"Any thief who tries to come will have climbed eighty steps first. I guarantee I'll hear them breathing from a mile away."

Yuki gave her a shadow of a smile. Reyna was not exactly careless, but she was assertive, as if the world would bend to whatever she wanted.

"How was your week?" Reyna asked, darting back into the kitchen to finish up the cooking. It was their tradition—Reyna cooked lunch on Saturdays in her apartments ever since they'd come to Grimrose, a day they spent together, sometimes reading, sometimes doing nothing at all but being in each other's company. "Classes giving you trouble?"

Yuki shook her head. "No. It's all fine."

"And the girls?"

Yuki didn't answer, leaning against the door frame. Reyna turned around to look at her, and there was light concern in her eyes.

"You had a fight?" she asked. Yuki hated that even though she did her best to hide it, it was still evident.

Yuki didn't fight with her friends, because that would mean she wasn't *perfect*.

Ella did not fight with her friends, Ella believed in what they had to say even when they didn't agree. Ella was always willing to help. And Ella kept believing, kept being kind, even when Yuki didn't deserve it.

Yuki was tired of trying to be something she wasn't.

"Small disagreement," Yuki said instead. "It's just with Ariane gone..."

Her voice trailed off, unable to finish her sentence.

"It'll take time," Reyna said, kindly, finally taking the lamb off the oven. It seemed to melt into the plate, with cooked garlic and the strong smell of wine. For a minute, Yuki wondered if she should tell her stepmother Ella's theories, just to have someone else agree with her. But she knew she wouldn't.

"It's not going to be easy," Reyna continued. "It'll always seem like something is going to be empty, no matter how hard you try."

Empty was a good word for how Yuki felt.

Empty, trying to fill herself with words and gestures that weren't her own. Empty, because no matter how hard she tried, she couldn't hold on to anything for herself.

She wondered, for a minute, what would happen if she'd let all fall away. Let them see what Yuki looked like underneath, the color of her longing, the shape of her want.

The problem was Yuki didn't even know what she longed for.

What she wanted.

What she was afraid of.

"A letter from Cambridge arrived today," Reyna said, changing the subject as they sat down to eat. "It's for the interview. They're thinking May."

Yuki's blood froze in her veins, the approaching date hitting her rather harder than she thought it would.

"That's very early," she said. She'd sent the applications, but it hadn't even been something on her mind. She had sent them because she had to. Because it was expected.

"It's never too early to think about your future, Yuki."

"But they have already sent all the letters, haven't they? Now it's time to just wait and think."

Reyna narrowed her dark eyes toward Yuki. "Are you sure you want all this? There's a lot of things that can change before this interview comes up."

Yuki shifted in her seat. "I'll be fine," she muttered.

They ate the rest of their lunch in silence, though Yuki mostly just poked at her food, having lost her appetite. She thought of what next year would look like, because no matter how hard she tried to push it away, next year was still real.

Next year Yuki would be leaving, or everyone would be leaving her.

Reyna dark brown eyes fixed on Yuki as if she could figure out what was going on in her head. Yuki doubted it. They always did a careful dance around each other.

They were close, but not too close. Yuki liked Reyna, but at the same time, she never felt like she truly knew her stepmother. Like Reyna was always guarding a part of herself, like she had never allowed herself to feel more than the spoken words that were expected of them.

Not that Reyna knew Yuki either.

"I have a surprise for you," Reyna said, smiling, and went back to the kitchen, returning with a delicious-smelling apple pie. "I promise I didn't burn this one. You okay? You look pale."

Yuki realized she was staring at the pie with uncertainty. If the fairy-tale book was connected to the girls, Yuki didn't have a doubt which was her own.

But this was ridiculous.

"Yes," Yuki managed to say, after what seemed like ages.

Reyna slid a piece of pie into her plate, the crust crumbling as the apple pieces, red as Yuki's mouth, started sliding off the plate.

"I wanted to ask you something," Yuki said, her voice small, and she tried to make it stronger. To shape it into strength. "It's about Nani. I know there are other rooms you could have put her in, so why ours? After what happened?"

Reyna pressed her lips together, uncertainty dancing behind her eyes.

"I didn't want her to feel alone," Reyna said. "Her father worked here for us, but he quit before she came here. I promised I'd take care of his daughter. I thought it would be good for her to have a home."

"Why is it so important for her to fit in, anyway?" she asked, feeling the question more about herself. "I don't see why having friends makes any difference."

Reyna hesitated, her expression almost sad. Then she smiled gently at Yuki and took a bite of pie. "You have no idea."

CHAPTER TWENTY-SEVEN

RORY

Rory tried to clean her room on Saturday, *tried* being the key word. She'd never been especially good at staying organized. But between Ari, and Ella when she came up, helping out, Rory could kind of manage the mess. With Ari gone now, and Ella distracted, there wasn't anyone to kick her into cleaning the room—and it showed.

With a sigh, she pulled back all her hair into a ponytail and started digging through the pile of shirts and uniforms, sorting things. She found Ariane's bag under the bed, but she didn't have any will to sort it out. Besides, who would she even give it to? So under the bed it stayed.

Saturday had always been the day she'd spent with Ari. She'd go for a run in the morning, and then they'd sit down by the lake, or in the gardens, or Ari would organize her perfume collection for the hundredth time while Rory listened to her talk. That's what Rory loved the most about Ari. She talked.

It's what she loved about Ella too, even though she teased her about it.

Rory never had to feel inadequate for not having something to add to the conversation. She never needed to find an answer when she was with Ari. Listening was enough, and Rory missed it.

Yuki walked into the room at that moment, doing a double take when she saw Rory straightening up.

"What's happening here?"

"Cleaning," Rory said, raising her head slightly from her position in the bed.

Yuki frowned. "Should I take you to the infirmary?"

Rory gave her the middle finger. Yuki smiled, amused, sitting down on her own bed. The sky was already darkening outside, the glass windows of their room turning rosy pink as the sun slid behind the mountains. The light streamed across both sides of her bed.

"Where's Nani?" Yuki asked.

"I don't know," Rory said. "I haven't seen her all day."

They fell into silence, and Rory noticed Yuki staring at Nani's bed with such intensity that in a minute more she might burn a hole through the mattress.

"Do you trust her?" Rory asked.

Yuki blinked, turning to Rory. When she first learned she'd be bunking with the headmistress's daughter, Rory thought her life was going to be hell at Grimrose. She thought Yuki would be demanding, but the only person Rory had seen Yuki be demanding of was herself. It was almost tiring seeing her always working late, the way she scheduled her life down to the second.

Rory and Yuki were completely different, but there was something both of them shared: the weight of what people expected from them both.

"Nani?" Yuki asked. "I don't know."

"Me either," said Rory.

More silence, but that was the thing about Rory and Yuki—unlike with Ari, Rory always felt like she was the one who had to be saying something, to coax Yuki out of her shell, and Rory never really knew how to do that type of delicate work. Even after four years, there were still things Rory didn't understand about Yuki.

"What about Ella's theory?"

Yuki set her jaw. "What about it?"

"Do you think there's a chance it's real?" Rory asked.

Yuki hesitated, folding her fingers together. They had so many conversations that way. Each girl in one bed, meters apart, not looking at each other, but not needing to, either.

"I don't know," Yuki repeated, and Rory heard the annoyance in her voice.

"You didn't have to be a bitch about it."

Yuki's breath sharpened. "I know, okay. I'm sorry. It's just... What if going down that road ends badly? What if we don't find any of the answers? Do you even think about that, Rory?"

"Do you?"

"All the time."

Rory straightened up to lean on her elbows, to really see Yuki, who was still staring at Nani's bed. Rory almost felt bad for hating Nani at first. Even with a new duvet and new books, the place was still Ari's, and Nani was never going to be able to change that.

Yuki wrung her fingers in her lap, her head shaking slightly. "I don't want you and Ella to be disappointed."

"You don't have to protect us."

"I do, though," Yuki said, turning her eyes to Rory, and there was a fierce determination, a burning and hurt that Rory almost never saw coming from Yuki's cold eyes. "I *do*."

And in that moment, Rory realized what she'd been truly afraid of.

That now that Ari was gone, she wasn't going to have a place among them. Yuki and Ella were who they were, and they'd been there first, and Rory was the intruder. Rory was the sore thumb sticking out, and any day now, they'd realize that, and Rory would be alone, friendless.

But no. Yuki was a pillar, and she wasn't going anywhere. Like the old stones of Grimrose, Yuki was unmoving, and Rory didn't have to worry about her ever leaving.

"We're big girls," Rory finally said. "We'll handle it."

"And if the answers hurt you?"

"Well," Rory said. "You'll be there right with us."

"Yes," Yuki replied. "I'll be there."

CHAPTER TWENTY-EIGHT

ELLA

Ella was used to walking in Constanz alone, but she wasn't used to knocking on strangers' doors. She felt a chill in the air as she stood in front of an overgrown garden, trees starting to get yellow leaves as the winter approached faster and faster. Ella couldn't wait till spring came around, and not only because it would bring her birthday.

She knocked on the door again, bracing herself, shrinking inside her old *Star Wars* dress. It was too short now. Her father had given it to her on her twelfth birthday, only months before he died, and now it was one of the few things she had left of their shared love for the space saga. She counted the Vader masks on the skirt, getting to fourteen before the door finally opened to reveal a woman.

She had natural gray streaks in her black hair and crow's-feet around her dark eyes. She looked, above all else, tired, and eyed Ella with suspicion.

"What do you want?"

"Are you Mrs. Vãduva?" Ella asked.

The woman continued to glare at her. "That depends on who's asking."

"I'm Ella Ashworth. I study at Grimrose."

At the sound of *Grimrose,* Mrs. Vãduva's eyes widened, and she moved to close the door—but Ella was fast and slid her foot right in the opening.

"I promise it won't take long," Ella said, and then, her voice cracking, "I need your help."

The woman looked her up and down, taking in the state of her worn dress, her combed hair, her face, covered in a thick slab of foundation and concealer. The only new thing about her was her pair of shoes—beautiful pink ballet flats, which Rory had given her.

Mrs. Vãduva opened the door a bit, ushering her in.

It had been easy for Ella to find her. The town whispered words like *witch,* but towns were never particularly kind about old and lonely women. She was, however, a psychic, a word that meant witch, but in a politer sort of way.

"That's not what it means," Ella muttered.

Mrs. Vãduva looked over her shoulder. "Did you say something?"

"No," Ella answered, looking up at the ceiling while she walked into the living room.

The house was cleaner than outside, orderly in a rustic sense. There were wicker chairs, a coffee table in the middle of the room with a softly flickering candle, and bright light filtered in through the old window.

"Would you like tea?" Mrs. Vãduva asked.

"No, I don't want to bother you," Ella replied. She scanned the rest of the living room and found a picture, someone she recognized from school from years ago, the year she'd arrived.

"It's no bother." Mrs. Vãduva went to the kitchen, bringing back two cups of steaming tea. The smell was spicy, like cinnamon and pepper mixed together, and Ella inhaled it gladly. In the distance, Grimrose's imposing clock struck three. It echoed all through the town.

"Sit down," Mrs. Vãduva said, gesturing to the couch, and Ella obeyed, her knees pressed together, her nervousness growing.

She didn't think she'd have the courage to come here by herself, but now that she did, she didn't know what to say.

"I'm here to talk about a friend." Ella took a gulp of tea for comfort. "She had dyed red hair, really big green eyes. You would remember her, I think."

Mrs. Vãduva frowned, sitting herself in a wicker chair in the darkest corner of the room. "Get to your point, girl."

"I know a lot of girls come here," Ella said.

"Girls are young and like to entertain themselves trying to know their future. Is it not what you're here for?"

Ella shook her head. "No. I came here to talk about something else. I didn't come here to ask you for a reading, I came here to ask what you know about what's happening at Grimrose."

Mrs. Vãduva's expression soured suddenly, her eyes darting to the door, to the portrait on the mantelpiece, then back to Ella.

"I don't know what you have heard," Mrs. Vãduva said, "but there are things best left alone."

Ella didn't falter, knowing she'd already come this far. "You're afraid."

"Death pursues all the girls from the Académie," Mrs. Vãduva said darkly. "I will not take part in it."

Ella didn't budge, continuing to gaze at Mrs. Vãduva. She put her tea on the table.

"She came here," Ella said. "Ariane, my friend. I think she wanted to get answers about what she'd found."

"I don't have the answers you're looking for."

"But you know something about it," Ella insisted, her voice turning sharp. "Your daughter was a victim too, wasn't she?"

There was a hanging pause in the air as Mrs. Vãduva looked at the picture. Ella followed her gaze. The one other thing the town talked about other than the witch? The witch's daughter, the one who'd died.

"That was her, wasn't it?" Ella asked, pressing forward.

"Yes," Mrs. Vãduva said. "My Camelia. She was a beautiful, bright girl, and that school took everything from her."

"What happened?"

"She hung herself," Mrs. Vãduva said simply, barely masking the pain in her voice. "I was the one who found her. I cursed myself for leaving our home to come here. It was my husband's idea that he work in the school gardens, and that Camelia could study there."

Her lips trembled, and then she looked away from the picture, back at Ella.

"If you know what's good for you, you take your friend and you leave."

"I can't leave," Ella said. "Ariane is dead."

Mrs. Vãduva's shock was clear on her face. She didn't know. Grimrose had hid it well enough.

"Please," Ella said, her voice failing. "I don't know what's going on. I thought you might have answers. She left a list, but so many of the girls on it, they're dead. Your daughter's name was on it. I need to... I need to talk to Ari."

Ella hadn't let herself entertain the thought for long. They were things meant for silly girls who could not accept the truth. Ella didn't believe in ghosts, and at the same time, she desperately wanted to. She wanted to ask Ari what happened, what she'd learned.

"You don't know what you're asking for," Mrs. Vãduva said, not unkindly. "You do not even believe in such things."

"I believe in *her*," Ella answered. "I believe that she found something important and that she couldn't tell us. And I believe that we have to finish what she started."

Mrs. Vãduva wet her lips. Ella didn't know if she could push any farther. She only wanted answers, she wanted closure. She needed something meaningful.

"Your friend did come here," the older woman finally said. "It was a few months ago. She had a book with her, and I could not tell her what it meant. I could feel some sort of power in it, however. She said the girls were in the book. She wanted answers I couldn't give her. I'm not a witch. I only have my faith and the belief my ancestors gave me. I could not help her, because I'm not a part of that story."

Ella clung to every word, understanding. "But I am."

"You might be," Mrs. Vãduva agreed. "The answers lie at Grimrose, not in the outside world. And perhaps in the book."

"Do you think I can talk to her?" Ella asked, her voice trembling. She hated how she sounded—half hopeful, half broken, trying to reach for answers that were beyond this world.

But if she believed in Ariane, the answers could only be found there. On another side of the story, on a place where the normal rules didn't apply. A place where magic was very, very real.

Mrs. Vãduva got up, searching her drawers for something. She turned around, carrying four different crystals of varying colors and four thick white candles.

"Here," she said, handing them to Ella. "You'll need to come back with friends. Four is the ideal number."

"I thought that magic things were always in threes. Three brothers, three rings, that sort of thing."

Mrs. Vãduva let out a small smile. "The tales will have you believe that. Three is a good number, but there are four cardinal points. Four elements, four seasons, four ways to guide you home. On the next full moon, get your friends in a circle and light the candles. Try to find a way to make sense of it."

Ella took the crystals in her hand, heavier than she thought.

"That's it?" she asked. "No more instructions?"

"This type of thing is not like a recipe, girl," Mrs. Vãduva said. "It's based on feeling. It's based on soul. Only your soul knows the path it wants to follow."

Ella put all the items in her bag, trying to remind herself why she was doing this. It was honoring Ariane. It was believing she had died for something, and not just about finding out the culprit. Ella cared about the truth, but more than that—she believed that to honor something meant carrying on after their death, whatever their work was.

Ariane had died trying to find the truth.

If Ella wanted to honor that, she'd have to find the truth herself.

"Thank you," Ella said sincerely. She moved toward the door, opening it and letting the light in. "Do you really believe I can change anything?"

"Who knows?" Mrs. Vãduva said, still sitting in her chair. "The important thing is that you are trying. Find your happy ending. For my Camelia too."

Ella smiled. "I will."

CHAPTER TWENTY-NINE

RORY

When Rory woke up on Monday, it struck her that it had been more than a month since Ari died. She felt a pang of guilt, knowing that her life was still going on. And that she didn't know what to believe anymore.

She hadn't slept well these last weeks, her body rebelling, trying to push the boundaries of where it could go. She ached all over and was certain she wouldn't be able to get up. She used the bed as a crutch, breathing hard, the pain shooting up until she saw nothing but the stars in the dark.

She got up all the same.

She wasn't about to let her body beat her into submission. She wasn't going down without a fight.

The pain lingered all day, but even so, she was excited to go train, to make her body work for her again. Fencing practice was always on Monday and Wednesday afternoons, but the sessions against Pippa only happened on Friday. She wished it was Friday; she could use the distraction. Her friends had still seemed on edge during lunch. She'd shared a look with Yuki over the table, but they'd stayed on the safe topics.

She'd done what she could. Done what she knew. She'd even found Ari's old essay on the school, but it had just been a load of useless information about the castle grounds—nothing on the students. Whatever she'd found in the book, she hadn't put it into the report.

When Rory finally got to the gym, the team was already there with their instructor. Instead of their swords out, though, the instructor was talking to them in a huddle.

Rory met Pippa's eyes on the other side of the room. She looked like a vision all in white, a knight with her erect posture and dark skin, her hair braided to keep away from her face. Rory approached her and asked, "What's going on?"

"Have you not been paying attention for the last month?" Pippa asked, one eyebrow raised. "It's practice for the tournament."

Rory had completely forgotten about the tournament, or anything that didn't have to do with Ari's death.

"All right, everyone," the instructor said, clapping. "Break off into pairs."

The fencing team wasn't particularly big, but it contained all of twelve people who Rory could often boss around, something she personally enjoyed. Rory adjusted her uniform, the tight white pants, the gear that kept her in place.

Once Rory was on the floor, everything else faded away. Who she was, her responsibilities, everything that had gotten her here. She was what she'd honed herself to be—fast, brutal, deadly.

The fencing team spread out in the room, which had wide glass windows that looked into the mountains. Light filtered on the black and white tiled floor that made it almost seem like a ballroom.

Rory slipped on her mask and tightened her hand around her saber, the Belgian grip familiar and comforting. Pippa preferred the épée, but they all trained in the different modalities, especially Pippa and Rory, who'd been training seriously ever since they'd arrived at Grimrose. Rory cracked her neck, feeling the weight of the protective jacket over her.

And then they began. Rory forgot all things beyond the duel, the here and now. Ari's death, the book, her friends, everything took a step back as the world blurred into her hand holding a saber, the white dance of the crossing blades, feints and parries and lunges and flicks. Everything dimmed into the world was all black and white, and she saw it all through the holes in her mask.

She fought each of her classmates, beat them with her saber swinging left and right, her instructor shouting corrections, making her try another feint, another counterattack, a new footing she needed to work on. By the end, when everyone else was tired from the practice, Rory was still going, until even she couldn't stand a moment more.

She took off the mask, putting the saber and the rest of the equipment back in place. In the locker room, Pippa and Rory undressed with their backs turned to each other. Rory would catch a glimpse in the mirror sometimes, Pippa's bared shoulder, the wing of her back, flashes of naked skin that Rory tried to wipe from her mind as she focused on changing.

The notice for the European inter-school tournament was posted on the wall, and Pippa stared at it for a moment as they both left the locker room.

"Are you going to sign up?"

"For the tournament? No," Rory said. "You know I don't do the whole traveling-around thing."

"Rory, you're one of the best on our team."

"What, you don't want to say best?"

"You could be if you competed."

"Tournaments are a waste of time. You can have a couple of my medals, as a treat."

This time, Pippa didn't take the joke. She pushed Rory against the wall, holding her against the marble pillar of the empty ballroom, one arm under her chin, another gripping her arm. Rory felt the touch like a burn, and she looked into Pippa's eyes, and it was like her whole body was scalded with hot water, heating up her muscles and bones. Rory couldn't look away, her heart beating fast, anger rising, but also something else that she tried to bury.

"Let go of me," Rory said, her voice low.

Pippa didn't. "I don't win because you're not there. I win because I *deserve* to. Because I work hard. Because I'm not wasting my time while I'm here, because I *want* to do something with this. Do you?"

Rory felt a blush creeping to her cheeks. She noticed

Pippa's brown lashes, a tint lighter than those of her eyebrows, and lighter still than the brown of her hair. Her smooth skin did not have a single flaw up close, while Rory was still struggling with pimples that insisted on showing up on her chin. Pippa, every muscle a trained weapon, was everything polished and powerful, and Rory wanted to melt in her hands.

Finally, Pippa let her go, and Rory dropped down to her feet, trying to suck in air without making ridiculous gasping sounds as she massaged the back of her neck.

"You can't keep hiding, Rory," Pippa finally said. "One day, you'll have to fight for something."

Pippa turned around, and Rory was left there, staring at her braid as it disappeared beyond the door.

CHAPTER THIRTY

NANI

Nani had stayed in the library for most of the weekend. Svenja told her they'd go to the archives on Monday, so Nani spent the Saturday and Sunday reading and trying to sort out what she could from the book, holding it between her hands. Tūtū had taught her to hold books like this, so Nani stopped trying to munch on her cuticles with only one hand, keeping her hands busy so she wouldn't rip her nails open. More than one of her books was tainted with blood, the red edges on the page from when Nani forgot herself and started biting her fingers again.

Instead of more questions about Ari's death or where her father was, Nani sorted out the deaths in the book. She read the fairy tales, most of which she knew by heart. They weren't her favorites. She'd liked the stranger ones from the start, "One-Eye, Two-Eyes, and Three-Eyes," "The Devil with the Three Golden Hairs," and her favorite of them all, "Blue

Beard." Nani would never forget reading it for the first time, when the princess had seen the dead wives, knowing she would be next, determined to survive it, no matter the cost.

The deaths waiting at the end of each story were gruesome. Nani didn't like the happy endings of the usual fairy tales. They failed to acknowledge what Nani thought was most important in the story: the path, the darkness that they had been through. Happily ever after never covered what came after that, how half the heroes could be scarred for the rest of their lives. It was a falsehood sold to keep little girls dreaming about something that didn't exist.

The book was still strange, though. None of them had any promise of good to balance it out, and it was eerie how hopeless all of it was.

She didn't believe in Ella's theory that the book somehow predicted death, but Nani couldn't help but notice that the coincidence of it all was too close for comfort.

Nani didn't believe in magic, even though she admitted there were weird things happening at the Académie. Tūtū would say to keep her mind open, just like her eyes, but Tūtū was an old grandmother who loved wives' tales too much for her own good. Nani had grown up hearing stories of the islands, of volcanoes and battles, fish gods and shark men, but magic didn't change their reality. It didn't change who they were, the color of their skin, the language that had been taken from her ancestors and through which Nani stammered through, forbidden to be passed on for so long. A barrier to all her people.

Nani suddenly wanted to slam the book and throw it at the other side of the room. Maybe the book didn't offer real answers. The tales remained the same, keeping their secrets, and Nani was tired of things with secrets, including herself.

Or maybe that was the real magic. The ability to make everyone who touched it very, very pissed off.

She shut the book hard, startling someone else at the table. She hadn't noticed the other student come in, a girl who she'd seen before but whose name she could not recall. The same girl who'd been talking about the deaths so casually in class the other day, while Nani was pretending not to pay attention.

The girl frowned at the book. "What book is that?"

Nani cursed herself inwardly for her carelessness.

"It's mine," Nani said. "I brought it from home."

The girl narrowed her eyes a little. "I've seen it before."

Nani remembered her name now. Michaella or Mickaylee or something equally full of unnecessary letters. She resisted the urge to respond to her in a rude manner. Plus, if she'd seen the book before, maybe she knew something.

Nani let her see the cover, and the girl pouted.

"Oh, never mind," she said. "I thought they were the same."

"It's just a book," Nani said, gesturing to the rest of the library. "Plenty of those around."

The girl frowned, but decided to ignore Nani.

Nani put the book back in her bag, eying the other girl carefully, wondering if she knew more than she was saying.

On Monday, Svenja showed the way to the archive room.

It wasn't exactly what Nani had envisioned, but she was glad to have Ella following along after lunch.

"You sure it's safe during a weekday?" Ella asked as Svenja climbed a set of stairs, voicing the same thoughts Nani had.

"The teachers are too busy in class," Svenja replied without looking back. "Having second thoughts already?"

Ella didn't answer, giving only a huff as a response. Nani walked right behind Svenja, keeping an eye on the elegant curve of her neck, the way her shoulders were perfectly balanced, the way there was a dimple right behind the right side of her neck. Svenja turned around as if she sensed Nani staring. Their eyes met, and Nani looked down quickly, pretending an intense interest in the floor. She didn't know if she could trust Svenja. Correction. She definitely couldn't trust her. Like all the other students in the school, she might have had something to do with Ariane's death. No one was above suspicion.

They slipped into the underbelly of the castle, evading a cross and unhappy Mrs. Blumstein coming out of the teachers' quarters. Svenja did it with such ease that Nani couldn't help but wonder how many times she'd done it before. When they came to a door, Svenja stopped and turned to them both.

"This is it," she said. "Now would be the ideal time for you to tell me what you're looking for."

"We have to get into the room first," Nani said.

Svenja rolled her eyes and turned the doorknob. The door opened with a creak.

"It's open?" Nani gasped.

"This is the archive room," Svenja said in a tone of disdain. "It's not a top-security prison."

Nani hesitated in the doorway. "But—"

"It's forbidden for the students, sure, but it's more a question of privacy than anything else," Svenja said. "No bodies in here, promise."

Svenja went first. Nani looked at Ella, who hesitated.

"You don't have to come," said Nani, "if you don't want to break the rules."

Ella curled her hands into fists. "This is more important than rules."

She marched in before Nani could stop her, leaving Nani to follow.

The archive room was surprisingly normal and dull. Nani thought she was going to get a rush of adrenaline, a feeling that she'd find answers, and what she found instead were dozens of cabinets of paper files, all lined up in neat rows, relatively clear lighting.

It was the most boring sight Nani had seen in Grimrose yet.

"Student files are at the back," Svenja pointed, making her way there.

Svenja walked past rows of cabinets, finally arriving at the last one. She pointed to a single archival tower.

"Those are for this year," she said. "They get moved if you stay here to the next year, left alone if you either graduate or leave the school, so you just have to work your way back."

"I'm going to start at the back," Ella said, pointing to the other side of the room. "Might be hard since they'll be under surnames, and we don't have those."

Svenja raised an eyebrow at Nani, but Nani said nothing as Ella disappeared from view.

Nani tested one of the drawers, and it opened with ease, revealing dozens of paper files with students' names on it.

"How do you know all this?" Nani asked.

"I came here before," Svenja said, and then paused, hesitating, something Nani knew she didn't do. "My file had my deadname on it."

"Oh," Nani said. "I hope you tore it to pieces."

Svenja grinned. "Couldn't burn down the whole building, so that had to do. I know they keep it for organizing purposes, but it's not my name. Has never been my name. It's not me at all they were keeping down here."

Maybe it was a good thing she wasn't down here, when all they expected was to find a list of dead girls.

"How did you choose your name?" Nani asked instead, opening the cabinet file, trying to search the names to see if any matched Ariane's list.

"It felt right," Svenja said. "It means swan. I thought it would be like the story, you know. The ugly duckling who in the end learns who they were all along."

A chill climbed over Nani's spine. An ugly duckling? No. Impossible.

Except impossible wasn't a word in their vocabulary anymore.

"Yeah," Nani croaked, not trusting her voice. "It suits you."

"It *is* my name, after all." Svenja smiled.

Nani opened more cabinets, thumbing through the files, discarding them as soon as she saw they didn't hold the names she wanted. There were deaths, but all of them seemed normal. No mysterious accidents anyway. She found Flannery's file, the one Ella had mentioned, but the rest of the names didn't match.

"You sure I can't help?" Svenja said. "Don't get me wrong, the view is fine from here, but I think I'd be more useful if you filled me in so I didn't have to just stand around."

Nani looked up, just as Svenja stepped close. She pushed back one of Nani's curls behind her ear. The touch froze Nani in place, Svenja's long fingernails brushing against the sensitive skin of her neck. Nani forgot she was supposed to answer. She stammered, clearing her throat.

"Like I said, we're just poking around about deaths in school," she mumbled.

"Oh, so you're investigating Ariane," Svenja said. "Don't you know that it's dangerous to do that sort of thing?"

Nani tensed at that. "That sounds like a threat."

Svenja laughed. "What, you think I had something to do with it?"

"I don't know," Nani said. "I just got here, remember?"

"And yet you're already involved," Svenja mused. "For a girl with no secrets, you're very mysterious."

Nani ignored her, going back to the files. All they needed was to confirm the names on the list, make sure that the connection to Ariane's list was real, and that they were indeed connected to the book.

Nani kept going back, and she found one. Camelia Vãduva.

And then she found more.

Bianca and Siofra. Kiara and Alice. Lilia and Neva. Diane and Irena. Liesel and Willow.

Drowned, lost in the woods, attacked by a rogue bear. Fallen from one of the towers, food poisoning. Freak accidents that weren't supposed to happen more than once in a lifetime, but that lined up eerily with the stories, over and over again, dating back years. Years of history of the school, deaths that had been forgotten.

Ella appeared around the corner, her face pale and concerned as she clutched the list in her hands.

"You found some too?" Nani asked.

Ella nodded. "From the very beginning."

Svenja looked between both of the girls, her expression curious. "So are either of you going to tell me what this is really about?"

Ella turned her hazel eyes to Svenja. "Trust me. I think it's better if you don't know anything at all."

CHAPTER THIRTY-ONE

ELLA

Ella had kept the crystals and candles hidden in the loose board underneath the bed in her attic.

The attic wasn't big, but it was the only thing in the house that belonged to her and no one else. The few things she'd kept after they moved—some figurines her father had collected, some dresses and coats for winter, all mismatched, old, and repaired more times than she could count. The sewing machine that had belonged to her mother, which she'd smuggled among kitchen things so Sharon wouldn't notice she'd kept it.

Underneath the bed, hidden deep under the floor, were Ella's more precious things. The money she kept hidden, the small amount she'd managed to get when she was paid for sewing something, for baking cookies in the kitchen on a weekend when nobody was there. She also hid her mother's button collection, with big white ones and small green ones in the shape of strawberries or bearing coats of arms, all different from one another. There were gifts she'd received from Rory, Ari, and

Yuki over the years, all kept far away from reach, because that was the only way Ella was allowed to keep anything in her life: tucked away where not even she could see them.

On Monday, Ella spent all day counting the chairs around her, counting the steps she took up and down to go to different rooms, counting the windows on the opposite side of the castle. Counting kept her calm, because even though there were numbers that she didn't like, which, in her anxiety, she'd stumble over, numbers were still infinite. They stretched forever, and if she just kept counting, everything would be okay.

And then Nani asked if she wanted to go to the archives, and Ella couldn't say no. Couldn't say no to confirming the thing she already knew was true.

The infinite list of dead girls kept running through her mind as she and Nani made their way back to the library to meet Yuki and Rory. Staying at school longer would make her late, and she feared what would happen at home if that happened, but this was more important.

Nani didn't wait for them to be settled around the usual library table they'd claimed before she burst.

"All the girls on the list are dead," Nani announced, throwing her notebook on the table toward Yuki and Rory. "We've just came back from the archives."

Ella darted her eyes in the direction of Yuki. Ella hadn't really spoken to her since their last argument, except to exchange notes in class. It felt strange, fighting with Yuki.

"And?" Yuki said, her voice ice-cold as she looked up.

"There are too many coincidences," Nani said.

"Several girls have drowned," Yuki stated. "This is not new, or are you saying there's more than one story where that happens? We can make anything fit into the theory if we want to."

"So you're saying you think these deaths are only coincidences," Ella said.

"I'm saying over the course of a hundred years accidents will happen," Yuki replied. "You're saying that what happened to Ari is some conspiracy theory that the book predicts? That the students' deaths connect them to some magical fairy tale?"

Ella knew it seemed like she was trying hard to believe in something, in what Ari had left behind, but that didn't mean her theories were wrong. Ella looked at Nani for help, but Nani didn't offer any.

"I know how hard it is to believe this," said Ella. "Even if there was a killer using it as inspiration, this goes back ages ago. And no one even seems to remember the deaths."

"It's just..." Yuki stopped. "We need to look at this the other way around. We find proof, and *then* we form theories. Maybe the deaths are connected, but what does it mean?"

Ella took a deep breath. It was a good question. What *did* it mean? When she'd talked to Mrs. Vãduva, she'd asked the same thing.

As far as Ella was concerned, it meant something was wrong with Grimrose.

She just had to convince everyone of that.

"Did you find anything?" she asked finally, trying to approach the subject another way. "Did you try to figure out where Ari could have found the book?"

"No, but that won't get us anywhere anyway," Yuki answered. "Ariane was our closest friend, and now we know how she liked to keep secrets."

"You must have seen her with the book at one point," Nani said logically. "Just looking at the amount of things she's written down, she must have been working on this for a while."

Which meant, she would have worked on it while Edric and Ari were still dating. She remembered how heartbroken Ari was when it came to an end, how much she'd cried even though Ella couldn't really understand what it was with Edric in the first place, what they liked about each other, how it worked. Ella had rarely felt a romantic pull toward anybody, but when she did, it was a person who she could like first and foremost as a friend, someone she could talk to, someone she admired, no gender specified. Romance and attraction were wildly diverse experiences for everybody, and it was hard enough figuring them out without added judgment, so she never said anything to Ari.

"She was out of the room a lot," Rory said, musing out loud. "Like, you wouldn't see her for hours. She was always searching for all the unexplored places of the castle. Ari had a checklist of rooms and secret passageways her mother knew back in the day."

Nani blinked. "Passageways? And you know those?"

"Ari never showed them to anybody," Yuki said, and Ella thought she detected a hint of bitterness in Yuki's tone, but maybe she was only imagining it. "If you figure out one of Grimrose's secret passageways, it's yours to keep, and you have to let people discover for themselves."

"So is that like...a rule?" Nani asked, her voice uncertain. "I'm sorry, I'm really trying to understand. Is this some rich people thing?"

"How should I know?" Yuki snapped.

"You all go here," Nani pointed out. "If anything, you're the ones who know about the world of a school of rich and privileged kids where everyone lives in a castle."

"You don't know anything about us." Yuki turned to Nani. "I study here because my stepmother is the headmistress. Ella is here because she got a scholarship."

Ella blushed at the mention, but Nani paid no mind, turning to Rory. "And you?"

Rory shrugged, putting her feet up on the table while she leaned against her chair with a grin. "Oh, I'm absolutely the rich and privileged kid."

Nani sighed, one that sounded half angry, half tired. "I can't help you if you can't help yourselves."

"Well, there's another way," Ella said.

Every head whipped toward her, and Ella felt herself almost shrinking in her seat. "I talked to Mrs. Vãduva," Ella said. "She's the psychic in Constanz. Ari had been to see her too. Her daughter is on the list."

Yuki blinked, those big raven eyes fixed on her. For the first time, Ella saw something she did not recognize there—something that made Yuki look different, strange, like Ella didn't know her at all. "You told a psychic what was happening here?" Yuki asked. "What were you thinking, Ella?"

"She lost a daughter," Ella said. "And Ari went there first."

"And?" Rory said, her eyebrows rising. "What did she say?"

"She says that whatever is happening, it has to do with Grimrose, that much she's sure, and it has to do with the book. Exactly like the list of deaths proves."

"That much we figured out," Nani muttered, discontent.

"This is a lot bigger than just Ari," Ella insisted. "It's not just about one or two girls that died. It's about all of us."

"We aren't dead," Rory said.

"But Ari still put us in the list," Ella snapped back, surprised at her own insistence. "She figured out something."

Ella's last words fell into the silence, and she took a deep breath, feeling her throat lump again. It was like shouting at a wall.

"I told her I wanted to talk to Ari," Ella finally said. "She gave me things. So we can do a ritual in the light of the next full moon."

The silence around Ella was deafening.

And then Yuki started laughing. "You've got to be kidding me," Yuki said, disdain dripping from her voice. Her eyes were sharp, angry, unrecognizable. "You want us to talk to Ari's ghost."

Ella blushed. "Well, not exactly, but..."

Yuki got up. "This has gone too far," she said, and her words were cold. "I know we're grieving. I know we miss her, but we can't keep doing this. A ritual, Ella? Really?"

Ella felt her cheeks burn, half in shame, but half in indignation too. "We have to try! We can't fail her."

"Wake up!" Yuki shouted, gesturing wildly to nothing. "We already have! She's dead!"

The words echoed around the silence of the library, reverberating through the edges and the spaces between the books, and all that Ella could think was: *We did, we failed her, she's right, there's nothing we can do now.*

"This has to stop," she said. "No more fairy-tale talk. We grieve Ariane like normal people. And even if someone did come after her, we're not going to be the ones who find out who. We are done with this."

She picked up her bag, swung it over her shoulder, and brushed past Ella, who still had words stuck in her throat.

"I expected better from you," Ella said quietly.

Yuki heard her. She stopped, turned, and looked directly at her. "Then you expected wrong."

Ella was at the bus stop, already late.

She kept looking at her watch to stop the tears from coming again. She didn't know how to help. And helping was the only thing she'd ever been good at.

The inside of her cheek was raw from biting it; Ella could taste blood. She deserved this. Deserved every piece of it. It's what she got for thinking she could find a solution when no one else could. It's what she got for believing.

The bus wasn't coming either, adding insult to injury. If

she'd just run faster, if she'd left five minutes earlier, if she hadn't kept arguing, if she'd just been *better*, none of this would have happened.

When she looked up from her watch, a horse was staring her right in the face.

Ella jumped back, and the horse backed off. The rider, though, continued to look at her, grinning a half-amused smile.

"You afraid of horses?" Frederick's voice rang from above, interrupting her inner thoughts, the anxiety loop that was forming in her mind. She tried finding her voice.

"I'm afraid of horses that stand in the way of me being able to see whether the bus is coming."

"Ah, I see."

Frederick maneuvered the horse so it stepped aside, the road free. Ella felt dizzy as she followed the horse's march. Her head was beginning to ache from holding back tears, from worry and restlessness.

"What are you catching the bus for?"

"I need to go home."

"I'd forgotten you lived in town."

He smiled at her.

"What are you doing?" Ella asked.

"Exercising the horse," Frederick answered. "It's Monday, which means we get to pick an irrationally stupid hobby that only rich people care about and practice twice a week."

Ella laughed at that, being suddenly reminded that Rory had once said the same thing about fencing. Grimrose had a fencing team, a horse-riding team, a gymnastics club, and a ballet class. Ella avoided anything that made her truly exercise—running was absolutely out of the question for her—so she'd never even looked properly at the list of activities Grimrose offered.

"I didn't know you liked riding," Ella said.

"There's a lot of things you don't know about me, Eleanor Ashworth," he said, his smile smug. With all his freckles, the only effect he accomplished was making Ella laugh. "Right. No more pretending to be the mysterious tall dark stranger."

"You're nothing if not tall."

"That's my only quality?" Frederick asked, sighing dramatically. "Shows you what I know about what girls like."

"Dark brooding guy is overrated," Ella told him. "And honestly, 'mysterious' is slightly creepy. Would you date a girl you knew nothing about?"

"Not a girl or a guy," Frederick said, making her smile again. "Are you okay? You looked a little worried there."

"Who, me? That's just my face."

He laughed. Ella looked again at the road, wondering if the bus was coming, how much longer she could hold herself together for the sake of someone else.

"Do you really need to get home?"

Ella turned her attention back to Frederick, nodding. "I have a curfew."

"I can take you."

The offer took her by surprise, and Ella looked up, feeling her throat bob. Not that Ella was afraid of climbing up behind him to get on the horse. She knew how to deal with horses; she had Carrots back home. She was more afraid of the consequences.

Here was Frederick, probably thinking she was someone else completely. Someone who came to the school and studied there like all the others, someone whose life was not a farce, not a part to play. And sure, he had invited her to the ball, but because they were friends. Because they were partners in class, because he was the nicest boy Ella had ever met, and there was nothing more to it.

And just by having him believe that, she was betraying him every step of the way.

"Come on," he said. "Are you really afraid of the horse?"

"I'm afraid of the boy controlling it."

Frederick blinked, but he offered his arm nonetheless, his hand outstretched so she could reach it.

She had faced worse than this.

She took his hand, and Frederick pulled her up. It was one smooth movement, and she settled behind Frederick, her knees beneath her skirt brushing against his legs, and she looked away, face hot. His back pressed against her, and her heart fluttered.

"You all right?"

Ella nodded, her head swimming again, not trusting herself to speak.

And then they were off. The horse galloped beneath her, his hooves beating against the ground. Ella felt the rush of wind against her face as she held on tight.

Soon enough—too soon—they neared her part of town,

and Frederick slowed the horse to a walk. Ella touched his arm slightly.

"I think it's better if you leave me here."

Frederick turned his head slightly, and their faces were so close she could feel his warm breath on her face.

"You don't want me to see where you live?"

"A girl's gotta keep her secrets," she replied in a light tone.

Ella felt like he was about to push for more, but she shook her head. She didn't want him ruining this—she wanted to live this dream, at least for a while. *Let me have this,* she thought, selfishly. *Let me have this, this one thing, this one small paradise.*

"You sure you're okay here?" he asked, and Ella felt her muscles relax.

"Yes," she replied. "Thank you. Really."

"Anytime you need, Eleanor."

She smiled, and her hands gripped his as she slid off. His fingers were sweaty from holding the reins, but smooth. Not like hers. Ella had little scars over most of her hands, from scrubbing the floors or washing the curtains or from cleaning out the stables. More scars than she could count—they appeared, seemingly out of nowhere, already reddened, with the blood dry on her knuckles.

Frederick looked at her hands and said nothing.

"Thanks for being the white knight," Ella said, looking up at him, hiding her hands behind her, afraid of what he might think.

Frederick nodded his head again, and Ella watched his horse turn around before she ran the rest of the way home.

CHAPTER THIRTY-TWO

YUKI

Yuki lost her temper.

She hadn't thought it through, didn't realize it was coming. She'd just stood there for a minute, listening to Ella talk about Ari, about a damned *ritual*, like all of it was supposed to make sense and was perfectly normal, and then she couldn't take it anymore. Couldn't find her way through, couldn't hold herself together, and had simply exploded.

The worst part was that Yuki had liked it.

She'd imagined doing it before, letting it all go, but not like this. She'd always pictured herself drowning in her daydreams, swallowing down everything until her lungs grew so heavy it would feel like she'd sunk to the bottom of the ocean, and there, just there, in her last moment of consciousness, she'd burst. Explode out into the water, create ripples and seams and recklessly, joyously spill out until she covered everything that was within her reach.

But even in her imagination, it never felt this good.

Yuki stood in the stairs, her hands shaking, breathing hard, trying to get back in control of herself. Trying to stand up straight, to have her hair be smooth and her face be kind, and all those things that she was supposed to be, had yearned to be, because when she looked at Ella, she wanted it desperately. It was so easy for Ella to be good. It was in her nature, in her heart, and Yuki loved her for it with every fiber of her being, and she wanted so *badly* to be the same. She stood in front of the mirror trying to control her impulses, to forget her inner darkness, to be selfless, willing to do anything for someone else, willing to go to the ends of the universe because she was too gentle, too kind to be anything else.

So Yuki had shaped every single one of her edges, turning them smooth, wearing them against her inner nature, against her heart, to the point where she wasn't sure what she'd find if one day she decided to let her edges be.

"Yuki?" a voice called, and Yuki closed her eyes, fearing it would be Rory or Nani, or worse, Ella.

She willed her body to stop trembling, for everything to be back into a composed image of herself, a whole girl, not sharpened by knife edges.

Penelope appeared on the steps behind her, her green eyes glowing like a cat's in the dark. Yuki took another breath, desperate to steady her body that was still craving a release, craving more of wherever that explosion had come from.

"You okay?" Penelope asked, concern lining her voice. "I saw you running down the stairs, and I just wanted to check."

"I'm fine," Yuki said automatically, her voice so controlled she wanted to laugh. She was a mess inside, and yet, here she was, pretending everything was normal. Never one to disappoint. Never one to drop the mask.

"It's okay not to be fine, you know," Penelope said. "Not after what you've been through."

"Stop pitying me," Yuki snapped. "I don't need it."

Exploding. Again. It was easier after the first time. It was easier to be a hurtful, sharp thing, poking others so that she didn't have to think about what it was doing to herself.

"Great," Penelope replied. "I hate pitying people. I was just telling you the truth."

Penelope's reply took her by surprise, and Yuki felt her shoulders relax, another breath that eased into her body as she tried to untangle the shape of her anger.

"I don't know why you asked, then."

Penelope grinned. "I won't next time."

Yuki shook her head, feeling the back of her neck damp with sweat. She'd lost control, but now she could pull herself together. Could regret the things she said. Could muster enough strength to really force herself to regret it, to feel the overwhelming guilt that was supposed to come later.

Penelope sat down on the staircase. Yuki sat down too, the shaking of her knees subsiding.

"Did something happen with Ella?" Penelope asked. "I just saw her leaving with Frederick on his horse."

"On his *horse*?" Yuki asked, and then shook her head. That's not what she should be angry at; it shouldn't be her concern, even though it was one of the things that was starting to bite at her.

"Yeah. I know how close you two are. It must be hard to see her with someone else."

Oh, Yuki realized. *That's what she thinks.*

Penelope thought she was in love with Ella.

"That's not how it is between us," Yuki said.

Penelope raised one of her eyebrows. "Good. Because you know you could have anybody at this school, right? I mean anybody. Have you looked at yourself in the mirror?"

Yuki's hand flew immediately to her face, because she knew. She knew what the mirror told her in the mornings, even though she didn't particularly care.

"You're the most beautiful girl in the whole school," Penelope said with another sincere smile, and for the first time, Yuki didn't feel like making excuses for her beauty, apologizing for taking up too much space or for looking the way she did. For being what she was. "Anyone would be lucky."

"I'm not interested in that. I'm not..." She struggled with the words, because they felt like a weight between her lungs, confessing it like it was a secret, because even the words seemed to say too much about her, and Yuki didn't want to say anything at all. "I'm asexual. And aromantic."

"Oh," Penelope said, then nodded her head. "Easier for you, then. You avoid all the drama."

Yuki laughed, because it was the natural response. Everyone assumed it was easier, that she wouldn't have to navigate the difficulties of love. Even her friends thought that, but it only came back to bite her in the end.

It's not like you understand what it's like to love someone, do you?

Because in the end, they would have someone, they would all have their counterparts, and Yuki was going to be alone.

That was the monster whispering in her ears when she saw Ella and Frederick. Because Ella would fall in love, and move to a new place, experience new things, and she'd have someone she loved and who loved her back, and Yuki was going to be here, with no one to love or choose her at all.

She ground her teeth, pushing all of it back inside, caging the lonely beast within herself. Ella hadn't deserved her outburst—and if she kept breaking like that, then none of her friends would want her around at all. They would have no reason to stay, no reason to love her when she could barely grasp enough to love them back herself.

"There really wasn't any drama," Yuki said finally. Talking helped. With Penelope, at least. She didn't have to keep Penelope close to her, and thus, she could be honest. No expectations, no disappointments. No responsibility. "We're just having a hard time adjusting to Ari."

"It's barely been two months."

"And it feels like a lifetime," Yuki confessed. "It's just... Ella and Rory want something, an explanation, something that makes sense. She died, and we failed her."

"It wasn't your fault," Penelope said.

Gently, Penelope reached to touch her shoulder. Yuki felt the comfort of the touch, drew a sharp intake of breath. Penelope's fingers were light, reaffirming. Yuki didn't realize how starved she was for that touch, like a peregrine that thirsted in the desert.

"It was, though," Yuki finally said. "We had a fight the day she came back."

Penelope blinked, eyes widening in surprise.

"We'd had fights before," Yuki said. "Ari and I didn't see eye to eye on a lot of things. And we had been fighting after Edric broke up with her. I said I didn't get why she was so upset, and Ari said I could never understand, because I didn't even know what love was."

Penelope's fingers squeezed her shoulder in sympathy.

"I'm sorry," she said. "She was supposed to be your friend."

"Yeah. But she wasn't."

Yuki took a deep breath, her shoulders sagging, her body relaxing while Penelope's touch kept her anchored in place, like it was her one tether to the rest of the world.

Yuki knew she didn't have to tell the rest of the story. How they blamed each other for everything, Ariane getting angrier each time, and then Yuki's last straw, the last thing she'd said to Ari when the fighting had escalated.

If you want everyone to suffer for you so much, then maybe it's just easier if you kill yourself.

Yuki had basically told Ari that she was better off dead than miserable, and that's exactly what Ari had done.

And they were all suffering for Ariane now.

The guilt overwhelmed her. She'd as good as killed Ariane. Ari was dead, and it was Yuki's fault.

"Ella is trying to make a game of connect the dots," Yuki said instead of taking the blame. Because she wasn't strong enough to admit her own mistakes. "She thinks the other deaths in the school have to do with it too."

Penelope blinked. "Other deaths?"

"You know, Flannery last year. Others too."

"It doesn't sound like closure," Penelope finally said. "That's what you really need."

"Closure?"

"Yes," Penelope said. "Like a ritual or something. Something you all should do to get rid of the bad memories. So you can move on."

Yuki felt the hairs on her arms rise. The words were too close to what Ella had wanted to do; it was like an eerie repetition.

"Like what?" Yuki laughed, trying to play it off.

Penelope shrugged. "My family used to do this thing after a person died. They'd all gather around in a circle, saying things they wished they'd said when the person was alive." She paused. "I know it sounds weird, but it helped. Maybe it would help you too."

"I thought you didn't talk to your family."

Something flashed in Penelope's eyes. "I don't, not anymore."

Yuki looked up. "You're still angry."

"Of course I am," she said. "You are too."

"No, I'm not."

Penelope laughed, and it echoed through the stairs, through the corridor. "You're allowed to be angry, you're allowed to be hurt. You're allowed all those things."

"I'm better than that."

"You think you're better than me?" Penelope said, and suddenly, the grip of her shoulder tightened, pressing so hard it had to have been leaving marks on Yuki's skin. And the pain, it felt good. It felt right. "Now you're just fooling yourself. No one is better because they're not angry, because they don't hurt people. It's just what you need to do to cope. You do whatever it takes. Whatever you have to do to survive."

Yuki's lower lip trembled, but she didn't like how close they were, how strange that she was hearing the words she'd thought so many times, like a call she couldn't ignore.

"You want to move on, you say the things stopping you from it. It's the only way you can let the past die," Penelope said. "If you don't, it's going to keep haunting you. You don't want your friendship stranded with the other girls because none of you can let it go. You're beyond helping Ariane now. She's gone, and it's time for all of you to accept that."

Penelope's words were kind at the end, and they echoed something inside Yuki.

Maybe it was the only way they could forget this once and for all. Forget the book, forget the tales, forget the mystery. Say their goodbyes.

Once and for all.

CHAPTER THIRTY-THREE

NANI

There was a reason Nani didn't trust other people, and the reason was that they fought too much.

Yuki's explosion in the library hadn't helped their cause, it had set them back. Nani was no longer benefiting from their knowledge. The list had yielded only dead girls. She might have cast aside the idea of finding out what happened to Ariane, but there were still questions left about Grimrose, and she was going to get answers.

So on the next Saturday, Nani knocked on Svenja's door.

Svenja took a moment to open the door, yawning and blinking at Nani.

"Why are you wearing your uniform?" she asked. "It's Saturday."

"It's the only jacket I have," Nani said. She was not prepared for winter at all, but she was leaving that for Future Nani to worry about. "Were you still sleeping? It's four in the afternoon."

"What are you, my mom?" Svenja said, waving her in.

Nani hesitated on the doorstep, not sure if she should cross it.

"Stop that," Svenja said, pulling her inside.

Svenja's room was overwhelming.

It wasn't just that there was a pile of clothes dropped onto one of the chairs or books and papers spread haphazardly across a desk or random shoes and boots strewn from one corner of the room to another.

It was the photographs.

They were glued to the walls, pictures of concerts and parties, and photos of Svenja herself, when she was younger, but Nani couldn't see her face in a single one because they had been drawn over with a Sharpie or scratched off with...something.

Everywhere she looked were faceless, headless Svenjas.

Svenja caught her looking, and Nani looked away, feeling guilty for searching for personal remnants.

"You have a whole room to yourself?" Nani asked.

"Yes, I do," Svenja said. "Grimrose says, trans rights! Yippee!"

Nani raised an eyebrow.

"It's just easier for them not to have to deal with shitty parents," Svenja explained. "The usual litany. I can't complain, though. I would hate to share a bathroom."

There were curtains around the bed and a vinyl collection of classical ballet music. There was a picture of Svenja standing in her ballet dress in front of a fountain in the middle of the town square.

"Where was this?" Nani asked, eyeing the photo.

Svenja looked over her shoulder. "Home. Budapest. My first ballet presentation."

Svenja was probably about thirteen, her face still childish, the hair so tightly drawn back that it contrasted with her round cheeks.

"So, to what do I owe the visit?" Svenja asked, leaning against her desk.

Nani turned, trying to bury the part of herself that was insisting on feeling awkward about this. Svenja was just another normal girl in the school. Nani didn't need to feel guilty talking to her.

Except of course there was a reason she was doing this. She wanted to know what Svenja knew.

"Can't I just come for a visit?"

"I know your game already, Nani, you don't fool me."

"I'm naturally curious."

Svenja huffed. "That's putting it mildly."

Nani decided to stop playing games. "I thought you were curious about it all too," she said.

A dark shadow crossed Svenja's face, a cloud hiding the sun. "I think I've got enough to worry about without having to think of some poor girl who killed herself."

"You think that's what she did?"

"Yes," Svenja replied. "We're rich teenagers in a boarding school. Every single one of us is miserable."

"I'm not," Nani said.

Svenja said nothing, pressing her lips together. "It's no use asking, no one is going to tell you anything new. It's not like they care either. People move on."

From what Nani had seen, that much was true. It was as if most students had already forgotten about Ari.

"Actually, I came to ask about something else," Nani said. "What do you know of Grimrose's secret passageways?"

A mischievous grin lit up Svenja's face. She covered Nani's hand with her own. "Why? Looking for a good place to make out?"

"What?" Nani asked, suddenly jumping out of her skin, taking her hand away as fast as possible. "No!"

"Oh," Svenja said, and Nani could almost swear she heard disappointment. "You're in boarding school now, Nani, you'll have to learn how to have fun."

"I'll read books for that."

Svenja didn't look very impressed. "I think you and I have very different ideas of what fun is."

Nani stepped up closer to Svenja, looking into her eyes. "Then maybe you can show me."

Svenja knocked over the chair behind her, making a racket. "Shit!"

"I had no idea you felt so strongly about the passageways," Nani said lightly, grinning now that she'd gotten the upper hand in the exchange.

"Shut up. You *know* how that sounded."

Nani laughed. The moment of easy banter felt surreal, something she had read in books, something that she always imagined friendship would be like. Easy conversation, jokes, laughter, where two people could share everything.

Except Nani couldn't share everything.

"I'll show you a place I know," Svenja said. "But we'll behave like society ladies in there, do you hear me?"

"Yes, ma'am."

Svenja blinked. "I want to murder your accent."

"Why?" Nani said, suddenly taken aback, not realizing she had one. Except she did—all of them at Grimrose came from different countries, different places. They all spoke differently.

"Because it's cute. Let's go."

Svenja left, and Nani followed. The wind had taken a sudden turn that afternoon, announcing what would undoubtedly come later—the winter beyond the mountains, making its first appearance. Svenja guided Nani toward the main courtyard, where there was a single compass rose painted into the stone. Svenja stood right in the middle of it, her back to the enormous clock on Grimrose's main courtyard wall. Its ticking was always present in the back of every class.

"This is kind of the whole secret," she said, pointing so Nani would get closer to her. "You have to know where to stand first."

Their shoulders brushed against each other, and Nani looked down at the old drawing that was at least two centuries old. North, to the mountains. Southeast, to Constanz.

"And?" Nani asked. "What then?"

"Then you gotta learn how to count. Come on."

Nani followed Svenja as she muttered under her breath. They took one step after the other. They came back inside the castle, climbed a set of stairs near the kitchen area, then turned right toward the gymnasium and the indoor pool.

Before they got there, Svenja turned again, into a long corridor of classrooms, and then down another set of stairs, practically running.

Svenja turned down another corridor, and Nani stumbled, stopping to catch her breath. "Are we close yet?"

Svenja looked at her, then she couldn't hold back a laugh. "Did you really believe that thing about counting and directions?"

Nani frowned. "You mean you just made me run all this way for nothing?"

"Cardio's good for you."

"I'm going to kill you."

Nani gasped for another breath, half wanting to laugh.

"We're actually almost there," Svenja said. "Come on."

Svenja walked forward, measuring her steps, and in the space between two armored stone guards, standing watch like ever-present sentinels, she pushed a single stone out of place.

Nani heard something click before a door opened on the opposite corridor, partially hidden behind a tapestry. It was like seeing magic at work, one click, and it opened up, revealing its secrets. Svenja pushed the tapestry aside, gesturing to the darkness beyond.

"Whoa," Nani said, mesmerized by the stonework, at the ease in which the door had opened, revealing a space between all the spaces. A world within another world. She wondered how many secret places like this the castle hid in its depths.

Nani took a deep breath, her fingers grazing the stone.

"In you go," Svenja pointed. "This one's pretty simple. There's stairs at the bottom, but mostly, it's straightforward."

Svenja took out her phone and illuminated the passage.

"This was a lot harder in the past," Svenja said. "They had to bring candles."

Nani stepped carefully into the passage. It was surprisingly clean. There were a few spiderwebs above them, but otherwise, the stone was smooth, and the air fresh. Svenja went up ahead with the light, and Nani followed.

"What do you think?" Svenja asked, looking over her shoulder.

"You've finally managed to impress me," Nani replied.

"Finally? What do you mean *finally*? My good looks and my castle weren't good enough?"

"It's not your castle."

"Sure it is. I live in it."

Nani laughed again, shaking her head, wondering how many of these tunnels existed, hidden behind the castle walls.

"Most of these were built for servants," Svenja said. "Back in the day. They had to move like they were invisible so the nobility wouldn't see them. Now the students just use them if we don't want anyone seeing us kissing ugly boys out in the open."

"You kissed a lot of them?"

"A regrettable amount," Svenja agreed. "Boys are better in the dark."

"And girls?" Nani asked, her heart skipping a tiny beat, not wanting to give in to her own fancies.

Svenja gave her a knowing smile, cocking her eyebrow. "I'm gonna let you find that one out for yourself."

Nani was glad that the passage was so dark because she was sure her blush was visible.

"Where does this one lead?" Nani asked, changing the subject.

"To the teachers' rooms."

"You can't be serious."

Svenja grinned. "This is the one we really keep a secret. I think Mrs. Blumstein might be on to it already, but we try not to use it too much. The door used to be locked, you know."

"What happened?"

"Micaeli broke in," Svenja said. "She used to break into rich people's houses, *Bling Ring* style. Ate their food, tried on their shoes, slept in their beds when they weren't home. This lock was easy for her compared to some of the others she broke."

Nani couldn't even fathom what that was like, so distant from her reality.

"Anyway, we had a pretty hard biology test coming up," Svenja continued. "So Micaeli came in through the passageway to take a look at the answers and then told everybody else."

Nani shook her head, still in disbelief seeing the life in a completely different world.

"We're almost there," Svenja said. "Only need to turn the corner."

As soon as they did, a noxious odor hit them full in the face.

"God, that smell," Svenja said, a groan escaping her throat. "Raccoons are probably nesting in here."

Nani could feel it too now, invading her nostrils, something metallic and pungent.

"What *is* that?" Nani asked, covering her nose with the sleeve of her uniform jacket, for once glad that she was wearing this thing.

Svenja frowned, holding her phone up high.

The first thing Nani saw was the figure on the lower stone steps, limbs splayed like a mannequin, a pool of a dark liquid gathering below it. It took another moment to realize that this was a person, and that the liquid, now that she recognized the acrid smell, was blood.

The last thing she noticed was the face of Micaeli, her head bashed in, blood dripping down the stairs slowly and an upturned bowl of porridge by her side, half of her brains mixed with the thick yellow paste.

Nani screamed.

CHAPTER THIRTY-FOUR

ELLA

The news of Micaeli's death spread like wildfire in the school.

The Swiss police swarmed the castle, sealing off the entrance of the secret passageway, now laid open for the whole world to see. Ella watched as they cordoned off portions of the school and took posts in the entrance gate, coming in and out while they investigated.

Ella was almost sure what they would say.

Micaeli must have fallen down the stairs and hit her head. Another accident.

Ella knew better, though. She'd seen the records of the school, dating years back to different girls. Micaeli wasn't on the list, but maybe Ari hadn't gotten too far connecting the current students to the tales. Ari wasn't the first, and she wasn't going to be the last. Not until they learned how to stop this, whatever it was.

And the only way that was happening was if they did the ritual. If they believed in what Ari was trying to tell them.

She managed to get to school a little earlier that morning and knocked on the girls' bedroom door. Rory opened it, her copper hair a mess, her bright blue eyes looking like she hadn't gotten any sleep.

"Where's Nani?" Ella asked.

"Still at the infirmary," Rory answered, yawning. "I think she should be okay to come back today, but they're keeping an eye on her."

"It can't have been easy," Ella said, her heart tightening a little just from thinking of Nani finding the body in the state it was in.

"No," Rory agreed. "Svenja said she didn't even look human anymore. Just a bunch of limbs, half her head bashed in."

Ella shuddered. "It must have been awful. I hope it was quick."

"That's all we can hope for."

Ella knew they were both thinking the same thing. Ari's death wasn't quick. She'd drowned, her lungs full of water, and it would have lasted several minutes before she succumbed, the water dragging her down. Ella dreamed of it, sometimes, that she was the one stuck in the lake, her arms flailing, trying to swim upward without ever reaching the light.

"This is dreadful," Ella muttered, starting to pick up clothes from the floor and piling them all up in the laundry basket.

"You know you don't have to do that," Rory said.

"Yes, but I hate you living in a pigpen," Ella answered. "What about all these water bottles? You're killing at least ten tortoises a year."

"Let them die, those wrinkled old hags."

Ella glared at her as Yuki came out of the shower. Ella felt the immediate tension in the room, but Yuki only looked tired. She sat on the bed with a sigh, still wrapped in her towel, looking at Ella.

Ella didn't know where to start.

"This can't be a coincidence," was the only thing Ella managed to say.

"How are you so sure?" Yuki snapped back, but it was half-hearted, like she was too tired for an argument.

Ella picked up the book from Nani's table and sat down on the bed next to Yuki, leaving space between, like Yuki preferred. Ella had been touchy at first—hugs and hand-holding, but Yuki was always jumping away, scared, and Ella had stopped. She'd forced her hands back, training them not to reach out. She'd noticed Reyna was the same way, never quite touching her stepdaughter.

"Here," she said, opening up the book on the right story. "Goldilocks dies from falling out of the window while she was trying to escape, her head gets bashed in."

Rory looked over her shoulder at the book, her face paling. "This has to be some sick joke."

"We're the only ones who know besides Ariane. Us, and whoever wanted the book in the first place."

"It's a message," Yuki said.

They fell silent, both Ella and Rory looking at Yuki.

"To see if we know," Yuki continued, her voice quiet. "To see if we figured out. It doesn't have to be magic. Whoever is doing this wants to scare us."

"Then they can have the book," Rory said. "I don't want it, not if it's going to keep happening."

"But if we give it up, maybe it won't stop," Ella replied. "Maybe it'll just continue, and we won't know how to stop it. Not unless we figure out who's behind this. This has been happening for a long time, and maybe Ari was close to finding out the truth."

Rory closed the book, handing it back to Ella.

"You know what we have to do," Ella said gently, her voice low.

Rory frowned again. "Ella, we..."

"Maybe Ella is right," Yuki said, which took them all by surprise. "I think we need this. Even if it doesn't get us anywhere, I think it might be good for us to say goodbye."

Rory frowned. "How are we even supposed to do this?"

"On the full moon," Ella said. "We can use the old, abandoned aviary tower. No one goes there anymore."

"Uh, it has no roof," Rory pointed out.

"So?" Ella asked. "We'll be safe there. No one will come for us."

"Can you even break curfew?" Rory insisted.

"Yes," Ella answered, not wanting to think about the consequences. That would come later, and only if she got caught. She'd have to trust that it would work. "Next Friday, it'll be

Halloween. Everyone is going to be busy at the party Alethea is throwing. We won't be noticed."

"What do we need?" Rory asked.

"I can arrange things," Ella said. "We'll just need four people. The three of us, and then we can ask—"

"Penelope," Yuki said.

Ella stopped in the middle of her sentence, glancing at Yuki. "What?"

"It makes sense," Yuki said. "She was Ari's friend."

"Only in the last couple of months," Rory said. "And the other day she was pretty rude. She doesn't know about the book either."

"I could talk to her," Yuki said. "She's having a hard time too."

Rory crossed her arms, and Ella couldn't give a solid reason why it couldn't be Penelope, other than the gut feeling that she was the wrong choice.

"What about Nani? She wasn't here when Ari died, which could be a good thing," Ella said carefully.

"What are you saying?" Yuki's eyes flashed. "You think Penelope had something to do with this? You wanted me to talk to Penelope, see if she knew anything. She doesn't. She lost a friend, same as us. She deserves to have some kind of goodbye."

"That's not what I said!" Ella exclaimed. "But Nani already knows about the book, and she's helping. She's a neutral party."

"Oh, so the made-up ritual has to be neutral now," Yuki said sarcastically. "You get your choice, I get mine. I'm saying Penelope would help us. She wants to help."

Ella pressed her lips together. "I just don't think..."

"It's because I'm hanging with her?" Yuki asked. "Rory has Pippa."

"I do not *have* Pippa," Rory said loudly. "She's just the person I practice with. My rival."

Yuki ignored Rory. "And you're hanging out with Frederick all the time."

Ella felt a blush creeping into her cheeks. "It's not about that."

"You don't like her," Yuki stated.

"Of course I like her," Ella protested. "I like everybody."

"But you don't like her."

Ella sighed, not wanting to admit that a part of her did not, in fact, like Penelope. Ella didn't truly think that Penelope was grieving in the same way. She seemed to move on with her life just fine.

"All I'm saying is, Nani already knows," Ella said, trying to ignore the creeping sense of jealousy. "Nani's read the book. We should give her a chance."

"You realize she's only helping because she has her own mystery to solve, right?" Rory said, her arms still crossed.

Ella bit the inside of her cheeks, her anxiety building. "Maybe. But if we trust her, maybe she'll tell us the truth. Maybe we can help her, as much as she can help us."

Yuki's frown deepened, and Ella felt like at any moment she might explode again. But in a flash it was gone, all back under control, and Ella was left wondering if she had imagined it.

"Fine, then," Yuki finally said. "We'll do it your way."

CHAPTER THIRTY-FIVE

YUKI

They met outside the aviary tower, a bitter wind blowing past the trees and the mountains. Yuki didn't feel cold, but she welcomed the icy autumn air that spoke of the snow that was coming. Rory came behind her, Nani huddled in a winter coat she'd borrowed from Rory, her teeth chattering loudly.

Grimrose had been busy on Halloween night, every student giggling as they prepared to go to Alethea's infamous party, one the teachers pretended they didn't know about. Yuki was always invited, but she never went. Rory had come home from it drunk last year, carrying a laughing Ariane in her arms like a bride, and they both collapsed into a pile of hearty laughter as soon as they came in through the door.

Tonight, as Yuki, Rory, and Nani waited for Ella at the door of the abandoned tower, that memory felt distant, nearly as distant the heyday of the aviary. The tower had long ago fallen into disrepair, and had been off-limits to students for years.

Yuki put her hands in the pocket of her coat and looked up to see Ella, walking the path, a lonely figure under the moonlight. Grimrose's clock rang out across the garden, a reminder of time passing.

"Let's go," Rory said, as if prepping the team for a fencing match instead of some nonsense seance.

Ella tried to door to the tower. "It's locked," she said, turning around, like that was a surprise.

"Step aside. While you were busy being heterosexual, I studied the art of the blade," Rory said, taking out one of her smaller training swords from her backpack and jangling it against the lock until half the door broke down. "There you go."

"None of us are heterosexual," Ella said, and Rory turned to look at Nani, raising an eyebrow.

"Don't look at me," Nani grumbled.

"Thanks for destroying the door," Yuki added.

"For fuck's sake, it was destroyed already."

Ella was the first to step inside, and Yuki followed close behind her. The tower opened to a spiral staircase, and they all started climbing in silence one after the other.

At the top of the stairs, the tower opened into an old room. Half of the roof had been rotted away, toppled over to the mountains, and the remaining debris was lit by the moon.

Ella gasped as she came in, sliding a finger on one of the abandoned shelves, and her face contorted in disgust as her finger came out blackened with dust. She looked perfectly horrified.

Rory stood in the middle of the room, looking around. "So what do we do? Chant in Latin?"

Nani sighed deeply.

"Wait a minute," Ella said. "I have to prepare."

She stood in the middle of the room, looking around. Through the open roof and one of the crumbling walls they could see the lake and the towers of Grimrose. Ella muttered something under her breath as she started taking things out of her bag. Four small bowls, four candles, four crystals. She set out the bowls in a circle, measuring so they'd be equally spaced. In each of the bowls she placed a candle and a crystal, and then it started getting stranger.

In one, she placed rocks and earth. In another, she poured in water from a bottle. In the third, she placed what looked like alcohol, and lit it like a candle, the bowl burning with the crystal inside. And in the last, she placed a feather.

Ella snapped her fingers at Rory, directing her to sit in front of the feather, and she gestured for Nani to go toward the bowl with the small pile of dirt. Ella took the place in front of the water, and Yuki was left with the fire.

"Light your candles," Ella instructed, as each of them reached out to spark a flame to the candles in front of them.

Yuki felt like an idiot. She could respect people that did things like this, connecting to their inner natures and whatnot, but she'd never believed in any of it, and especially not in some old woman handing out candles and crystals and telling them to believe in their inner strength.

"You brought the book, right?" Ella asked Yuki.

Yuki nodded, taking it out of her bag, placing it in the middle of the circle. Yuki's knees were touching Rory's and Nani's, and she sat opposite Ella. Ella's shoulder-length blond hair fell straight, and the light from the flames illuminated her freckles and soft brown eyes.

"Okay," Ella breathed, seeming unsure of herself. "Let's hold hands."

Yuki hesitated a moment before reaching out with her own pale hand to touch Rory's and Nani's.

Nothing happened.

"Are we supposed to say something?" Rory asked. "Close our eyes? That's how it works, right?"

"I don't know," Ella replied.

"You have to speak from the heart," Nani finally said. "That's what Tūtū always told me, when we did our offerings. Offer your love."

Ella nodded, taking a deep breath. Yuki remained silent, a part of her not wanting to join, a part of her still refusing to acknowledge this was happening.

"Okay," Ella said, breathing deep. "As the winter dies and turns to spring, as the summer comes with soft heat and is replaced by autumn, as the world spins and spins again, we're here with our hearts open, and we would like to—uh, talk to Ariane."

Ella looked to Yuki, their eyes meeting over the fire, and it almost seemed like she was trying to hold back laughter. Yuki tightened her lips, not wanting to break first.

"Yes," Rory echoed vehemently. "Ari, talk to us. What the fuck is wrong with the book?"

Nani opened her eyes and glared at Rory. "That's not how you talk to the dead."

"You talk, then."

"She was not my friend. She isn't going to listen to me."

"Guys," Ella warned, and Yuki sighed, looking down at her flames.

They were still burning, the red crystal intact inside. Red and bright, and she could feel the heat growing.

"We should have just gotten a board or something," Rory said. "That's how people do in the movies."

"That's how they get *killed* in the movies," Nani replied.

"Ari is not going to kill us," Rory replied. "I think."

Yuki felt a squeeze coming from both Rory and Nani, their hands clasped tight, sweating even though it was cold.

"All we need are the answers," Ella said, looking down at the book. "I need to know about the book."

Suddenly, a breeze came swooping into the tower, flipping the book open. Rory's eyes widened. *It's just the wind,* Yuki had the urge to tell her. The pages shuffled, the breeze turning the beginning faster and faster until it stopped abruptly. They all leaned forward, staring down on the book.

It had opened to the first one, "Cinderella."

Yuki finally felt the cold air stinging her skin as the cloudless sky and the soft moonlight were swept away, clouds rolling in from behind the mountains like an omen. She looked up just as thunder echoed on the horizon, shaking the foundations of the tower.

Ella looked up at her, and Yuki felt Nani's fingers tightening around hers.

"We need answers," Ella said, her voice soft, yet powerful enough to echo everywhere, down the stairs, through the stone walls. "Tell us why someone's after the book. Tell us what the deaths mean."

Another roll of thunder crashed close, the lightning cutting the sky open, their faces painted in blue as the darkness covered the moonlight.

The wind blew again through the open wall, and Yuki felt a sudden jolt of energy, and the pages on the book moved again, opening to another tale.

"This isn't working," Yuki said out loud.

Ella stared at her from across their circle. "We just have to figure out the right words."

Rory looked between Yuki and Ella, as if wanting to find something, but it was Nani who spoke.

"This is better than nothing," she said. "You didn't see Micaeli, Yuki. You didn't *see* her."

Nani's voice faltered at the end, and she swallowed, but even Yuki couldn't interrupt her now.

"That wasn't an accident," Nani said. "That wasn't like anything I've ever seen."

Her hand faltered, still in Yuki's, trembling slightly, but Nani didn't back off. Yuki didn't think Nani was someone who backed out of anything.

"So no, maybe it's not about the book," Nani continued, "but someone died, and she wasn't the first. Maybe she knew something, and her story ended. I'm not interested in it turning bad for *me*, and I don't think you are either."

Yuki wet her lips. "What you guys are saying, you realize what that is. Magic isn't real."

"For most of my life I lived in a small house with my grandmother," Nani said. "Nothing beyond that was real, but I'm here now. And this is the new real."

Ella looked at Yuki, supplicant, her lips in a tight line, but Yuki refused to give in, refused to believe, even though something was happening with the world outside, the sky cracking open, the taste of something wild and unknown in the air. And something building inside her, wanting to burst out of its containment.

Rory squeezed Yuki's hand, the touch both uncertain and encouraging.

The wind blew in again; the pages flipped and the tale changed. This time it landed on "Snow White."

Ella narrowed her eyes.

"Once upon a time, there lived a queen..." she started.

"What are you doing?" Yuki snapped, electricity sizzling in the air around them as she fought against herself.

"I'm improvising," Ella said. "Maybe it's going to tell us something."

Yuki panicked, her heart hammering, but Ella started again, her voice drowning the sound of the storm gathering outside, both firm and unwavering, and soon, Nani and Rory had joined her in reading too, their heads going forward as they looked at the words, as the tale progressed and their voices became joined in one powerful song, as the book drew them in, and Yuki couldn't think of anything but knowing it had to be a curse, it had to, and she wasn't going to escape it.

Their voices became louder, and Yuki kept her lips shut tight, not giving in to this madness, to whatever they thought they were doing, because there was nothing beyond this world for them. No ghosts, no magic, no salvation, nothing but their lives ahead of them, and Yuki couldn't take it as the tale went on, as Snow White ran, as Snow White bit into the apple, falling into eternal sleep.

Ella finished the tale as the rain started pouring, as it started to drench them, the candles miraculously flickering, and in that moment, the entire world went quiet.

They all looked at each other, waiting for an answer, waiting to see if anything had changed. If there was magic in the air after all, if their guesses had been right, if they were on the right path.

Nothing happened.

"This is bullshit," Yuki spat. Before she could think twice, she let go of her friends' hands, grabbed the book, and threw it into her fire, still burning strong despite the rain.

Thunder crashed above and lightning struck. The flames licked the book, and Yuki put her hands on it, feeling the heat, waiting for the book to start to burn.

Except it didn't. The flames came for her instead, digging under her fingernails, running through her bloodstream, and it was burning, burning, sharpening all her edges, making her aware of every tiny cell in her body as it ran through her arms and legs and to her face, as it cut deeper into her with every flicker.

As it took her shell and cracked it open to touch what she'd locked inside.

"Yuki!" Ella screamed, breaking the rest of the circle and running to her with her bowl, dousing the fire with her water. Yuki could barely see as the others crowded closer, shouting incoherently.

She let go of the book, and it fell to the floor, immune to the flames, but her body was still burning from the inside. Thunder roared above them, and then it wasn't fire—it was ice, cold and scorching in a different way entirely, creeping through her veins, freezing her arms, hands, fingers, until she was still and solid like a statue, and then finally it came to her cold heart and her lungs, and it stilled them too.

Yuki stopped breathing, and, with Ella above her, she passed out.

CHAPTER THIRTY-SIX

RORY

Rory carried Yuki back to the dormitory. She was lucky Yuki was so light. Ella hovered in concern, but in the end, Rory had sent her home—Yuki was going to wake up. Her hands hadn't been burned by touching the fire, and neither had the book. There was not a single mark on either.

When both Rory and Nani finally snuck back into the castle, Rory deposited Yuki on the bed, keeping her head on the pillow, checking for temperature. Cold as ice, but that was Yuki. Rory felt the muscles on her back protesting her arms aching and heavy by her sides like they begged to be detached from her body. Rory was used to that already, and she rubbed her temple, wondering when being in pain had become normal, and she couldn't fathom what it was like to not be in any.

She slid off Yuki's bed, hands on her knees, resting her head against the frame.

"It hasn't been touched," Nani said, examining the book in her hands. "It's as if there was no fire at all."

Outside, the rumbling thunder had stopped, and the rain went away just as fast.

"So does that mean we failed at the ritual?" Rory asked. "Or that we succeeded? Where are we at?"

Nani sighed, sliding to the floor in front of Rory. Rory noticed the distance she kept—a part of their group now, but still set apart.

"I don't know," Nani said. "It was weird, wasn't it? It wasn't...normal."

"Define normal."

"Thunderstorms don't come just because you light some candles," Nani said, her voice quiet. She picked up the book again, opening the pages. "Do you have a match?"

"You're going to try it again?"

Nani nodded. Rory sighed, getting up to search for a lighter she'd gotten as a gift a few years past. It was branded with her initials, and she handed it to Nani.

"A.D.?" Nani asked, frowning.

"My father's," Rory lied, wanting to end the conversation there.

Nani shrugged, adjusted her glasses, and flicked it open. The flame was bright orange, and Nani put the book to it. Rory admired the guts of the girl who loved books but wasn't afraid to wreck them.

The flame flickered, but nothing happened.

"You sure it's hot?" Rory asked, putting her hand to the flame. She yelped.

"It is," Nani said, unnecessarily. "But it doesn't affect the book at all."

Nani got up, went to the bathroom, turned the tap on the sink to let the water pour. Then she stuck the book right underneath it, letting it get soaked.

Except it didn't. When Nani took it out, it was dry.

Nani sat down on the floor again, cracking the spine of the book and lifting a page, yanking it hard to pull it out of the binding.

Rory looked on, horrified. The page never budged.

"It can't be destroyed. No fire, no water, not even ripping it. You can't do it," Nani said, her shoulders sagging. "Books are among the most fragile objects in the world. Their pages are thin, they are flammable, they get soaked and the paper turns soggy and unreadable. This does nothing."

Rory looked at the binding of the book, still intact, still perfect.

"It's magic," Nani said into the night, and the word changed everything.

Rory didn't know how to feel about that, so she just rested her head against the bed, where Yuki was still knocked out, her breathing steady.

"What the actual fuck," Rory said.

Nani laughed. Rory raised her head, looking at the other girl, and for the first time, she didn't feel like Nani was someone trying to replace Ariane.

"I think that about sums it up," Nani agreed with another laugh. "What the actual fuck."

Rory closed her eyes, her whole body angry that she

wasn't in bed yet. Not that sleep ever came easy. Or lasted long when it did.

"Sorry I've been treating you like shit," she said to Nani, eyes still closed. "I didn't—I just miss Ari."

Nani took so long to answer that Rory didn't know if would. Or maybe Nani was already curled into sleep. Rory couldn't muster the energy to open her eyes to check.

"I know," Nani said finally. "I'm not trying to replace her. I'm not her. I'm not even your friend."

"Fine," Rory replied. "You're only the girl going to magic rituals with us."

Nani snorted. "I guess I am."

Yuki stirred in her sleep, and Rory turned her face toward Yuki's soft groaning.

"I'm here," Rory whispered.

"All right," Yuki answered softly. Yuki was going to be fine. She was just asleep. Whatever had happened in the aviary tower hadn't really hurt her, and it didn't change anything.

"You sleep now," Rory said, adjusting Yuki's covers, pulling them properly over her.

Rory slumped next to the bed again. Nani was looking at Yuki through narrowed eyes.

"Why doesn't she want to help?" Nani asked, her voice low, still facing the sleeping girl.

Rory had been turning that over and over, but there was no simple answer, except that it was the way it always was.

"Ella takes care of us, but Yuki... Yuki has always protected us. No matter what happens."

"And she didn't protect Ariane."

Rory's lip trembled, and she felt like she was going to cry, but she held back her tears. "Yeah."

Rory closed her eyes once more, because it didn't matter now. It didn't matter if Ella was taking care of them, if Yuki was protecting them, and if Rory was making sure they faced what was ahead, because now Ariane was gone, and Ariane had kept all of them together.

"So what are you doing here, Nani?" Rory asked, hoping that this time, in the darkness, Nani would give an honest answer. Ari, the book, Grimrose, all of it connected in a web they couldn't decipher. Nani was a part of that web now too, whether she liked it or not.

"I don't know," Nani said, finally, and Rory knew she was telling the truth. "But I'd like to find out."

CHAPTER THIRTY-SEVEN

ELLA

Rory texted Ella in the middle of the night to let her know that Yuki had woken up and was doing fine. Even so, Ella couldn't sleep—she tossed and turned, and when the sun poked through the clouds, Ella gave up entirely and spent the rest of the early morning sewing the dresses for the winter ball. She knew Yuki's and Rory's measurements, but Nani's was a guess, and she was hoping it fit her right. She hadn't told Nani she was making a dress for her too, and she wanted to make it a surprise.

When Monday came, Ella had spent the weekend without really sleeping, and she'd stitched and sewn until her fingers started bleeding.

She didn't see Yuki at first period and didn't meet her for their second class either. Rory had reassured Ella she was fine, that there was nothing to worry about, but there was something about the ritual that unsettled Ella. She supposed it was important to find out that the book couldn't be destroyed, but they hadn't really gotten the answers they were looking for.

Ella didn't know how to accept that.

She hurried to third period, hoping to spot any of her friends, when Frederick caught her by the arm.

"Hey," he said, and Ella turned around so fast she almost bumped nose first into his chest. "Didn't see you at the Halloween party on Friday."

"You know how it is," she said as an excuse, her smile not really reaching her eyes. "I had to stay at home."

"Stacie and Silla were there."

Ella sighed. "That's just how it is."

Frederick's frown deepened, and it made his red brows furrow in a cute way. "All right. I wanted to ask you... There's going to be a gelato festival in Constanz next week before they close all the shops for winter. You want to come?"

Ella hesitated a moment, feeling her heart clench. "I—I can't."

"It's the weekend," Frederick said. "You're gonna be back before five o'clock, promise. I'll deliver you myself."

"Freddie, you don't understand. I can't."

"Not even if your stepsisters got tickets for a music festival in Munich Saturday and weren't home?"

Ella blinked. "They didn't tell me anything about that."

"Well..." Freddie's voice trailed off. "Think about it, all right?"

Freddie was gone before Ella could say anything. When

she turned around, she almost hit another student coming up the stairs.

Penelope caught Ella before she tumbled back down and steadied her, her grip firm.

"Sorry," Ella muttered. "I wasn't looking."

Penelope craned her neck to see Freddie's red hair vanishing around the corner. "I can see why."

Ella felt herself blush hard. "It wasn't—"

"You don't owe me an explanation, Eleanor," Penelope said. Ella shifted her feet, trying to avoid Penelope's piercing green eyes. "You think I'm a tattletale like Micaeli?"

At Micaeli's mention, the mood got heavier.

"Shit," Penelope said, looking completely miserable. Penelope had an empty bed in her room now too. "It's easier to make jokes. It's all so horrible."

"Yes," Ella agreed. "It is."

Penelope shifted her weight. "I know our last conversation went badly. I thought I'd better stay away, because I kept thinking that maybe all of you would blame me for stealing your friend."

"We acted like jerks," Ella said after a pause, surprised at Penelope's sincerity, and that got Penelope laughing.

"I talked to Yuki about it, of course, but..." Her voice trailed off. "It wasn't the same. I wanted you to know that I'm sorry, and that having to go through this again is just wrong."

"You too. I know what you're going through," Ella conceded. "Did Ari talk to you?"

Penelope frowned. "About what?"

Ella didn't know what to say. She knew Yuki had already asked, but she couldn't help but feel that something was being left out of the story. And would she even believe her if Penelope said yes? Ella wanted to ask questions, but she didn't know if she could handle the answers.

"Sorry, I'm rambling," Ella said instead. "I know you were important to Ari, and to Micaeli."

Penelope gave a tight-lipped smile. "Yes. I don't want anyone else losing friends."

"You're right," Ella said, suddenly feeling guilty. "I know Yuki likes you a lot. You're good for her."

Penelope's eyes flashed. "I'm glad. I think it's good she realizes she has other friends, if she needs it."

Ella frowned. "What?"

Penelope hesitated, her hands curling together, biting her lower lip.

"Look, I'll be honest with you," Penelope said. "None of us are having the best time with these deaths happening, but I think Yuki is... I think she's worried about you. About you and Freddie. I think she needs some space. To process all of it."

Ella shrank back, Penelope's words taking her entirely by surprise. "She didn't tell me that."

"She didn't want you to think she was jealous," Penelope said.

"Jealous of me and Frederick?" Ella repeated, a familiar feeling twisting in her stomach. "That's absurd."

"I just think she needs time to process that you're

allowed to have some things that are entirely your own. We all deserve that."

Ella didn't know what to think of that, wanting to march upstairs and ask Yuki what was going on. If that had been the reason she was acting strangely lately, or if it was once again Ella's anxiety, poking at her insecurities.

Ella was allowed few things of her own, and what she had, she loved with all her heart, and never let go. But she also knew Yuki—quiet, private Yuki, who never shared anything, but who was fierce and protective. Yuki, who she'd die for, Yuki, her best friend.

And if Yuki didn't understand that she'd come first, no matter what, it didn't matter how many times Ella repeated it.

"It's nothing, probably," Penelope reassured her, reaching for Ella's shoulder, giving it a tight squeeze. "You have been through a lot. You'll find your way."

Ella found herself reaching for Penelope's hand, surprised by how calloused Penelope's hands were too. Not soft like she imagined, for a girl who had never worked a day in her life, whose parents owed several of the best farms in Europe. She gave it a squeeze, feeling the sharp press of Penelope's ring.

"Thanks," Ella said. "For taking care of her too."

"No need to thank me," Penelope said with another smile. "It's my pleasure."

CHAPTER THIRTY-EIGHT

NANI

Nani was still having a hard time wrapping her head around everything that had happened. Every time she closed her eyes, she saw Micaeli's mangled body on the stairs, half of her head bashed, the blood mixed with the porridge, and the *smell*. The smell of the blood mixed with oatmeal, pungent, acrid, *wrong*. Her stomach turned at the thought, and Nani could barely eat without remembering it, her mind a swirl of screaming, of running away and calling the teachers, of Svenja with her in the infirmary, and all Nani could say was that she was fine, even though she wasn't.

Tūtū had called, and Nani lied to her too. She couldn't say anything about what really happened in school. What was still happening, with all the girls inside it, weaving their destinies together, a hedge of thorns keeping them close. More parents had called the school, and even a couple students had left—but no more than that. The death had been deemed another accident, and accidents happen.

Nani knew answers could only be found within Grimrose itself.

She tried not to look too desperate as she casually looked for Svenja in the halls. Walking alone felt strange now, especially because last time she'd been in the corridors, she had been with Svenja.

Last time, they'd found a secret passage—and a dead girl.

When she finally spotted Svenja, she was going out through the main entrance, down the stairs and into the courtyard.

"Svenja!" Nani called, and Svenja turned around, looking up. Nani hurried to catch up to her. "Just wanted to see if you're doing okay."

"Better than last week," Svenja said. "You?"

Nani nodded. Svenja looked past her, frowned at something, then turned her attention back to Nani.

"You going somewhere?" Nani asked.

"Yes. Constanz. I need some fresh air," she said. "I'm getting tired of this place. Wanna come?"

"I think I would need permission," Nani said, darting her eyes upstairs, suddenly aware that one of the teachers might see her.

"Bullshit," Svenja said. "Come on. I need to breathe."

They made their way to Constanz in silence, Nani walking besides Svenja, both with their hands shoved in their pockets.

Nani hadn't been to Constanz yet, but the town was basically what she expected. She'd seen it through one of the tower's windows in the distance, the matching brown roofs with white houses, a peculiar and provincial town that seemed straight from a storybook. Svenja kept looking behind from time to time, somber. She guided them through one of the main streets, and Nani took a moment to admire the quaint shops. Neither of them talked, because Nani knew they were both thinking about Micaeli's death.

Svenja sighed, and she looked as tired as Nani felt, with dark circles under her eyes. It was surprising the amount of sleep people in the Grimrose Académie seemed to lack.

"I'm..." Svenja stopped in the middle of a sentence, darting her eyes behind her shoulder. "Don't look now. Act natural."

Nani immediately swirled to look. She spotted Odilia, dressed in black, pretending to look at a boutique shop.

"What did I say about not looking?" Svenja asked, hands on her hips.

"That never works," Nani replied. "How long has she been following us?"

"Since we left school," Svenja said.

Nani hadn't noticed, and both of them kept walking down the sidewalk, side by side. Nani caught herself looking in the glass surfaces of the shops, seeing Odilia behind them, always following.

"What does she want?" Nani asked.

"Nothing," Svenja said. "She just thinks it's a good prank or something. It's like having a shadow."

They kept going, turning another corner. A few moments later, Odilia was behind them again.

"That's why I wanted to take a walk," Svenja confessed. "I just can't..." Her voice trailed off, sounding tired and desperate.

Nani leaned closer to Svenja. "Do you trust me?" she asked.

"No," Svenja replied.

She grabbed Svenja's hand and started to run. Nani turned right at the first opportunity, then crossed the street and turned left. She could hear footsteps behind them but she didn't stop. The wind rushed across her face, sweeping her hair in an unruly mess of curls. Svenja ran by her side, a smile on her face despite their mad dash. A car honked at them, but Nani ran by it so fast that she didn't even see it coming. Svenja swore, but she was too out of breath to actually complete the sentence.

Svenja tripped on the paving stones, falling hands and knees first, and Nani helped her get up, continuing to run.

They must have run twelve or thirteen blocks into town by Nani's count, by the time they finally slowed down. Nani checked behind them—they'd lost Odilia.

Svenja backed into the wall, using it for support as her breath slowly came back.

"This is payback for the secret passageway," Nani said.

"Have you completely lost your mind?" Svenja asked, between huge gasps for breaths. "We could've died."

"Oh, come on, nobody in Switzerland drives over ten miles per hour." Nani dismissed her comment. "This isn't America."

"Thank God."

That sent a fit of giggling through Nani, her whole body shaking in spasms as she doubled up and sat on the sidewalk. Svenja finally stopped breathing hard and started laughing too. Finally, when Nani slowly felt she could stop laughing, she looked at Svenja.

Then she frowned.

"I think you're bleeding."

Svenja looked down at her leg and the dark stain that was showing through her jeans.

"Oh, fuck me," Svenja cursed, rolling the hem of her jeans halfway up to reveal a swollen, bloody cut. She put a finger to the wound, only to let out another string of curses in a different language.

Nani examined it. "It's not that bad."

"It means I can't dance, Nani."

Svenja looked up, took a deep breath, and Nani searched her bag for the things she'd always carried with her—because she was, after all, Tūtū's granddaughter, and she hadn't changed just because she had moved all the way across the world.

"This is going to hurt," she warned, before putting disinfectant on Svenja's knee.

Svenja muffled a scream, digging her fingers hard into Nani's shoulders, but Nani ignored her grip, cleaning the rest.

"Stop behaving like a child," Nani chastised her.

Svenja glared as Nani started wrapping a bandage around Svenja's leg.

Nani hadn't realized they were so close until she looked up and met Svenja's brown eyes.

Nani's heart beat fast, heat rising in her cheeks, her stomach fluttery. She had read in books over a dozen descriptions, watched it happen in television over a hundred times. Girl meets boy. Girl falls in love with boy.

Happily ever after.

But sitting here with Svenja, her heart thumping as strong as the waves clashing against the rocks, she started to doubt.

Nani had never liked any of the boys in school. Always thought there was something wrong with her, because the other girls giggled and gossiped, but Nani hadn't cared. She thought she must be too weird, too out of place to ever fall in love. It had taken her the longest time to realize that there was nothing wrong with her after all, but she'd never spoken the word lesbian to describe herself out loud, even if she knew.

With Svenja, however, it was all she could think about.

"Thank you," Svenja said quietly.

"Don't thank me," Nani said. "I'm the reason you're hurt in the first place."

"I have a weird feeling this might not be the only time that happens."

Svenja smiled, and Nani wondered what it would be like if she leaned in, or if she only closed her eyes, but then she took a deep breath, pulling herself away before she could wander down that path. She was already too involved with the happenings at Grimrose; she wouldn't let herself get pulled into this.

"You're going to be fine," Nani said. "It's just a small cut. You'll be running and dancing in no time."

"You're a doctor now?"

"No, but my father taught me the basics of first aid. CPR even."

Svenja's forehead lined with a frown. "But you still can't promise that I'll be fine."

"Then you'll just have to trust me," Nani said.

Svenja's eyes glinted, and Nani wished she hadn't been so quick to pull away.

"Yes. That's what I'm afraid of."

After helping Svenja into her room, Nani headed back to her own room and tried not to linger in the breath that they had shared, that moment where the possibilities were endless before she turned away, and she almost wished she wasn't so stubborn. It was too late now.

Nani opened the door to her room, and only a second later realized it wasn't locked. Rory and Yuki weren't there when she'd left. Had she forgotten to lock it? Tūtū was always chastising her for this.

There was nothing out of place at first. Nani checked her drawers, and Yuki's organized side of the room. It wasn't worth checking out Rory's side—it was a mess, and Nani wouldn't know the difference even if someone had completely upturned the room. Nani doubted Rory would either.

She moved to her side of the room, checking if the book

was still hidden behind the false board of the drawer in her wardrobe. It was there, right where it should be.

She collapsed back on the bed. No one had come in, no one had found what they were hiding.

That's when Nani noticed the note on Yuki's pillow.

She walked over to it, and in red pen, red as blood, was written:

I KNOW YOU HAVE IT

CHAPTER THIRTY-NINE

YUKI

Yuki had woken up after the ritual well rested, but there was a strange fire that still seemed to run through her veins. She felt as if something was about to come undone, but she didn't know what.

Yuki spent all that week in class, distracted and on edge. The ritual had failed, but her attempt at destroying the book had yielded nothing, and Yuki couldn't understand that. Couldn't acknowledge what it truly meant.

When Yuki walked into her room on Saturday after another afternoon with Reyna, Rory was just coming back from a run. Both stopped when they saw Nani standing in the middle of the room holding a piece of paper.

She looked scared.

"What happened?" Yuki asked.

"I think..." Nani's voice trailed off. "We got a message."

She held it out to them, and Yuki snatched it from her hands. Rory's lips moved as she read it silently, her face paling.

"Where did you find this?" Yuki asked.

"It was on your pillow," Nani replied, her fingers trembling slightly. "I left not long after you, and when I came back, the door was unlocked."

"You left the door unlocked?" Rory gasped. "You know that's how people get murdered, right? I saw it in the movies."

"*Halloween* is not a documentary," Yuki said. "I already told you that."

"It might as well be!"

"I don't think I left it unlocked," Nani said. "Did Ariane have keys?"

Yuki exchanged one look with Rory.

"Yes," Yuki said, putting the piece of paper down in the bed. "She lost one set in the beginning of the year, but the school gave her a new one. It's the one you have right now."

"So someone could have her old set," Nani concluded.

"It's possible," Yuki conceded.

Rory huffed, putting her hands on her hips. Her neck was sweaty after running, and she leaned against the end of her own bed, staring at the two of them.

"What do we do?" Rory asked. "You still have the book, right? They didn't take anything?"

"It was the first thing I checked," Nani said. "Nothing seemed out of place."

"So they didn't search for it?" Rory raised an eyebrow.

"Maybe they didn't have enough time," Nani replied. "Or they didn't want to risk it. But the book can't stay here. It's too obvious. The first place they'll search when they have the time is this room. Especially if they have a set of keys."

"We change the locks," Yuki said. "I'll talk to Reyna about it. I won't tell her the details, just that we need the lock changed."

Yuki looked at the message again, the letters seeming to glow a bright red. *I know you have it.* The same writing on the note they'd found inside the book.

The more they dug into the book, the more Yuki felt herself crumble, her edges coming undone, falling apart, until soon there would be nothing left of her.

She wanted to burn the book, but she couldn't even do that.

The weirdest part about that night was that she felt her hands on the fire, but she hadn't burned. She felt the flames licking her skin, the pain, but it hadn't left a single mark on her skin.

She was used to it. She didn't have any scars. Not from scraping her knees as a child, not when she'd gotten into a car accident with her father's driver, and not from the other night. It was something she took almost for granted; she could do these things and not be harmed. Like her body was compensating for the mess it was on the inside.

"Maybe they know we have it now," Nani suggested. "Or they got tired of waiting around to see if we would tell anyone about it."

"How would anyone know we found it?" Rory asked.

"At least now we can be sure someone wants it," Nani said.

"But we can't be sure they killed Ari for it," Yuki reminded them. "Or Micaeli."

"We know what this note is about," Rory said. "And that it's happened before, according to Ari. It's been happening for a while, and someone knows the truth."

"What are you saying?" Yuki asked. "You think the school is cursed?"

Rory shrugged.

"It doesn't matter what we think," Yuki said. "What matters is what we know. And what we know is someone is after the book and now they know we have it. We have to hide it."

Yuki breathed through her nose, trying to keep herself calm, trying not to freak out again. The note kept staring at her, working its magic, working at her edges until she was sure she'd come undone at any moment.

"All right," Rory said. "So what do we do? We have to hide it somewhere."

"Ella's house," Nani said.

Rory shook her head. "We can't risk losing it, and Ella's house isn't safe. What else do we have?"

"The library," both Nani and Yuki said in unison.

Rory frowned. "But that just leaves it out in the open."

"With five thousand other books," Nani pointed out. "If the person wants to find it, they'll have to search through the whole place."

"It's a good idea," Yuki said. "We can check on it, move it when we need to. Agreed?"

Nani nodded her head, and Rory did too reluctantly.

"Okay then," Yuki concluded.

"We still need to know who's after it," Nani said.

"Good luck with that," Yuki said. "I'm taking a shower."

"Hey, I just came back from running—" Rory started to protest, but Yuki was faster, and shut the door to muffle Rory's fist banging against it.

She rested her back against the door, breathing hard, shutting her eyes to her reflection in the mirror, trying to breathe.

When she opened them again, she looked into the mirror and saw that she was covered in blood.

The blood washed over half her face, her clothes, more was spilling out from an open gash on her throat. Yuki tried backing away, putting a hand to her mouth, muffling her scream. Her reflection did not follow. It only smiled, then lifted a hand. In her reflection's hand, there was the reddest apple Yuki had ever seen. She could taste it in her mouth right now, juicy and sweet.

Yuki choked, running to the toilet and vomiting what she'd eaten for lunch. Her hands trembled, fingers shaking, and she felt weak. She reached out a hand to touch the mirror, to steady herself, but there was nothing there but her own face staring out.

"This can't be happening," Yuki muttered to herself. "This isn't happening."

Yet it was like a wave that she'd seen coming from far away, unavoidable. From the moment she touched the book, there had been that burning sensation, the crawling underneath her skin. The moment their hands had all connected, like the energy was flowing freely between them all, and Yuki could feel it, *really* feel it, and then it had crawled inside her, found her darkest and deepest corners, and nestled there.

Yuki walked to the shower stall, turning it on. The hot

water steamed up the room. She stood underneath it, letting it wash over her. She squeezed her eyes shut, wishing she could forget all of this, that there was a reason the note had made her feel what she felt.

The feeling was anger.

Yuki had tried to repress it since Ari's death, from the moment they'd found the book, maybe from the moment she was born. Because she had to be good, she was her father's daughter. Her father with his dignity, his love of great things, and wasn't Yuki a great thing? Polite, kind, good. Yuki had shut herself inside that shell, and she'd never dared to come out, and now, all of it only got harder. Every day, it was harder to hide. She didn't even know who she was underneath all that, and she wanted to scream.

She wanted to let it all out.

She was tired of being perfect.

Yuki banged her fist against the marble wall of the bathroom, a silent release of the rage building inside her. It ran through her body like a shock, and when she looked up, she saw that the water on the shower had stopped. There weren't droplets anymore, but instead, a white mist falling from the ceiling, and Yuki reached out.

It was snow. A flake rested in her palm for a split second before melting.

Yuki had made it snow.

She had done magic.

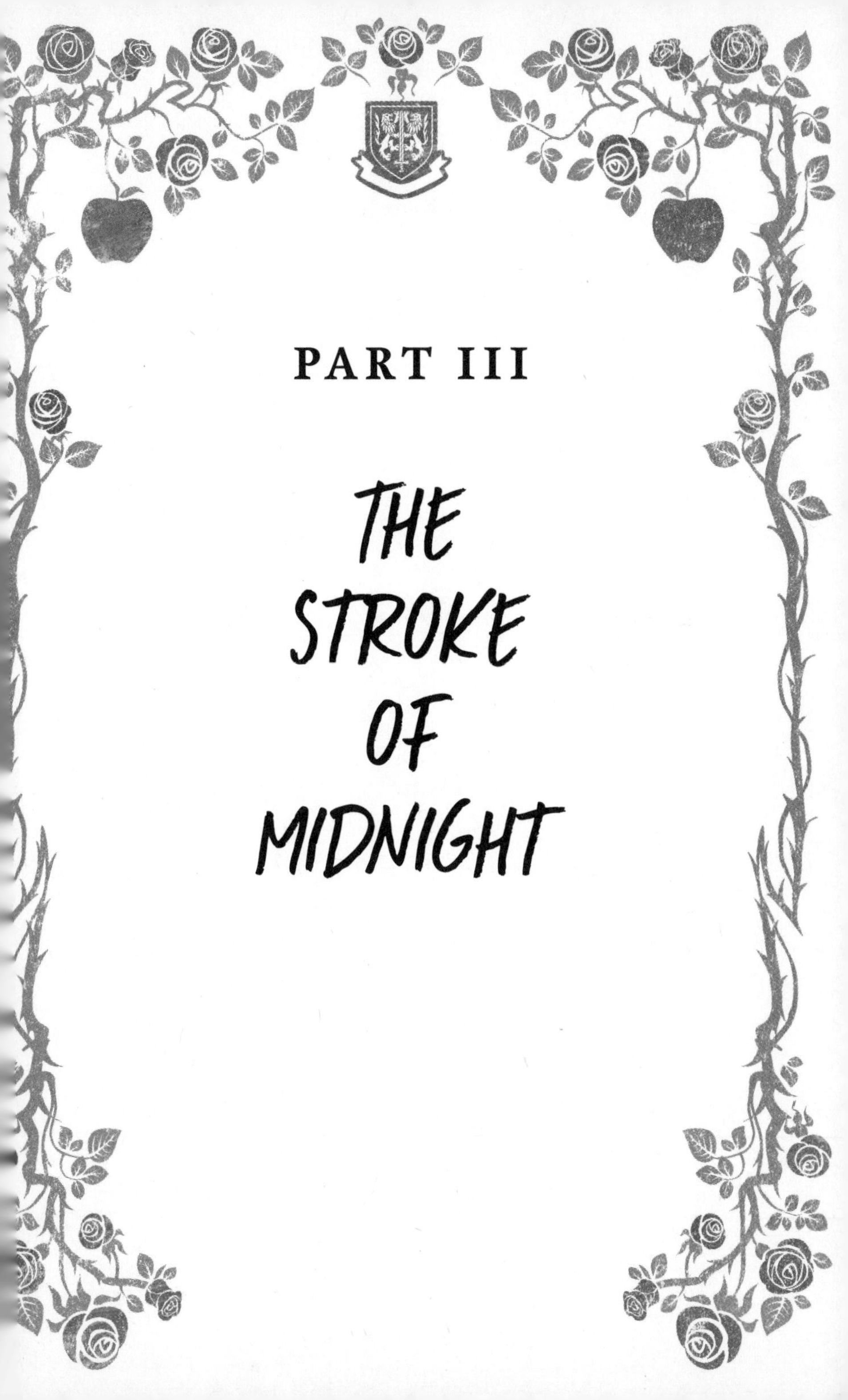

PART III

THE STROKE OF MIDNIGHT

CHAPTER FORTY

ELLA

Ella had waited to see if her stepmother and stepsisters were really leaving for the weekend before she texted Frederick. She had done most of her chores already, put an audiobook on, then pulled out the broom and started sweeping, letting the narration keep her company. When she finished, she showered and put on the usual amount of makeup, carefully covering any hint of purple or green from marks on her face. Most had faded from last time, and there were times Ella could go weeks without having to put makeup on.

The gates were closed, of course. Ella didn't have a key. If she didn't have any tasks in the garden or cleaning the stables, Sharon would lock her in the house, the windows padlocked. She had to get out through the window in the attic, slide down the roof, and drop into the garden. In the first year, she'd taken a fall and twisted her ankle. It had bloated, and Ella limped for almost three weeks but said nothing, lest Sharon lock the attic too.

Ella started to climb the tree next to the gate, trying not to tear her dress or her coat. The wall faced the back street, which made it the safest route to sneak out. She made her way up the branches and then jumped over the wall, feeling a rush of adrenaline as she dropped onto the pavement.

"So the song was wrong," a voice said behind her. "It's raining girls."

Ella jumped, whirling around to face Frederick. "What are you doing here?"

"I came to get you," he said. "Is the gate too convenient for you?"

"No challenge there," Ella said, looking up, still feeling uneasiness at Frederick's presence so close to her house. "How did you know where I live?"

Frederick smiled. "I have my ways."

"I'm serious, Freddie," Ella insisted, looking over her shoulders, expecting to see Sharon any moment. "You can't be here."

"I cornered Silla, got her talking," he admitted. "Wouldn't dare try to get anything out of Stacie."

"Oh, so she scares you too, huh?"

"To death," Freddie agreed. "Luckily, I know both of them are on their way to another country to enjoy a music festival that will get canceled at the last minute."

Ella opened her mouth, taking a moment. "What did you do?"

"Me?" Freddie asked, innocently. "Nothing at all. Just mentioned it was very exclusive, and a friend had tickets but I wouldn't be able to go."

"You *didn't*."

"I must use my skills for something, even if it's to beguile two poor innocent girls into leaving their house."

Ella looked up in disbelief that he'd do something like that. For her. She tried to push her mind away from Sharon's inevitable reaction toward the twins when the show got canceled. Even if it wasn't their fault, Ella knew the consequences of Sharon's ire all too well.

"I have something for you," she said finally, taking a sturdy package out of her bag.

Freddie looked at it for a second, confused. When he ripped it open, he found a yellow scarf. Freddie took it out, looking at it with wide eyes, open mouth, and Ella found herself stuttering.

"It's not a big deal," Ella said, hurrying her words. "I already had the wool at home, so I just had to do a few rows."

Freddie was silent, clutching the scarf.

"If you don't like it, you don't have to wear it," Ella said quickly.

"No!" Freddie said, as if he suddenly remembered how to speak.

"No, you don't like it?"

Freddie stopped. "Why do we keep doing this?"

"Really, it's no—"

Frederick put it around his neck, looking comfortable.

"How do I look?" he asked.

Ella looked up. "Like the embodiment of autumn."

Freddie looked up to the withered red and yellow trees around them on the streets of Constanz and let out a curse.

"It's the damned red hair," he replied.

"I like it," Ella said, feeling herself blush just as she said it.

Frederick offered her his arm. "Let's go before all the ice cream runs out."

Ella took his arm, and they walked together through the streets of Constanz. At first, Ella kept looking behind her, conscious that someone she knew, or someone who knew Sharon, would notice them, but after a while, Ella started to relax. She hadn't been able to do that since the night of the ritual.

They arrived at the gelato festival, and she tried to put all thoughts of Grimrose or deaths or the book out of her mind.

"Last time I came here, it was with my mother," Frederick said. "She had an absolutely horrifying sweet potato salad gelato."

"Ew," Ella said in disgust. "Does your mother come to visit a lot?"

"Once a semester. My father comes sometimes too, but his visits are quicker, only when he's passing through for work."

"What does he do?" Ella asked.

"Movie producer," said Frederick. "Works here and there, but when he's in Europe he tries to visit."

"Is that why you're studying here?" Ella asked.

Freddie shrugged. "I know it sounds harsh when I say it like that, but his business takes a lot of time. And so does raising children, so he had to make a choice."

"Oh."

"I don't blame him," Freddie said, and there was a twinkle in his eyes that Ella recognized from miles away.

"So that's what you want to do too."

Frederick laughed. "That obvious, huh? My father used to take me out to the sets when I was younger. It's like seeing magic right in front of your eyes. I want to study film, and then go make some of my own."

Frederick's hand brushed hers as they walked. It sent a buzzing through Ella's body.

"And you?" Freddie asked. "Your parents?"

Suddenly, there was the abyss between them.

"My parents passed away," she managed to say. It was so long ago, but sometimes, it felt like it was yesterday. If she closed her eyes, she could still feel the warmth of home, the soft touch of her mother's velvet cushions, where she laid her head to sleep while her father read out loud.

Frederick's face collapsed. "I'm so sorry. I didn't mean to bring it up. I thought..."

"It's okay," Ella said sheepishly. "Not a lot of people know. It's why I live with Sharon. She's my father's second wife."

Frederick nodded, and Ella was eager to change the subject again.

"And you?" Frederick asked. "What do you want to do?"

Ella thought about giving him an answer, but nothing seemed real until her eighteenth birthday, until she was able to leave the house. Until she was free.

Ella had a hard time thinking about what came after that.

"I don't know," Ella answered truthfully. "There's still time."

Freddie agreed, and it was finally their turn to order. Ella was going to get the smallest cup, the one she had money for, but instead, Frederick ordered seven different cups so they had all the weirdest flavors to taste.

They sat at a table and ate and talked about school and about their lives. Ella listened while Frederick talked about his family. She shared what little she remembered from hers, and she felt like by the end, they were old friends. They shared from the same cups, and sometimes, Ella's hand would brush against his, and her heart would beat just a little faster.

They both got up as the afternoon started getting darker.

"Maybe we should go back for round two," Frederick said. "I think the peanut butter and Belgian chocolate was special."

"Round two might ruin things," Ella said, even though that had been her favorite flavor too.

"Why?" Frederick demanded.

"Have you never heard of the expression 'too much of a good thing'?"

"Well, I happen to think we deserve good things."

Ella smiled at him, but her heart was already far away with her thoughts. She supposed that there was nothing wrong with wanting good things—especially for people who could get them. To Frederick, and to most people at Grimrose, they had never wanted for anything.

"It's nice that you think like that," Ella said.

Freddie shrugged. "Why not? Sure, it's lucky that we get this...all of this. We should enjoy it, every part of it."

"Sometimes," Ella said quietly, "I think I don't deserve it."

Frederick stopped in his tracks. "Ella, you deserve the entire world. Don't let anyone tell you otherwise."

Ella looked up at him and wondered what she'd done to deserve this. Perhaps she only had to be patient, because in the end, her happy ending would be waiting for her.

She wouldn't have to change anything at all.

Freddie leaned in a little closer, stooping down. Ella tiptoed closer to him, feeling his warmth, inhaling his cologne that smelled like flowers and vanilla. A sweet smell like this sweet boy, and if he tasted like that too, she'd be glad of it.

Just at that moment, thunder cracked above them, and Ella jumped. The sky opened up and rain began to fall.

"I have to go," she said.

"Back before midnight?" he joked lightly, looking down at their intertwined hands, and Ella felt her heart might burst.

"You know, gotta jump a couple of more walls."

Frederick nodded, smiling at her.

"Thank you," she said, as the rain fell harder. She'd have to hurry. "I had a great time."

"Except maybe for the corn ice cream?"

"No, I loved that one too," Ella said, laughing.

Ella turned to go, but Frederick held onto her hand, his fingers warm in hers for a moment before Ella left through the rain.

She could wait a little longer for her happy ending.

She was very good at waiting.

CHAPTER FORTY-ONE

RORY

They put the book in the library. Nani had done it in the middle of the night, risking the ire of Mephistopheles, but that was the only advantage they had—the cat wasn't going to let anyone else in its library without making a fuss. The book had been slipped between the shelves, hidden in plain sight, but Rory still felt uneasy.

The note didn't help. Yuki had talked to Reyna and they changed the locks, but Rory couldn't help imagining someone turning the doorknob in the middle of the night, feeding her nightmares.

Yuki had scoffed at the word *curse*, but Rory was a believer now. Things like that couldn't be a coincidence, and if there was a magic book, there could be a curse.

I know you have it.

The person knew what the book did or what it really meant. They had the key, and the girls had nothing.

It was another Friday, another week of training. She'd skipped the last session with Pippa, but she missed the challenge. She also didn't want Pippa to think she was a coward for not showing up just because they'd had a fight. That wasn't it at all. Or not all of it, anyway. She just hadn't the time to think about it, not since the seance and the threatening note.

Rory left class that afternoon and made her way to the gym.

To her surprise, Pippa was already there, but she wasn't running or even in training clothes. She was wearing her regular uniform, the skirt spreading around her, her shirt buttoned up to the last button on her neck, pressing against her elegant throat. Rory's never was, with always at least two buttons loose, not to mention the fact that they were often lopsided, with the sleeves folded up. Rory saw no point in sleeves, since wearing them meant she couldn't show off her arms.

"You're here," Rory said.

"The more surprising thing is that *you* are," Pippa pointed out.

"I've had a lot on my mind," Rory said as an excuse, the understatement of the century. "Why aren't you in training clothes?"

"I didn't know if you were coming," she answered, her arms folded. "So, you want to beat me, fair and square?"

Rory felt a rush of heat to her cheeks. "You know that's not what I meant."

"What did you mean, then?"

Rory blinked, surprised at her question. It didn't seem like Pippa to ask for clarification on anything Rory did. Rory and Pippa didn't rely on words. It had always been about the power in their muscles, the way they danced around each other. Even when she'd put Rory against the wall, it felt more right than this.

Rory wasn't good with words. She was always bound to disappoint.

"It's been a shitty year," Rory said.

Pippa nodded. "I know you're still grieving over Ariane's death, and it's your right. But that can't stop you from doing other things."

"Who says that's the only thing stopping me?"

"It isn't," Pippa said. "It's just your latest excuse."

Rory felt the words smack her faster than she was prepared for. Faster than she would have liked, in a way that she couldn't unhear.

Because the thing was, Pippa was right.

It was an excuse. Of course she was devastated over Ariane's death. Rory had never lost someone. But even Ariane's presence had been a shield Rory hid behind—Ari had been there to validate her in who she was and what she wanted. And even with Ella and Yuki, they never pushed her too far. Not like Pippa did.

And the problem was, Rory was realizing, that in a way, Ariane had been holding her back.

Ari was just another in a long series of excuses Rory had made up along the years, when she didn't want to confront her fears, when she didn't try anything at all, because it was better than the alternative: that she would try and fail.

"I know it's fucked up," Pippa said, getting up. "I know that whatever went on with these deaths, it's affecting us all. But we're still alive."

Pippa stopped right next to her. It wasn't an attack, and Pippa didn't touch her, but her dark brown eyes were still firm, not looking away.

"I'm not going to say what you have to do," Pippa said. "But you can't make excuses for all of it. I had to work so hard to be here, you can't imagine how hard, and you just think you can blow things off and come back like nothing happened."

"I know—"

"You don't," Pippa cut her off. "You talked about beating me like you know what it meant. Rory, have you noticed that I'm the only Black girl on the fencing team?"

Rory had noticed it. She had noticed that Pippa was one of the few in the entire school too.

"And sure, we're all rich and it's all the same, except that it's not," Pippa said adamantly. "It's not, and it is exhausting that I have to pretend it is. I didn't expect that from you. I don't care if you like me, but I want you to respect me."

Rory blinked, unable to reply.

"You have to work harder than this, Rory," Pippa said, and Rory's name on her lips felt like she was pulling her strings, ready for Rory to come undone. "You can't keep choosing to not do anything because you can't face the consequences."

With that, she left.

Rory went back to her room, and then she wrote a letter to her parents.

CHAPTER FORTY-TWO

YUKI

It started with the snow and went downhill from there.

Her body grew cold. Her hands trembled. She'd keep them in her pockets, because if she didn't, the surfaces she touched started freezing, and the water she touched would begin to frost. But that wasn't all.

Yuki would catch glimpses of herself in the mirror. Sometimes, she'd look so quickly she didn't have time to register before she looked away. But other times, it wouldn't be her at all. She'd be smaller, her eyes and cheeks rounder. Or she'd be covered in white scars. Each time though, she had skin as white as snow. Hair as black as ebony. Lips as red as blood.

So she did her best to avoid reflective surfaces, avoid mirrors, avoid looking in the wrong direction, afraid of what she'd see there. And still, always, there was this strange power underneath her skin, ready to break free at any moment.

The ritual had changed her.

Yuki had gone in as herself, and she came out a shattered monster, barely contained within her body, magic gluing her together.

For that was what it was; Yuki had no other word for it.

It was magic.

At least with the book tucked away at the library, Yuki could pretend that her answers weren't connected to the book somehow, and worse, that Ariane knew that this would happen. Missing Ariane had turned to blame, a growing resentment. She'd left them with this mess and was actually the lucky one; she'd left the clue behind and moved on to a better, easier place.

Yuki was losing her composure. She was losing herself, little by little.

She stood outside in the gardens, and she didn't shiver despite the encroaching winter. The green grass had turned almost brown, the trees had turned red, then yellow, then nothing at all, their branches twisting bereft while reaching for the sky. The world grew colder each day with December, its color slowly fading. Just like Yuki.

She kept her hands to herself as she watched the Grimrose students sort out decorations for the winter ball. The decorations were still being brought in, though half the school was already lit up for the holidays. Yuki watched from her place in the gardens as they passed through the main gates, her hands trembling on her lap.

"Are you sure it's comfortable to sit out in this cold?" a voice spoke behind her.

Yuki turned around to see Penelope. She'd already changed to her winter uniform, with wool socks and a big overcoat, a blue scarf tied around her neck, her blond hair falling over it.

"I like the cold," Yuki said, hiding her fingers in her pockets.

"I hate it," Penelope muttered, adjusting her coat to sit down. "I can't wait for summer."

Yuki scoffed.

Penelope looked sideways at her. "Haven't seen you around much," she said. "You look..."

"Like I haven't slept in a week?"

"I was going to say like shit."

Yuki laughed, and her lungs contracted, like she was trying to control all of it, keep it in. Yuki had years of experience. If magic thought it was going to burst out of her and live freely, it'd have to think again. Yuki had put on a mask early in life, and she'd never learned to take it off.

"What's wrong?" Penelope asked.

"Nothing," Yuki replied. "It's finals."

This time, it was Penelope who scoffed. "Right. You can give that answer to everybody else, but not to me."

"You think I'm lying?"

"I've spent enough time with you to know."

Yuki's trembling fingers kept gnawing at her edges, willing for her to do something, to let that nervousness out, but Yuki kept it in, kept her fear, her anger, locked up tight.

"And what do you know about me?" Yuki asked, raising her chin.

"I know everything about you, Yuki," Penelope said, and then Yuki had to laugh, because she didn't think anyone in the entire world would ever know what that was like.

"No, you don't," Yuki replied, getting up, but Penelope was faster, pulling her hand away, holding her in place, the same way she'd done on the first day.

Except this time, she didn't let go.

"You do what others want. What others expect," Penelope said. "And you're scared to death that if you stop doing what everybody wants you to do, they're going to leave you behind."

Yuki stopped in her tracks.

"I know what it's like to pretend to be someone you're not. The way you hide from the others, the way you never tell them what you're really feeling because you're scared they're going to think you're terrible?"

"Stop."

"Your friends don't even know you. You hide from them like you hide from yourself."

"Stop, Penelope."

"Have you even told them what you said to Ariane, that maybe you were the one that made her—"

"Stop!"

The word hung in the air like an echo, and in that word, Yuki saw what she had done. Penelope looked around, wonder lighting up her eyes.

Particles of icy shards hung around them like snowflakes, a bubble that had burst from within Yuki herself. Snowflakes like mirrors, reflecting on the surface before melting to the touch.

"This is..." She breathed out. "This is magic."

Yuki was too stunned to say anything, her hands trembling from the release she felt the moment she let her anger out. Her heart had calmed down, like it was begging for this, and the magic settled around her like a warm cloak. The magic that came out as soon as she let any emotion show.

"How?" Penelope asked, looking up at Yuki.

Yuki wanted to tell someone. Not the girls, who would turn this into some big conspiracy. She wanted the truth to be what it was.

"I don't know," Yuki replied. "It has to do with Ari's death, I think."

Penelope's eyes flashed, concern lining her face. "Ari was saying weird things to me," Penelope confessed, biting her lower lip. "Speaking in riddles. She kept going on about... You're going to think this is silly, but she talked about—"

"Fairy tales?" Yuki completed for her.

Penelope nodded, grave. "I don't know what she was really on about," Penelope said. "She thought we were under some kind of curse. That's one of the last things she said to me."

"Ariane believed that?" Yuki asked, her gut twisting.

"I think so," Penelope agreed. She reached out to touch a mirrored snowflake with her fingers, awe still in her eyes. "I thought she was going crazy. Talking about deaths and curses and magic. I thought she'd flipped."

"But now you don't."

"Now I think she might have been onto something," Penelope said, her eyes turning from the snowflakes hovering in the air around them. "Maybe we are cursed. This isn't normal."

"And you think believing in a curse is normal?"

Penelope shrugged. "You're the one doing magic, sweetheart."

Yuki shook her head vehemently, ignoring the sarcasm in Penelope's voice. "I don't want this. I don't know what it is, but I don't want it. I can't have it."

Penelope looked up at her again, kindness in her eyes. "Did you tell them?"

Yuki's silence was answer enough.

"I understand," Penelope said. "Hiding what you really are. Who you really are, because you're scared of what will happen if they find out. Believe me, I know." Her voice sounded truthful, almost hurt. "But you can't let that fear stop you," she continued. "Because then everything that happens will only be an illusion."

"My friends know me," Yuki said instead, hoping that somehow it was true. That her friends would know, despite all of it, despite her hiding, despite her fear, despite her desperate, crumbling loneliness. "Because I am—"

"You're not Ella," Penelope snapped, her voice harsher. "You're not some boring goody two-shoes—"

"Don't talk that way about her," Yuki snapped, her voice ice cold. "You don't know her."

Penelope met her stare. "Fine. But you're not her. You want to be like her, because everybody loves her, and you want everyone to love you too. But you're not her, and you're never going to be."

Yuki felt the tears prickling in the back of her eyes, but she didn't let them fall. Didn't let Penelope see that weakness.

"People may love you," Penelope said, finally, "but it's not real love if they don't know who you are."

"I don't think anyone will ever really know me," Yuki murmured.

"I want to," Penelope replied. "Let all of it out. Your anger, your fear. This world is pretty messed up already. It can take the weight of your feeling."

"What if I do? What if I only find out I'm terrible?"

Yuki had always known it, deep inside. It was the thing she saw when she looked in the mirror. The part of her who craved the pain, who craved things Yuki could not name, and who was always going to be reprimanded for it. Yuki had tried shaping herself like Ella, because otherwise, she'd be giving in to that darkness, and she didn't know how much longer she could take.

"Who even gets to define what terrible is?" Penelope replied. "That's just a thing to stop you from becoming who you're meant to be, because the world is scared of girls who know what they want."

Penelope reached out and squeezed Yuki's hand, the magic still hanging around them, stinging the air.

"Find something, and then make it yours. Make it true. You deserve that. That's the girl I want to know. And if other people can't love you for what you are, then they don't deserve you at all."

CHAPTER FORTY-THREE

ELLA

Two weeks before the ball, on a chilly December morning, Ella carried three separate boxes to the castle. Rory met her outside in the courtyard where the tree was being hauled up with its decorations. It was almost like a ceremony, and the students crowded the courtyard and upper corridors to watch.

"God, it's cold," Rory complained as they stood on the courtyard. "What are you carrying?"

"It's a surprise," Ella said. "You can open it the day of the ball."

Rory rolled her eyes, taking two of the boxes from her to help carrying the load; Ella still held onto Nani's. They stood shoulder to shoulder, watching as the tree was being pulled up, held by strong metal cables pinned to the four corners of the courtyard, the sound clinking as the thousands of ornaments rose in the air, a tumultuous musical sound.

As soon as the tree was up, there was clapping, and Ella's eyes trailed upward to see the top, and only then saw someone reaching out for one of the branches.

"Who's that?" Ella asked. She pointed to a student, and Rory's gaze followed Ella's finger.

A girl stood on one of the many balconies overlooking the courtyard. She leaned over the edge, trying to reach for something in the tree—a round, decorated fruit on one of the higher branches, her body precariously close to the razor-sharp cable holding the tree in place.

"What is she doing?" Rory asked, frowning deeply. Ella recognized Annmarie, her face straining in effort as she extended her arm.

"Rory, we have to stop her," Ella said, realization dawning on her as she ran for the stone steps beneath the balcony. It was like she'd somehow seen the scene before. Dread spread across her body. "Annmarie! Annmarie!"

"I don't think she can hear us," Rory said behind her. "There's too much noise here."

"We have to go up," Ella said, heart drumming against her rib cage.

As a hundred students looked on, Annmarie's fingers clutched the fruit in the tree, green nails gripping triumphantly. Except that it didn't budge from its branch, and Annmarie moved forward, her mouth dropping open in a silent scream as her body faltered and as she fell, the metal cable holding the tree in place slid across her soft neck, splitting head from body.

Ella put her hand to her mouth to contain her scream.

After Annmarie's body was recovered, the school called all the students for an emergency assembly. The room was packed. Alethea was sobbing loudly in the front row, consoled by a tired-looking Rhiannon, their group now down by two.

Ella's stomach twisted in pity and guilt, because maybe if the ritual had worked and they'd gotten answers from Ari, they could have stopped this from happening. Nani and Yuki rushed in, Yuki looking pale and sick, her eyes ringed with black. Penelope was with her, and offered Ella a tight-lipped smile as she bumped her shoulder, moving away to find a seat somewhere else.

"I thought it would take more time," Ella said. "After Micaeli... Two in the same semester. The others weren't as close."

"Are you sure it wasn't an accident?" Nani asked, saying out loud what they were all thinking.

"It looked like one," Rory said, uncertain, her voice a whispered rush. "But that's in the book too, isn't it?"

"'The Juniper Tree,'" said Nani beside them, her voice dark. "It could have been worse."

"How could this be worse?" Rory muttered.

"You didn't read the tale?" Nani asked, but Rory just shrugged and Nani let out an exasperated sigh. "Stepmother decapitates her stepson, and then cooks him in a soup, feeding it to her husband. Trust me, we were lucky."

Ella's stomach churned in response, her heart twisting, because Annmarie hadn't been lucky. Nor had Micaeli or Ari.

"We have to do something," Ella said.

"We did enough," Yuki snapped by her side.

Her tone was resentful, and Ella understood where she was coming from. The list wasn't complete—Ari had the past names, and theirs, and no one else. They couldn't get ahead of it if they didn't know who it was targeting. Ella spotted Frederick in the crowd, waving to her, standing tall above the other students and he came forward to where they were standing. Ella rushed to meet him, throwing her arms around him.

Freddie's arms wrapped around her too. His chin rested on the top of her head, and at least here, she felt safe. Warm, with her cheek pressed against his coat.

"You okay?" Freddie asked, gently.

"No," Ella said in a whisper, and he couldn't offer her any words of comfort for that, but he squeezed her even tighter.

She let go of Freddie's embrace, and looked behind her, but Yuki had turned her head, her hands shoved deep inside her pockets.

"You both better sit down," Yuki said, her voice rough. "It's about to start."

Ella sat next to Yuki. Freddie's hand had slipped into hers, and his grip was comforting.

Reyna's voice echoed through the speakers as she told the students not to be afraid. Ella drowned half of the speech out with her own inner monologue, trying to fit the pieces they knew into the story. Girls had been dying before Ari, years and years ago, some in the same pattern. The book predicted the unhappy endings, and all of it was connected.

And then Ari's list, she had figured it out. Matched past names with past stories. Discovered which girls had met a fairy-tale end.

But she hadn't said what the book really meant. And was it just predicting the deaths, or was it binding the girls' fates to it? Did the book decide who lived and who died? Or was there someone using the book to set up the girls?

Freddie squeezed her hand throughout the speech. Ella smiled at him. Yuki eyed their intertwined hands but said nothing, turning her eyes to her stepmother almost immediately.

The assembly ended, but Ella wasn't comforted by Reyna's warm words of reassurance. She slipped her free hand into her pocket, and there was something there. It must have happened in the rush to get into the assembly, and she'd only noticed it now. A crumpled piece of paper.

She opened it and gasped at the words.

ONE OF YOU IS NEXT

CHAPTER FORTY-FOUR

NANI

The assembly had been a waste of time.

Reyna had gone over safety measures and stated that most balconies were now off-limits, and so were the secret passageways inside the school, and if students respected these rules, there would be no more losses.

Nani doubted it. According to the book and Ari's list, this had been happening for hundreds of years now. They all had something in common, something tying them to this fate and Grimrose.

And if Nani stayed any longer, if she dug deeper, would she end up the same way? She had felt a strange energy connecting them at the ritual, and it hadn't been the same since. It wasn't a bad feeling though, just something she couldn't recognize. Something that almost felt like peace.

The weekend arrived, and Yuki vanished like she usually did. Nani had fallen into a routine with the other girls, and now it was strange when they weren't around. The room felt empty without Rory's loud complaints, without Yuki's cutting comments, with the laughter that had started bubbling naturally between them when they were feeling like themselves. Nani had watched it, even laughed along, and for a moment, she'd forgotten.

Forgotten that she still hadn't uncovered any of the secrets of Grimrose or why her father had left her there or where he really was.

Her phone rang, and she picked up, trying not to be disappointed that it was only Tūtū.

"Hi, Tūtū," Nani said.

"Hello, moʻo," Tūtū said on the other side of the line. "How are you doing? Your school called me this week."

Nani sat up straighter. "It what?"

"They wanted to make sure I knew you were safe there," her grandmother's familiar voice told her. "That poor girl. What a terrible accident."

"Yes," Nani agreed, her voice coming out dry. Nani hadn't told her grandmother about Micaeli or Annmarie, or the fact that Nani had taken over a dead girl's room. "It was."

Tūtū's voice seemed to hesitate on the other side of the line, and Nani tensed.

"Was that the only reason you called?" she asked. "Or did you, did you—"

"No, I haven't heard anything," Tūtū replied with a sigh. "I'm sorry, moʻo. I know you're still waiting, but he hasn't called me either. You know how he is."

"It's been so long, Tūtū. Why did he even send me here if he wasn't going to be around?"

"It's no use trying to sort out why your father did anything," Tūtū said, and it was the first sensible thing Nani had heard her say about her father in all these years. "He comes and goes as he wants. It's no different this time."

"But he left," Nani mumbled.

He'd left. He'd chosen to leave her.

Again.

Just like he had done to Nani's mother all those years ago, left her looking at the horizon, wondering when he was going to come home. For all her trying, Nani was exactly the same.

"I do have something for you, though," Tūtū said. "I've been looking into flights, and I have money saved. If you want, as soon as classes are over, you can come home. I've already talked to your old school, and you can finish the school year here."

An offer to go back home.

Tūtū continued over the speaker, "You'll be here before Christmas. Come home, mo'o."

Nani hung on the words for a long time, hearing her grandmother's breathing on the other side, the offer in the air. She wanted to. She wanted to leave it all behind.

"I can't," Nani said, and she realized it was true.

Not only because she couldn't leave this business unfinished, but because she didn't want to. Because in the end...

In the end, the girls had become her friends.

That truth hit Nani like a lightning bolt. She wasn't expecting it, she wasn't even sure when it had begun. She had told them no secrets of her own, hadn't shared her books, her father's promise. And yet, there had been that growing feeling within her bones—Rory asking to copy her homework and Ella guiding her through the corridors and Yuki sneaking chocolate to their bedroom. Those things had been tiny, but they had grown within her, like seeds taking root, and they blossomed into something new, something rare and precious that Nani had never experienced before.

And it wasn't just her curiosity moving her now, her desire to know why her father had left her there, or the true mystery of Grimrose. It was more than that. It was a shared commitment; they were in this *together*. She wasn't just a stranger to Grimrose anymore. She was a part of this story too.

She couldn't abandon them before they fixed it. Couldn't leave before she found the truth.

"I can't," Nani repeated. "I have something here. I don't know what it is yet, but I want to stay. I can't just leave it unfinished."

She could feel Tūtū's smile from the other side of the line. In the end, even if she wanted to see her granddaughter for Christmas, there was a part of her that was proud that Nani was choosing to stay, choosing to commit to something.

It was time she left her father and his empty promises behind.

No good would come of dwelling on it.

If she waited for other people to fulfill their promises, then she'd end up exactly like her mother and make no choices of her own. Nani didn't want to be like her, and she didn't want to be like her father either.

"I'll send you your gifts in the mail," Tūtū said. "And you stay right there, mo'o."

"I will," Nani said, her smile coming through in her voice. "Thank you, Tūtū."

CHAPTER FORTY-FIVE

RORY

Rory had been so worried over Annmarie's death that she'd almost forgotten to worry about the reply to the letter she sent her parents, until it came. She read it twice, making sure she hadn't read it wrong in her rush to get an answer. Letters were easier between them because it made things official. Besides, Rory was sure that her parents didn't even know her cell number.

She'd read it right. They were coming to see her, and they would discuss her proposal.

Rory shoved the letter into the bottom drawer, hiding the wax seal beneath a forgotten pile of schoolwork.

She hadn't seen her parents since before school started. Even though she'd barely left the house all summer, they hadn't been around much—off dealing with foreign affairs or other important things they didn't feel the need to tell her about. The one time she had gone out, slipping through the gates and into the city, they'd dragged her home after a few hours, three security guards on her tail.

Her parents had given her another stern talking-to about her responsibilities and not putting herself in danger. Rory mostly ignored them. She was used to it, but this time, she wasn't going to let them win. They'd listen to what she had to say.

On Saturday, she set out to Constanz to meet them. Her parents had set the time and place, an inconspicuous coffee shop in the rich part of town. An early winter storm had come during the night, the first of the season, painting the thickets of grass white with snow. Her boots left imprints in it as she made her way down through the gardens, into town, going over her plan in her head. She'd explain about the tournament. She'd say she wanted to compete. She wouldn't give them a chance to say no. She'd bargain her way out, even if it meant taking more responsibility. She'd do anything.

She didn't want to disappoint Pippa again.

More than that, Rory didn't want to disappoint herself.

The cold made her muscles ache, her knees stiff. She'd taken her pills that morning, already predicting she'd need them, but she was going to show her parents she was doing just fine. She would show them that she could compete in the tournament, that she was strong enough, that she could do this one thing, even when her body did everything it could to turn her into a liar.

She got to the café, scanning the windows for the sight of red hair that matched her own. Or for her father's tall frame, wearing glasses now that he'd gotten older. She moved to the next window and still didn't see anything. She checked her phone; she was only a couple of minutes late. Her parents were never late.

She opened the door, searching again for the familiar faces of her parents, but she saw someone else instead.

Sitting in the café was Éveline Travere. Her parents' secretary.

Éveline perked up when she saw Rory, giving a small wave. She was younger than her employers, in her late thirties, her blond hair tied back in an elegant ponytail. She gestured for Rory to take a seat, and unwillingly, Rory did so, taking off her coat and draping it on the back of her chair. Éveline noticed her clothes, and her lips thinned, but the rules were that Rory could wear whatever she wanted while she was in school. That included a loose checkered shirt and black cargo pants.

"What are you doing here?" Rory said by way of greeting.

Éveline raised one elegant eyebrow. "Where are your manners, Aurore? It's so nice to see you—"

"Don't call me Aurore," Rory said. "You know I prefer Rory. What are you doing here? Where are my parents?"

Éveline shifted in her seat. She made a gesture to one of the café's waitresses, ordering two hot chocolates for them both with a smile.

"They send their apologies, but they couldn't come," she said. "You know how busy their schedule is. His Majesty—"

"Yes, yes, whatever," Rory cut her off. "I asked for one thing, and they said they'd be here. They never visit me.

We're practically neighbors. They couldn't make a two-hour car ride?"

Éveline's smile was strained. "You know it's not that simple."

"It is," Rory insisted. Un-fucking-believable. "I asked for one thing, and they couldn't even come."

"They love you," Éveline said, "and they're deeply sorry they couldn't make it to discuss this in person."

"So what?" asked Rory, taking a sip of the hot chocolate Éveline had ordered. "I'm supposed to talk to you instead of them?"

"You can't be angry with them, Rory."

"Of course I can," Rory said. "They're never here. Do you think my mother still remembers the color of my eyes or only because of the ridiculous portrait in the living room?"

Éveline didn't rise to Rory's bait. "They explained the situation; it's about some kind of fencing tournament. You want their permission to participate, is that it?"

"Yes," Rory said moodily, crossing her arms. "I was supposed to talk to them about it. This is important to me."

Éveline took a sip of her own chocolate, red lipstick staining the rim of her cup.

"Rory, you know the rules," Éveline said calmly. "You're not allowed to leave Constanz and the school grounds, not allowed to compete in tournaments—"

"Why?" Rory demanded.

"Things haven't changed since last time," Éveline said, giving her a once-over. "The rules are always the same."

"I've trained for this," Rory said. "I've been training for the past three years. And I'm *good,* Éveline. I'm good, I can hold my own, and besides, we're all going to be wearing masks in the tournament. It's not like anyone will even know it's me."

Éveline set down her cup with a small clink.

"Your parents wanted me to give you the news in person because they knew you'd take it this way," Éveline said. "They are concerned for your safety, your future. They don't want you to get hurt. You're so fragile that—"

"Fragile?" Rory exclaimed, loud enough that other people in the café turned their heads to look at her. "Is that all they think I am? A girl made of glass?"

"That's not what they think," she replied. "Please, Aurore, don't make a scene."

"Don't call me Aurore," Rory snapped. "I'll make a scene if I please."

"Someone may recognize you," Éveline hissed from across the table. "And then—"

"Who's going to recognize me?" Rory laughed. "I'm never in any pictures. People don't know who I am, because of this obsession with my safety, thinking I'm so fucking *fragile.*"

Éveline wrinkled her nose at Rory's swearing, but Rory didn't stop there.

"You can tell them both I said that," Rory told her. "You can tell them I'm doing the tournament because I'm done with hiding out of some paranoia they've harbored since the day I was born."

"Your birth—" Éveline started.

"I'm not done," Rory snapped, and her tone was so

imperial, so majestic, that she felt like her parents might have been proud of her. "What they do doesn't make me feel safe or protected. All I've done is change schools all my life, hide my face, hide my name, until I'm not even their daughter anymore. And guess what that made me?"

Not their daughter, Rory repeated in her own mind. Her parents had locked her up in the palace, in different schools, never letting her do anything at all, because they wanted her to be safe. Because they didn't want their daughter, who suffered from a chronic pain they couldn't even bother to understand, to ever feel like she could be something bigger than what they had made her to be.

Rory was not safe. Her best friend had been murdered. Girls were dying in her school. There was no such thing as safe.

"I'm not fragile," Rory said again. "I'm not some *thing* to be locked away in a vault. I'm a person. I want a life, and I'll have it."

Rory got up and put on her coat, preparing to go back to the cold. Her muscles ached in pain, but she ignored it, because she was not going to bend. According to her parents, to Éveline, Rory had no right to her life, to her face, to anything at all. The only thing that was truly hers was her body. She was not going to let it be a servant to her parents' will.

"I'll send the medal home when I have it," Rory said. "Merry Christmas, Éveline."

CHAPTER FORTY-SIX

ELLA

The note was on Ella's mind for the rest of the week. When it wasn't the note, it was Annmarie's head, her dead eyes staring ahead, her body lying completely severed, and the blood didn't even spill because of the shock. A warning of the destiny that seemed to await them if they didn't figure out what was wanted.

She'd taken her things out of her secret attic hideout, looking at one of the oldest pictures of Ari she had, back when they started at Grimrose. They were all thirteen, all bony with limbs too large to be part of their bodies, still growing. Except Yuki. Yuki always looked beautiful, no matter her age. In the picture, Ariane had an arm in Rory's, another in Penelope's, back before she switched schools. Penelope had a gap-toothed grin and a mole under her right eye. She looked nothing like that now, entirely grown out of it.

One of you is next.

One week before the ball, Ella arrived at school so distracted she didn't notice the chocolate truffle lying in the hall until she'd almost stepped on it.

She spotted more candy on the opposite side of the hall, a trail of them, exactly like in the story.

Her blood ran cold.

Heart beating in her ears, unable to stop herself, even when there was a voice in her head warning her not to, she followed them step by step, candy by candy. The trail took her down the corridor, then down a staircase. The last piece of candy sat on the threshold of one of the old classrooms in the northern wing of the castle.

She knew what she had to do.

The door creaked as she opened it the sight before her filling her with dread. Her hands shook, and she stumbled back. Even though she'd thought she was ready, she still wasn't.

Two bodies sat in the chairs inside the room, hands clasped together in rigor mortis. Molly and her young brother, Ian, mousy brown hair hanging limp over their pallid faces, empty eyes staring at the ceiling. Chocolate frosting ran down their mouths, sugar dusted their clothes, the sweet smell of it filling the entire room.

In an opened candy wrapper, there was a message, just for her. She didn't want to move farther into the room, didn't want to get closer to the bodies, didn't want anything to do with any of it.

But she went anyway, because she had to know what the message said.

GOT YOU.

The wrapper fluttered from her numb fingers, landing like a flower petal on a pile of sugar at her feet. Ella backed out of the room, glancing back and forth wildly to see if there was anybody there, anyone could help, taking step after step away...

She tripped on something, and screamed as she tumbled down the stairs.

She landed on the floor with a thud, her back smashed against the floor, everything hurting at once. A particularly fierce pain shot through her ankle, and she groaned. From the corner of her eye, a shadow approached, but when she whipped her head to look, no one was there.

Ella had been to the infirmary only once in her life, when Rory had broken an arm in fencing and had to spend a whole afternoon studying for a test there. Ella had helped her memorize what she needed, and Ella had paid the price for that disobedience later too, and she hadn't returned to the infirmary for those consequences. She knew all too well how to take care of her wounds.

She'd been ushered there by Mrs. Blumstein after she'd limped all the way back to the main hall, her left ankle swollen and blue. She hadn't even processed what she'd just seen, her tears dry even before she shed them, focused on what she had to do next, her brain overwhelmed. The nurse had given her a painkiller and a dose of medicine for sleep, but the dose was nowhere even near what she took every day to control her anxiety and OCD. She hadn't broken anything, but was bruised all over from falling down the steps. She couldn't shake the feeling that it had been a trap, and she'd fallen for it.

Ella had been left to rest all day, but she preferred to do it in the girls' room rather than the infirmary, where the bodies were being taken. The three came back after class, and Ella sat up straighter on Rory's bed.

"They've just removed the bodies," Rory said. "Allergic reaction, according to the nurse."

Ella closed her mouth, but she could almost taste the chocolate in it—rich, sweet, covering her tongue in thick syrup, and Ella wanted to throw up everything she had for lunch, even when she couldn't afford to because it was the only decent meal she'd get in the day.

"What happened?" Rory said, leaning against her bed.

"There was candy in the middle of the hall," Ella replied, her hands clenched in fists in her lap. The pain in her leg had dulled to an ache, but her entire body still felt like it'd been put through the wringer. "There was a trail of them, and I... Well, I followed it."

"You had to know where it was leading," Yuki said, her voice angry, but Ella didn't think it was directed at her specifically. "Why did you?"

"I couldn't stop myself," Ella said. "Someone would have found them. It might as well have been me."

Yuki's gaze snapped up.

"It was a trap," Ella said. "It wasn't an accident. Someone had put a wire there for me to trip. There was a message for me."

Ella took a deep breath, remembering the sight of Molly and Ian looking younger in death, hands united in their pallidness.

"What message?" Nani asked.

"It was written on a wrapper. It just said 'got you'," Ella said. "I dropped it. Someone else must have found it."

"The person knew you were going to follow the clues," Nani said. "And we all know by now that it's just too many accidents to not be done on purpose. Dozens of girls before, and this can't be a coincidence. Even if whoever was threatening Ari didn't kill these people, they still had to know it could happen."

"Someone was there when I fell. Someone was watching."

"Are you sure?" Yuki asked, her tone even. Ella only nodded. She'd just seen a shadow, but she had no doubt someone had been there.

"So if they know about the book," Nani mused, starting to pace around the room, hands on her round hips, "and if they know about the deaths, and how all of it is connected... But it doesn't make sense. There are deaths decades before on Ariane's list. Deaths that also fit the pattern."

Ella couldn't give an answer, but she knew there was a connection.

"They're not unrelated," Rory said. "You said it yourself. There's one for each of the tales in the book."

Nani ran to her drawer and to her papers, picking up the list of all the dead girls, drawing lines that connected each of the names to their respective tales.

"So Ari's death is here, and these are all in the last five years," Nani said. "Then we stop for a while, and then about twenty years back, we have another cycle. Two years ago, Flannery got mangled in her grandmother's house, and twenty years ago, there's Sienna, who cut classes to go to her grandmother's house and a wolf attacked her on the way. Same story, different girls."

She continued to connect them through red lines, picking up speed as she went.

"But isn't that weird?" Rory said, tilting her head.

"There are more than two. Look at this one, back in the sixties, a girl drowned in the lake, ruled a suicide," Nani said. "It has to be the book. It's magical. It's leading us to these deaths, somehow. We are bound to it."

The answer had always been magic.

"The story repeats," Ella said, and a sudden calmness came over her, a deep understanding. "Over and over again, until we get the right ending. The happy ending. Except we can't, because something is wrong. That's what the book is saying. That's the curse. We're cursed not to get the happy ending."

The deaths kept repeating, never getting to their true ending.

"The book has to be the key," Nani said. "That's why they want it. Maybe because we have it, we can break it."

"Slow down," Yuki snapped, her arms crossed. She was standing farther from them, Ella noticed it now. Ella, Rory, and Nani were all huddled around Nani's notes, and Yuki was on the other side of the room.

"Explain this with logic," Nani said, gesturing wildly to her notes. "Explain the book. We can't destroy it. It doesn't matter whether you're calling it a curse, a plague, or whatever it is. It doesn't change the fact that there are deaths, and the book has predicted them, over and over again."

Nani's and Yuki's stares met, but it was Rory who tried to lighten the tone.

"How do we break it then?" she said, jamming an elbow into Ella's ribs. "True love's kiss? Who's volunteering?"

"Looks like Pippa will finally have her chance," Ella joked, and that made Rory glare at her.

"Maybe for you," Yuki said. "But if any of you let a man near me when I'm asleep, I will burn this castle to the ground."

Ella looked up at Yuki with a smile, Yuki wasn't smiling back.

"So the book predicts the deaths, but we can't just choose who is connected to each story," Yuki snapped again. "You want your answers to fit your hypothesis, but it has to be the other way around."

Ella frowned, thinking again, a thought just out of reach.

Fairy tales were history in a manner of speaking, and history repeated itself. They all shared the same elements in a hundred different cultures. Cultures that had never been in contact with one another, but the reflection still rippled: mistreated girls who fled their homes, the dangers lurking in the wilderness, the wit and kindness needed to survive. They were different tales, but they held the same truth in them for hundreds of years.

Ella put her hand to her mouth, realizing all the implications. That they were cursed, all of them, doomed to repeat their worst endings. And if she didn't find a way to break the curse, that version of life would be her destiny too.

All she would know was what she had already known: living in a home that was never hers, where she had to work every single day just so she could eat, dreaming about the day she was getting out, but only dreaming, never actually fulfilling those dreams. Scrubbing the kitchen, washing the curtains, sweeping until her hands were blistered and bleeding, until her mind was screaming at her to stop. To have another life than the eternal cycle of the abuse at her home.

"It's not random," Ella said finally, lowering her hand, looking at the scars on her knuckles. "It's who we are."

Yuki's gaze sharpened, and now Ella understood it all with such clarity. Ari's simple message, the warning she'd left behind. *I'm one of them.*

"Our lives are not our own," Ella said quietly, trying to express what she knew. Her invitation to Grimrose, the only thing that had ever mattered, the thing that she'd been most proud of, all that was a lie. "We are drawn here because we're meant to fulfill it. Play out the story until it gets to the bad ending. We never had a choice."

She looked at her friends: Nani's eyebrows drawn tight, Rory's hand covering her mouth. And Yuki, motionless, standing like a statue.

"That doesn't make sense," Yuki finally said, her voice rising.

"But it does," Rory said, looking up at Yuki, and even Rory was serious now, any trace of laughter gone. "It all fits."

Yuki shook her head, stepping away from them. Ella got up instinctively, ignoring the pain in her ankle.

There was panic in Yuki's eyes as she looked between them. "I know you're trying to find answers, and—"

"We just did," snapped Rory. "So what if it's all magic? Maybe it is!"

"No," Yuki said. "We can't go on with this nonsense forever."

Yuki's hands were trembling now. Ella saw them, and an instinct made her recoil. Yuki looked down at her hands, breathing hard, and then she looked up again, her eyes dark, wide, desperate. Warning of danger.

"Yuki, let me—"

Yuki pushed her away, and then the room shattered into tiny pieces.

CHAPTER FORTY-SEVEN

YUKI

This time, there weren't any snowflakes.

She had created mirrors, jagged broken points floating in the air like sharp stalactites. They hung in the air for a moment, and Yuki looked on in shock, all pieces pointing to Ella standing with her outstretched hand.

In every flicker of the mirror, there was a version of her staring back.

When she realized what she'd done, when she blinked, all the mirrors clattered to the ground. They fell, the glass shattering in a million tinier pieces, the mirrors covering the floor in their glittery form, like they were standing over a fairy cave as they started to melt like ice.

Ella lowered her hand, taken aback in surprise. Blood trickled from a wound in her arm, the only mark the mirror left on her. Ella clutched it, turning away so it wouldn't show, but Yuki saw.

Yuki opened her mouth and then closed it, and her heart broke in two.

"What the hell was that?" Rory said, her feet moving, crunching the mirrors under her boots.

"Magic," Nani answered simply, her gaze unflinching.

Yuki's hands stopped trembling, like they often did when she let all her anger out, when she released the part of her that she was fighting to keep hidden. When she gave in to her feelings and the magic poured out.

"How—" Rory started, then stopped herself, still frowning. "Since when?"

"Since the ritual," Yuki answered, finally managing to find her voice.

"So it did work," Ella said quietly.

"No, it didn't!" Yuki snapped, irritated. The glass on the floor flickered under her shoes, and she wanted to dissolve all of the broken pieces, all the small and ugly parts of her that were reflected in the tiniest fragment. "It didn't tell us anything about whatever you think this curse is."

"We have to find whoever is causing this, all of this," Ella said. "There have been too many deaths. Someone is using the book for their own purposes, and they've been threatening us all along."

"Someone is just hurrying up the inevitable," Nani said, tapping her fingers rhythmically, thinking. "And if they know about the book, they know about the curse. That's what they're after."

"That's why Ariane had the note," Rory said, turning to them. "Because the person promised to tell the truth. Ari went without the book, so the person killed her, but still couldn't get their hands on it."

"And then—"

"Ari wasn't murdered," Yuki interrupted. "Ari killed herself."

The three girls turned to her, waiting. Expectant.

"We had a fight," Yuki said, her throat dry, her essence spent. "The day she came back. And I said if she wanted everyone to pity her so much, she should go ahead and kill herself."

The silence echoed within Yuki's own empty heart.

"You don't know that," Ella said.

"I know how much you want to believe in this," Yuki said. "In the curse, in Ari's death. But maybe she did it because of me."

"I don't believe that," Nani said simply. "We only have to find a way to break the cycle. Find out who's been killing the girls, get them to tell the truth. Maybe they know how to stop this."

"No," Yuki said. She took a deep sigh. "We're done here. I don't care where the magic comes from. I don't care what the book says."

"But we could be cursed," Ella said. "Either the school, the book, ourselves. It's not *right*."

"Hand them the book, for all I care. Let them have it. I don't want to be a part of this anymore."

Nani raised her chin. "You don't get to choose that."

Yuki laughed. Rough, sharp, full of disdain and scorn, and it was so *goddamn freeing*.

It was the sound of everything she was, without having to hide.

"Funny you're the one to say that." She turned to Nani, intent on having all the truth before them, because that's all they had left. The truth. "You think you're so much better than all of us. From the moment you got here. You think you're so superior."

"You know nothing about me," Nani said, and there was true hurt in her eyes.

"You're only using us to get your answers," Yuki accused. "You don't want to help, you didn't even tell us why you came here, didn't do anything that wasn't for yourself. If you want to leave, do it. We're not stopping you."

"I—"

"You don't want to be here," Yuki continued, "and we don't need you here either."

Nani looked like she was going to cry, but she only shook her head, her shoulder bumping against Yuki as she left through the door.

"Great," muttered Rory, but loud enough that Yuki could still hear. "Just what we need."

Yuki turned her glare to Rory. "You don't even know her," she said. "She's not even interested in the curse."

"A second ago you weren't either," Rory said, raising an eyebrow.

Yuki threw her hands in the air, and Ella flinched—a reflex. Yuki lowered her hands, feeling the gesture like a stab to her broken heart.

"If it's a cycle, then what use is it?" Yuki finally said. "No one stopped it before. Maybe it's just better if we let it play out." There was nothing left of the careful, perfect Yuki, and for once, her shoulders didn't feel heavy. "Maybe Ari knew that," Yuki said, looking straight at Rory. "Maybe she did what she did because it was the easiest way out."

Yuki wanted to be left alone, so she turned on her heel and left. They could deal with the mess.

Ella was the one to run after her.

Of course she was.

"Yuki, wait!" she said, and Yuki could hear the trembling in her voice, like she was trying hard not to cry.

Yuki wasn't sure she could hold on to enough of herself to even have any kind of conversation. She felt her broken edges slipping, turning sharp, a girl made of shards of ice and broken mirrors, ready for anything the world threw at her, ready to hurt it back.

She was tired of pretending. She was tired of doing what everyone expected of her. Every single person in her life had put expectations on her, and Yuki had wanted to please them all and do want what they wanted, but none of them saw Yuki as a real girl, who could want things for herself, be upset and tired and angry, and all that anger had turned inward, isolating her from the others, because she couldn't be like them.

She had so many things, but she was still *so* lonely.

"What?" Yuki demanded.

"It wasn't your fault," Ella said. "Ariane dying."

"I don't need your help. What use is it? You can't even help yourself. You can't even walk out of that house."

It was all spilling out of her, all her anger, all her impatience, all her meanest thoughts, and she wanted to let them come. Let it be like a flood.

"You know that's not how it works," Ella said, her jaw set. "I'm just trying to survive there. My father—"

"Don't defend him."

"Defend him?" Ella asked, stunned. "Are you accusing him of something?"

"Yes," Yuki spit. "Your father knew what he was doing when he married Sharon, and he didn't care that his daughter was going to suffer for it. He asked you to be brave, he asked you to be kind, but he didn't care what happened to you. And now look at you."

Yuki let it all out, all at once, all the words she'd been thinking all this time. Ella thought her father was a saint, but he watched his daughter's pain, and he did nothing, and Yuki was never going to forgive him for it, and she wanted Ella to know. She wanted Ella to *see*.

She wanted Ella to know the truth, the same as she did, even if she was hurt by it.

It was the cruelest thing Yuki had ever done.

Ella held back her tears with all the dignity she could muster.

"It's his fault too," Yuki said, quietly. "He chose his own happiness over you. He's as much at fault as Sharon is."

Ella shook her head. "That's not true," she whispered.

"It is," Yuki said, easily. "Or else you wouldn't be crying about it. Stop waiting for people to come save you, Ella. They aren't going to do it."

Yuki didn't let Ella say anything else, and she turned her back on her best friend, walking away.

CHAPTER FORTY-EIGHT

NANI

Nani went to the only place she thought she'd find comfort.

Yuki's words echoed through her mind and through her heart, and she tried to push it all away. She didn't need them. She didn't need Ella, Yuki, or Rory. She could figure things out by herself, like she'd always done, and she was not going to fall prey to a stupid curse.

She thought about what Ella said, how they were all in the book. Ariane hadn't know her, but Nani was afraid that she might be one of them, that if she searched, she'd find herself in the pages, folded between the letters of a story, her essence fragmented and made raw so that she'd matched the tales she'd heard a thousand times.

She'd forgotten her true objectives, dismissed everything in the name of a stupid magic book, all because she wanted her answers, wanted them to be grand, wanted them to be out of this world, so she could forget how little her life mattered at all. Because she'd been promised an adventure, and she wanted to believe in it.

No more.

She wasn't fooling herself into that ever again.

Nani knocked, and waited outside.

Svenja opened her door. She frowned when she saw Nani, and Nani saw her eyes were a little red.

"Did something happen?" Nani asked, concerned.

Svenja sniffed, looking up. "Yes," Svenja said, without opening the door further. "What is it this time? You want us to rob the headmistress's office?"

Nani frowned, looking into Svenja's room. It was the same as last time, nobody in there with her.

"No," Nani replied, standing awkwardly there, her hands shoved in her pockets.

"Dig a grave?" Svenja suggested. "I know the cemetery."

Nani's frown deepened, not catching on. "Why are you angry with me?"

"I'm angry because you're an idiot."

"I can't help being an idiot."

"So I've noticed," Svenja said bitterly. She sighed, her shoulders sagged. "I'm tired, Nani," she said instead. "I thought we were friends, but you only ever come to my door when you need something, and I'm smart enough to figure out when I'm being used."

The words were like a stab to the gut. Svenja was right. She'd used her, and even after Nani had started caring for her, she said nothing. Nani wanted to be comforted, but she had only lied to Svenja.

"I'm sorry," Nani said.

"Are you?" Svenja asked, eyebrow raised.

Nani's cheeks flushed, and she swallowed hard once, twice. She wasn't going to cry about this. It had been enough with the girls accusing her of wanting to leave, of not caring. She wasn't going to have that again. Nani wasn't sure she could listen to what her heart was telling her, but there was something here that she believed.

"Svenja, you don't understand—"

"Of course I don't, you haven't told me anything!" Svenja replied, throwing her hands in the air. "Since the moment you got here, we've had dozens of conversations, and I know you're scared that you're in a place where you don't know anybody, a place you don't understand, but what I offered was a place of safety."

Svenja blinked, and Nani realized she was trying not to cry too.

"I know what it's like to feel alone in a place that doesn't understand you," Svenja said, and she extended a hand, wrapping her fingers around Nani's wrist. "I don't want anyone to ever feel like that. And maybe we don't have to share everything. I can't understand what it's like to be you, and you can't understand what's like to be me. But I know how horrible it is to not belong anywhere."

Svenja looked up to Nani's eyes.

Nani wished she could find her words, but she had none,

her throat clasped tightly shut, her body turned inward into a temple of vast emptiness as Svenja's words echoed around her pillars, around her bones. Around the emptiness that she'd created for herself, the fear of someone truly, truly knowing her.

She had waited on her father's promise. Waited for the day he'd bring her with him, to have adventures, to live in a different world.

And her father had given it to her. Here, at Grimrose.

Nani had been too stupid to see it.

"Ever since you came here, you treated everyone like a jailer you can't wait to escape," Svenja concluded, tears falling down her cheek. "My friendship doesn't have to be your prison."

Svenja stepped back and let go of Nani's arm. Nani felt alone, like that had been the only thing still was connecting her to the world—for a moment, she had someone.

"We're not your enemies, Nani," Svenja said, taking another step back. "Don't make me into a monster I'm not."

She shut the door on Nani's face, and she was left alone again in the empty corridor.

She hated it.

CHAPTER FORTY-NINE

ELLA

Ella decided to head home, trying not to cry. On the way out, she looked at herself in one of the mirrors and saw she was a complete disaster, her eyes blotchy, and half her makeup running down her cheeks. She sniffed, wiping her nose on the blazer of her uniform, trying to count the steps she would take to her to the bus.

Crying, at least, helped with her anxiety, simply because it overwhelmed her brain into not thinking about anything else. She was not far from the gate when she heard footsteps pound after her.

Ella had a good idea who it was, and couldn't bear facing him like this. She ran faster, even though her ankle was still in pain, but Frederick was a lot taller than her, and had more practice exercising, which Ella herself had none, not for lack of everyone reminding her of it.

"Oh, shut it," Ella said to herself.

Frederick reached her. "You all right?"

Ella looked up at him, her eyes puffy. "Yes."

"Oh. Didn't realize we had a new standard for that."

"Now's not the time to be funny," she replied, holding in a sob that tried to shake her entire body.

"I won't ask stupid questions," Freddie promised. "Want me to take you home? Here."

He handed her a tissue from his bag, and Ella took it gratefully.

"I heard about your accident," Freddie said gently, gesturing to her limping leg. "It's been quite a day for you, hasn't it?"

"I just need to go home."

Freddie offered her his arm. "Come on."

Freddie didn't ask any questions on the way. He hopped on the bus with her even though he didn't have to, and just sat with her and held her hand as the events from the day ran through her head.

Ella didn't want to acknowledge that what Yuki had said had the ring of truth. Acknowledging it meant that her father had his faults, that he had chosen Sharon over her safety. Ella understood he'd been lonely since her mother died, that he wanted company, that he was a romantic at heart. She knew people could be like that, the way they attached themselves to a new love like nothing had ever come before that.

She excused him for it. Excused what he'd not seen, and then he died, and it was so much easier to forgive him when he was gone.

"If you want to talk about it, I'm here, Eleanor," Frederick told her quietly as he slipped his arm around her, and Ella rested her head on his shoulder.

Ella didn't want to talk about it, but she smiled at the sound of her full name. She wasn't just plain old Ella with him. Eleanor was sophisticated and tasteful, and she went to grand parties. Eleanor didn't have a bedtime or a curfew, and she didn't wake up early to do the house chores. Eleanor didn't have a savings jar she kept under her bed. Eleanor had a thousand different possibilities.

Ella liked being herself, but sometimes, she wouldn't mind trading her life for Eleanor's.

They got out at her bus stop, and then he took her almost to the corner of her house. He stood on the sidewalk, with the snow from last night around him, out of place. The prince in a story.

More than ever, Ella felt the urge to lean in. To be taken by this particular storm, to be saved.

Stop waiting for somebody else to save you.

Ella had done all the waiting. All the days she'd counted on the calendar until her freedom, because she didn't know how to fight back. Because in the end, she was comfortable with her situation, because she knew what it was. This house was safe, even when it wasn't. She knew this evil. She didn't know what would wait for her on the other side.

For all her words, Eleanor Ashworth was a coward.

"Thank you," she said to Frederick.

Freddie nodded, pressing his lips together. "I'll see you at the ball, then?"

Ella nodded, but even thinking about it made her heart sink.

Of course they hadn't canceled the ball, even if they'd just found two new dead bodies in the school. Canceling meant that something was wrong, and nothing could ever be wrong at Grimrose.

She left Frederick and slipped quietly through the front gate, unlocked for her during school days. The house was quiet, and she tiptoed her way around the living room to the kitchen. Sharon had yet to make an appearance, and she felt safe washing her face in the sink, getting off the last residue of makeup from her eyes.

Sharon wasn't there, but Stacie was. She was a shadowy presence, her arms crossed, her jaw set.

"Didn't I warn you in the beginning, Ella?"

Ella said nothing, biting her lower lip, trying to find a way to calm her beating heart.

"Always dreaming of a happy ending, aren't you?" Stacie said, but there was no mockery in her words, only bitterness. "Do you think Frederick really cares about you? That you're not just a silly girl he's playing with?"

"That's not true," Ella said. She wouldn't doubt Frederick. Couldn't doubt it.

It didn't matter that she liked him. It didn't matter that her heart beat a little faster when she heard him talk, when he ruffled his red hair with his hands. It didn't matter that she wanted to run her own fingers through it, that maybe something more could happen at the ball. Some kind of magic.

A *good* kind of magic.

"Does he know your secret?"

Ella's hand lifted involuntarily to her cheek, and Stacie wet her lips.

"No one in the school gets it," she continued. "Do you think I can tell *my* boyfriend about it?"

Ella tensed, because Stacie never talked about the way Sharon treated them. She'd always pretend they were the favored daughters and nothing was wrong. They didn't talk about their shared experience, because Stacie liked to pretend she was nothing like Ella.

"None of them understand," Stacie said. "Spare yourself the heartache. People don't like things they can't fix."

Stacie's words dug deep. Too much. Too much trouble, too many problems—she had anxiety and OCD, a dead father and a dead mother, still living under Sharon's shadow. She was far too much trouble, and she knew it.

No one was going to save Ella. Because her only way out was if someone else offered a hand, a way to save her, a way to forget all the hurt. She'd kept being kind, kept trying to compensate for every single of her traumas, being the best person she could be despite it all. Because one day, someone was going to come and save her, and she couldn't give them a reason to turn her away.

"You'll get over it," Stacie said, not unkindly. "But we're alone. It's best if we don't forget it."

Stacie turned away and climbed the stairs back into her room. Ella's hands trembled, but her tears were spent.

No one would come for the broken girls, the girls who had too much of their troubles, the girls who kept trying. No one was going to let them forget what they'd been through.

No one was going to save them.

CHAPTER FIFTY

RORY

Rory stared at the bulletin board with the dates of the tournament.

She'd missed the sign-up. Of course she had.

After all her bravado with Éveline, after the fight with Pippa, and she couldn't still do one single thing right. It hadn't even occurred to her that the tournament would have a deadline, because this kind of thing didn't even enter Rory Derosiers's mind.

She stared at the sign, shoulders sagging, trying to figure out a way to get past it.

"You missed it." Pippa said as she breezed into the locker room. Rory continued to stare at the sign like an idiot. The only thing that she maybe *wanted* to do in her life, and she'd missed it.

That served her right. It wasn't like she deserved this chance.

"I know," Rory said quietly, her voice surprisingly even.

Rory didn't cry. She'd mastered her body on the most painful nights, back when she hadn't even been diagnosed yet. Her parents had taken her to the best doctors in Europe, but even they had a hard time diagnosing something that only comprised of unending, tearing pain through the muscles and the body, and that ultimately had no cure.

She shoved her hands in the pockets of her uniform jacket, turning around to face Pippa. "I was going to sign up," Rory said.

Pippa raised an eyebrow. They were still a bit off, and Rory missed what they had shared before, when they first started. Swords clashing, the unending teasing, the way they would smile at each other after the day was done. Rory couldn't find it within herself now, even though she desperately wanted to.

"It's complicated," Rory said, her head hanging low. Her copper hair fell in waves over her shoulders, beautiful and silky. "I had to get permission from my parents. They're... overprotective."

Pippa's ears perked up at that, and she turned to Rory. Rory never willingly talked about her parents. Never willingly talked about the life outside Grimrose, because that life was not really hers to claim. It had been set for her from the day she was born, and she had no choice but to follow it.

Her real life was here, at Grimrose.

"And what did they say?"

"They wouldn't let me," Rory replied, sucking on the inside of her cheek. Pippa's dark eyes were attentive, drawing her in. "I was still going to sign up because fuck them."

At that, Pippa laughed, her white teeth flashing, her whole face changing into something even sharper, even clearer, and Rory's brain could not register anything but this—she was beautiful, she was excruciatingly, painfully beautiful, and Rory was an idiot for thinking that she could just shove away that information.

Rory knew she was a goner even before Pippa entered the playing field.

"Good for you," Pippa said. "You still missed it."

"Yeah," Rory said, her feet shuffling from side to side on the locker room floor, dancing an invisible dance. "I'm sorry I said that to you before. Really. I know how hard you fight for this."

Pippa blinked, her face becoming serious again. "Is this a real apology?"

"Yes," Rory said, sighing. Instead of her usual jittery nerves and restless nature, all she felt was calm. The calmness that came with the defeat.

She approached the bench where Pippa had put her bag and sat down, running her fingers through her hair.

"It's not that hard to acknowledge it, you know," Rory said, and she didn't look directly at Pippa. Didn't dare to. She had to let it all out, break her own rules. "I know most of us are all rich beyond reason to come and study at this ridiculous school, but that doesn't change how things are in the world, and I know people are..."

"Weary?" Pippa suggested.

"I was gonna say racist pieces of shit," Rory said, and Pippa laughed again. She sat next to Rory, her elbows on her knees. Her perfume smelled of alder and white musk, mixing the scents of autumn. Rory hated that she knew the exact perfume because she'd once been with Ari to a perfume shop and she'd scoured everything until she found what she was looking for. Only a scent of what she wanted, but that was all she could ever have. "It didn't give me the right to say I was going to beat you. Because I might. But that doesn't mean I'd do it easily."

Pippa waited, sitting still.

"It wouldn't be easy," Rory said, looking up to meet her eyes, pain in her chest at every confession. "You're the best fencing master I've ever seen, and I've seen Olympic competitions. You put them all to shame. When you get out of here, you're going to take the world by storm."

Pippa pressed her lips together, and Rory smiled at her. "And I'm lucky to count you as a friend," Rory finally said, her breath coming out in a hitch.

"A friend?" Pippa asked, her eyes darting toward Rory, biting her lower lip. "That's all?"

"Yes," Rory reassured her, forcing her gaze away from Pippa's plump lips. "A friend."

Pippa looked at her and nodded. Their shoulders were brushing, and Rory felt her own heartbeat accelerate just a tiny bit. She forced it down. She respected Pippa too much to drag her into her life.

"Fine," Pippa said, and her voice was a little strained. "Want some friendly advice? Now that we can stop this nonsense of not talking outside the field?"

"So you noticed that."

Pippa gave her a pointed look. "Rory, I know you," Pippa said, sighing. "I've seen you fight, and I know we don't talk about personal things. And I think you were right about signing up for the tournament."

"It's too late now."

"But it's not too late to do everything else," Pippa urged her, her fingers brushing against the back of Rory's hand, and all she wanted to do was grab her, grab Pippa and to hell with the rest. "You're living a half a life. Trying to please your parents, trying to still have something for yourself. But you're not living the life they want, and you're not living the life you want either."

Rory sat, stunned, suddenly afraid that Pippa had read her so well, that even between all the words of their non-conversations, she still had known. That if she stayed a moment longer, Pippa would unravel her from top to bottom.

And maybe, just maybe, she'd enjoy it.

"This one tournament isn't the end," Pippa said, getting up. "It's the beginning. Start making your own choices, and you'll see how much better you are for it."

CHAPTER FIFTY-ONE

YUKI

Yuki didn't care that her friends weren't speaking to her. She really, really didn't.

She had finals to worry about and the winter ball to get ready for. She'd found the box that contained her dress in her bedroom. The boxes all had different colors, and Yuki imagined the dresses inside did too. She hadn't opened hers yet, knowing she couldn't look at what Ella made for her.

She didn't regret telling the truth, but the consequences scared her.

She'd seen Ella with Frederick in the halls, and saw Rory training by herself, running laps around the frosty garden when no student dared to step outside. Yuki didn't even want to think about her own birthday approaching at the end of the month. Turning seventeen didn't seem like something worth celebrating.

Yuki concentrated on her studies instead and avoided every mirror. She wanted to get rid of all that was happening, forget all of it, let the curse take her once and for all.

She supposed that's what Ari had done in the end.

Penelope came to find her in the library after class, in Yuki's usual spot.

"Are you alone?" she asked, and Yuki nodded. "Are you going to tell me what happened or not?"

Yuki blinked.

"I can see it written all over you," Penelope said. Her eyes hovered over the library shelves, probably looking for Mephistopheles, in case he decided to leap for a surprise attack. "What happened?"

Yuki bit her lower lip. "I lost control," she said. "Of... whatever is happening to me."

"You can say the word. It's not going to hurt you."

Yuki rolled her eyes. "We had an argument," Yuki said. "It all exploded into bits and pieces."

"Snow again?" Penelope inquired. "Or something else?"

Penelope spoke as if she knew. She touched Yuki lightly on her shoulder, and Yuki didn't flinch away. It was as if Penelope had guessed what exactly had happened for Yuki to lose control.

"It's getting worse, I think," Yuki said. "I have to control it."

Penelope frowned at her. "That's one way of putting it. Or you can just...let it go."

She winked, and Yuki groaned, sighing inwardly. "Please don't."

"I know you have this thing about control. You're

struggling with yourself, to give away no emotion, and what do you think will happen to you?"

Yuki didn't know how to answer it. She couldn't control it. She could feel it, running through her veins, through her body, a spark of something unknown, something that had always been there, waiting, and now it was awake.

For the first time in years, Yuki was afraid of herself.

Of what she was capable of doing.

Of what she was capable of becoming.

"I can't," she said. "I could hurt someone."

"So you think repressing it is the best way to go," Penelope snorted. "Refusing to acknowledge it. Just like you've done the rest of your life."

"You don't know much about my life."

Penelope shook her head. "You're wrong. And you know why? Because you're *exactly* like me, Yuki. It's just that you're too scared to admit it. Too scared to want things for your own."

Yuki looked down at her hands, her steady hands, with skin as white as snow. Still perfect, still untouched. Her body like an impenetrable armor. Nothing in, nothing out.

"It's a gift," Penelope said after a while. "Not a curse."

Yuki blinked. "What did you say?"

Penelope turned her vivid green eyes to look at Yuki. They looked vast, like green fields of emerald, and in them, the inherent coldness that came with that. Yuki shivered.

"It isn't a curse," Penelope repeated. "It might actually be a way of breaking it. Of freeing yourself. I told you this."

"And what you told me made me fight with my friends."

Penelope snorted. "Sure, blame it all on me. I'm the bad influence. Isn't that what your friends said about me?"

Yuki's fingers turned to ice, the air around them growing cold. Penelope grabbed her hands, and Yuki could feel the chill seep into Penelope's skin, turning it cold, but the girl didn't flinch. She took it all in, an invisible dare as they held each other's gazes.

"You wanted this all along," Penelope said. "But you're just too afraid to admit it. Some people won't mind that you hurt them, Yuki."

Penelope held on until Yuki's magic flared in a last burst. Yuki pulled away and flexed her fingers, color returning to the pale skin.

"It's time you accept who you are," Penelope said. "You just showed them all the truth. Don't turn your back on it now. I don't care what they all think and want. What do *you* want, Yuki?"

CHAPTER FIFTY-TWO

ELLA

Ella spent the last week of classes before winter break writing her essays, completing her finals, and concentrating on things one step at a time. If she stopped for one moment, she'd spiral back again into the curse, into their discovery, and she couldn't do it on her own anymore. When she was not studying, she was cleaning, doing last-minute adjustments to her dress, sewing one of her mom's old buttons on for good luck right on the inside of the fabric, like her mother always did when she was a child.

Ella didn't feel like talking to her friends anymore, which felt wrong, desperate, like the clock striking midnight and the story coming to an end before the ending was due.

When she finally got home the Friday afternoon before the ball, she was glad there would be a three-week break from school afterward. Ella didn't want to think about the curse, about the girls dying.

But if she didn't believe in the curse, that meant the girls were dying for some other reason. By their own hands, by the world being a cruel and terrible place that dealt a horrible fate to young girls with a cold and unfriendly embrace. Ella refused to believe that. Refused to believe that their stories had such a harsh and abrupt ending.

The house was in disarray on Friday, with Stacie and Silla locked in a screaming match on the second floor. She heard the tearing of clothes, Silla's yelp, probably from Stacie pulling her hair. Sharon sighed as she heard it, looking at Ella, massaging her temples.

"They're such strong-minded girls," Sharon said. She looked tired, a streak of white in her usually perfect brown hair, and she headed upstairs and left Ella alone.

Ella didn't know how she was going to sneak out yet. She'd kept her dress well-guarded, but it was going to be hard to climb the tree wearing it. The screaming continued upstairs as Sharon intervened.

Sharon came downstairs again.

"Don't bother cooking a full meal. Only salad for them both," she told Ella. "They wanted those dresses, they better fit in them."

Ella nodded, her lips pressed together. The twins looked fine, and the dresses fit. She'd seen Stacie sneaking food when Sharon wasn't looking, after she'd imposed a diet on the house for a week.

Ella rested her hands against the kitchen counter, sorting out the newspaper.

"Mother, I am going to throw Silla out of the window if she doesn't let me wear the pearl earrings!" Stacie bellowed.

"I asked first," Silla complained, her voice small compared to her sister's. "They go well with my mask."

"The mask is the most important part, since it's hiding your ugly face."

"Did you forget we are twins?" Silla replied. "We have the same face, you idiot."

This went on for a while, as arguments between sisters often did, especially when the argument was made only for argument's sake. Sharon came back downstairs and downed three sleeping pills at once, and Ella couldn't believe her luck.

Her stepmother would be out cold this evening. She could leave after the twins. Get some money from her jar, maybe even get a cab. Then she could come back like nothing had happened.

She served lunch, then sorted the things in the kitchen again. The newspaper had caught her attention, nudging her back. She read the headline only to find it was another horrible story of a girl turned up dead, murdered and left near an abandoned house next to the train station, her body half buried and eerily undecomposed. They'd only found her because the house had been sold. The girl had been dead for about a year and a half. No identification. The gruesome photos were splashed on the first page.

There were not a lot of remarkable features, but there was some strange resemblance that Ella couldn't quite place. When she looked closer, she noticed that there was something familiar about the blazer the girl was wearing.

Most of the breast pocket had been cut off to purposefully mask what had been before, but there was a single and elegant embroidered G left.

The Grimrose Académie crest.

Ella's face went pale, and she picked up the newspaper, running upstairs. She took out the floorboard which hid her things, searching for the old photo she kept of the year Ari came to the school. The one with Ari and Penelope.

She'd spent so long thinking about the list, trying to figure out which fairy tale belonged where, that she hadn't realized something obvious. She never had thought about what happened to the tales after they ended.

Ella considered texting Yuki, but this would only stir up more trouble—and besides, it was a guess. A good guess, but she had to confirm it.

She'd have to do it tonight.

She'd go to the ball. She'd get the whole truth. It was the only way, even if she didn't think it was going to be that simple. Even if dread was already climbing through her throat.

But Yuki had been right.

Ella couldn't stay in the same place, waiting for somebody else to come.

She was done with waiting.

CHAPTER FIFTY-THREE

RORY

Rory really didn't feel up for the ball that evening.

Not that she'd felt up to any ball ever in her life—the ones she'd attended she'd been stuffed inside a dress, couldn't eat anything, had to dance with people who stepped on her feet, and then the next day she'd wake up sore from the corsets. Still, there wasn't anything else to *do* in the last day of school before break, because everyone else was busy attending the masquerade.

Rory hadn't showed up for training that week after she'd missed the deadline of tournament, and she'd canceled the usual Friday meeting with Pippa—now that they'd exchanged numbers after three years, Rory kept checking her phone just to make sure that she had it right, that Pippa's name really popped up when she opened up her chats. She kept tapping the screen to zoom in on the picture, only to close it again, and Rory felt like an idiot. It took her one hour to work up the courage just to say that she wasn't up for training that week.

Rory sighed, throwing her phone onto a pile of dirty clothes just so she wouldn't look at it. It was already dark outside, even though it was barely six. She should get ready. She searched for the box Ella had left for her, with Ella's ugly scrawl over the card. The only thing Ella didn't do beautifully. Her writing was a mess.

They hadn't even looked at the dresses after Annmarie's death, the boxes lying forgotten. Yuki had taken hers up to Reyna's tower to get ready and left without saying a word. Rory stared at hers with the lid closed, wondering what kind of dress Ella had sewn for her, even when she didn't feel like wearing a dress.

She would, though. For Ella. Because Ella had made this, staying up for who knows how long, using her mother's old sewing machine, making masterpieces. Rory opened the lid.

Ella hadn't made her a dress. Ella had made her a suit.

She hadn't asked Rory what she wanted, and Rory didn't say anything because she'd get whatever she got, but Ella had still known.

Rory took it out of the box gingerly. The suit was rose gold, with a sheer pink undertone, and it was the least discreet thing Rory had ever seen, and she *loved* it. The trimming was perfect, and when she tried on the jacket, it fit beautifully. The buttons were golden roses, and the lapel had been stitched in a golden thread that formed thorns. The pants matched the jacket, and the sleeveless shirt, just as she liked it, was half transparent, a sheer material that changed with the light.

Ella had outdone herself.

Rory showered quickly, her hair hanging heavy and wet over her back as she changed into the suit, looking in the mirror in wonder. She looked at her face—her pale skin, her big blue eyes, and that hanging princess hair. The hair that she kept because it was the only thing her parents had always complimented her on when they saw her, the hair that made her even more like a princess, the hair that people told her made her look beautiful.

Rory took off her suit jacket, and then she found scissors.

The blade snapped over the first waves that fell to the marble floor. Rory had a full moment of panic when she realized what she was doing, and then, screaming all the while she did, she cut off the rest of her hair. She chopped it first close to her shoulders, and then started chopping off all the rest, closer to her head, until her scalp was just a mess of bright red hair sticking up every which way.

It looked awful, but she looked like herself.

All it needed was some pomade to slick it down, and it would almost look manageable. Rory knew there was some in the bag that had stayed behind, under her bed. Ariane's bag. The bag she'd shoved away.

Taking a deep breath, she crouched underneath the bed, digging into the mess of clothing and shoes, pulling the strap of Ariane's bag.

Rory took a deep breath before she opened it. These were Ari's things, but they were everyday things, and she didn't need to make a fuss. There was nothing personal there, nothing to make her break down at the loss that had already happened. For better or worse, Ari was gone. She might as well use the things she'd left behind.

Rory rummaged for the pomade that Ari carried to help with her bangs. She threw aside a hairbrush and a couple of lipsticks, a new perfume bottle, and then at last, she found what she was looking for. And then something struck her. Someone else had known about this bag.

Except Penelope couldn't have known about the *garish little aquamarine bag*, because Ari had just bought it on the way back to the school.

She couldn't have known unless she'd seen Ari had taken the bag with her when she met her killer. Someone had a key to their room. Someone could have brought the bag back, to make sure it looked like a suicide.

She dropped the contents of the bag on the floor, searching for anything amiss, but there wasn't anything that looked out of place—receipts, a mirror, sunglasses, and then, finally, she spotted something. Evidence.

A single, golden strand of hair.

CHAPTER FIFTY-FOUR

NANI

Nani didn't give a single flying fuck about the ball.

She'd spent the last week alone in quiet rooms of the castle, avoiding her bedroom, reading books at the library. She could trust books. They had been her friends ever since the day she was born, and their smell and their worlds were familiar. They didn't disappoint. Even if they did, she could just throw them out of the window and grab another one. Nani couldn't really do that with people.

She couldn't do it to the girls she had begun to think of as friends. She couldn't do it to Svenja, who she'd wronged.

She was completely miserable, and she only had herself to blame for it.

Nani decided to go to the library, straight to the place where they'd hidden the book. Thankfully, it was still there. No one had come to steal it. She took a step forward to take it off the shelf, and when she did, huge yellow eyes were staring at her from the darkness.

Nani yelped as Mephistopheles pounced, and she put the book up as a shield. The fat cat hit his face on the hardcover and dropped down on his feet, hissing.

"Jesus Christ!" Nani swore, but the black cat did not move.

He stared up at Nani with his yellow eyes fixed on the book, his scrunched-up face still annoyed, his ears perked up. Nani stared at him, but he didn't try to attack her again.

"What, you're going to tell me you're a magical cat too?" Nani asked it, eyebrows raised and hands on her hips. "If you're gonna talk, you better start."

Nani stared at Mephistopheles. Mephistopheles stared at her.

Finally, the cat meowed and climbed on the table, licking his front paws. Nani carefully tiptoed around him, keeping an eye on the monster in case he moved.

She leaned against another table a safe distance away, eyes still half on the cat, adjusting her glasses. Mephistopheles seemed more than content to stare daggers at her from the other side of the room.

Nani flipped through the tales and the pages. By now, she'd memorized the order they were in. She had guessed the one she belonged to, though she wouldn't dare say it out loud, for fear of making it more real. She was a girl who loved books and reading who was stuck in a castle because of her father. Nani hadn't met any beasts, though, let alone fallen for them. She did have a crush as a child on the fox version of Robin Hood, but she was sure that was common at best, and at worst, it just made her a furry.

"I wish I didn't have only a cat for company," Nani said. "If I kiss you, will you turn into a prince?"

Mephistopheles tilted his head. Nani imagined that if she tried kissing the cat, she'd either get her face scratched off, or he'd turn into the Prince of Darkness himself.

She turned her attention back to the book, flipping through the other pages.

Ariane, dead like her counterpart in the tale, drowned. Molly and Ian, their mouths stuffed with the sweets, the candy trail unmistakable.

And then Micaeli. Micaeli, who'd told Ella about the other girls dying. Micaeli, who'd gossiped, and even—

Nani stopped suddenly. She hadn't thought of Micaeli as she had lived in the castle, just as the dead body on the stairs. She had seen her more than once, though, at the library, where she'd told Nani about another book just like hers.

Maybe Micaeli just hadn't died as a warning, to be part of this tale of tragedy, but because she knew too much.

Suddenly, Nani was running down the library stairs. All around her people were already getting ready for the party, girls slipping out of the rooms wearing ball gowns. Nani fought past them, practically flying down the corridors. She had to talk to the girls.

Nani burst into her room, where she found Rory holding an aquamarine bag, and all her hair chopped off, thick streams of wavy copper hair covering the bathroom floor.

Rory opened her mouth to say something, but Nani raised her hand before she could be interrupted.

"Who shared rooms with Micaeli?"

Rory frowned. "Penelope," she said, her jaw straight, her eyes darkening.

Nani felt her breath steady, the shock not surprising. Somehow, she'd known. "I have something to tell you."

"I do too," Rory said. "I know who killed Ariane."

CHAPTER FIFTY-FIVE

ELLA

Ella had snuck out through the front door after the twins were gone. She managed to button up the dozens of small blue buttons she'd sewed into the back of her dress, and then called a cab, her heart racing all the way to the castle.

It was cold outside. It had been snowing for the past week, the white obfuscating. She'd taken a coat, but Ella was still shivering as she made her way through the gates in her silvery shoes, the light blue georgette of the skirt falling behind her. Her dress was the simplest of the ones she'd made—the upper bodice was a silk crepe, and the sleeves fell over her shoulders. On the flowing skirt, hundreds of tiny butterflies had been embroidered, in pastel yellow and pink. Her mask, too, had butterfly's wings.

Her heart was in her throat. She didn't know what she'd say when she found Penelope. Demand the truth? Ask her why she had done what she did?

She had to find either Rory or Nani. Maybe Yuki, but Ella wasn't sure Yuki would believe her.

She walked into the ballroom, and it was even more beautiful than she imagined it would be. There were dangling branches of crystal near the chandeliers and banners of blue and silver strapped to the walls; it all felt like a dream. The Grimrose Académie crest was flying next to the windows, the elegant G swirling against the dark blue velvet. She couldn't get past the throng of students and was deciding on her next move when a someone's hand caught her own.

She turned to look and saw Frederick. He was wearing a gray tux and a simple black mask over his eyes.

"I thought you'd take longer to find me," Ella said.

"I wouldn't want to spend another second without you," Frederick said, and a blush crept to Ella's cheeks. She looked around, trying to find Penelope or the girls, but there was no sign of them.

"I hope you didn't have to wait for too long," Ella said.

"You're worth waiting for," Frederick told her, and then he extended a hand. "Dance with me?"

Ella hesitated. Dancing with Frederick was the reason she had wanted to go to the ball in the first place. To have a night out, to have fun, to forget herself. She hesitated, but she wanted this too much. She could spare time for a dance.

This was still the ball, after all.

When Frederick offered his hand again, she took it.

Frederick guided her first, a hand behind her back, and the other held firmly in hers. His eyes danced behind his mask, and Ella found herself smiling, found herself enjoying the song. She imagined a world full of long dances and starry nights and other things that didn't belong to her. But tonight, they did.

They spun around until she was out of breath, and then finally, Frederick pulled her aside, guiding her to the open night on the balcony. It was quiet out there, the music muted, and even though it was chilly, she was still feeling the warmth of dancing. They leaned against the marble rail, the lake and the garden visible just below them.

For a brief second, she wondered what he would say if she tried to tell him about what was going on. If he would even believe her.

She shook her head, leaving those thoughts to the moonlight. She had enough on her mind tonight, enough to keep her on edge, to know that this part of her story was approaching the end, fast. She hadn't spotted Rory, hadn't spotted Nani. She hadn't seen Penelope either, so maybe that was lucky.

"I wanted to talk to you," Freddie said, his fingers ruffling to his hair. "It's something I've been thinking ever since we went out...and kind of a little before that."

Every thought vanished before her, and Ella could only look up at him.

He took a deep breath, the said, "I understand if this isn't what you want. If you'd rather I stopped coming around."

Ella felt her stomach sink. "What?"

His eyes came back to hers. "I don't want to be in a place where I'm not really wanted."

Ella's heart beat faster. "You thought I didn't let you in my house because I don't want you there?"

Frederick opened his mouth, closed it, opened it again like a goldfish, lost.

"I want you here. My life is complicated. I just... I don't want anyone to see where I live, what I have to do," she said.

She couldn't tell the whole truth, of course, words couldn't come even close to describing it. Her throat bobbed, but she kept on, because Yuki was right—Frederick was not going to miraculously save her from something, no one was, and she had to face her own life.

"I didn't want your pity," Ella said. "That's all people have for me. Everyone looks at me like I'm just some poor little thing that can't handle herself. I'm more than the ashes on my clothes."

His brown eyes were warm as he watched her, and Ella could hear the soft in and out of his breath, so close to hers.

"I know, Ella."

"You do?"

"You think I'd be your friend out of pity?" Freddie asked. "I wanted to be your friend because I saw someone who was kind and smart and who everyone underestimated. I want to know you, Ella. Not pity you."

"Even if my life is a mess?" she asked, her throat bobbing. "Even when it's too much?"

"Even then," Frederick said, his hand slipping into hers, squeezing it tight.

And then, before she could stop herself, Ella said something she didn't know she could say out loud.

"I *like* you, Frederick."

Frederick blinked. "You like me?"

"I thought it was obvious," Ella said, her blush intensifying.

"I have a very hard time with obvious things," Frederick admitted. "What a mess."

"Yes," Ella agreed with a laugh.

"But what I wanted to tell you is that I like you too."

Ella stared at him. Frederick stared back.

"So what now?" Ella asked.

"I think this is the part where I kiss you," he said, and Ella felt her heart flutter inside her chest like the butterfly wings on her dress. "Can I?"

"I don't know, *can* you?"

"Actually," Freddie said, "I can."

He leaned in first, and the heels on Ella's shoes made up for the difference for the rest of the way. They hovered face-to-face a second, without touching, their mouths close, and in that space between them existed eternity.

His lips touched hers, his hot breath against hers, and she pressed her whole body against his. Her hands pulled his tie as she opened her lips to his, exploring taste. The only thing she could think about was how she wanted more of him.

His hand grabbed her and pulled her closer and tighter, the sound of the music wrapping around them as they kissed. Frederick stopped for breath first, and Ella pressed her head against his chest, hearing his heart hammering just like her own.

And then, the clock started ringing. She counted the

chimes. The stroke of midnight. When Ella looked out into the gardens, she saw the flash of golden hair.

She could try and find the others on the way, tell them what happened.

Penelope was going out to the gardens by herself, and it couldn't be good. She didn't have much time.

"I have to go," Ella said quietly.

This time, Frederick didn't ask her to stay, didn't ask her why. He'd learned to know when she'd give him answers.

Frederick kissed her forehead, his lips soft against her skin, and then Ella slipped out of the ballroom, the clock still chiming.

CHAPTER FIFTY-SIX

YUKI

Yuki couldn't bring herself to look in the mirror. She'd been trying for the past few minutes to work up the courage.

When she finally looked, there were no circles under her eyes from lack of sleep. Her marble skin was perfect, her eyes were dark and her lashes long, and her hair fell over her shoulders in a smooth cascade. There was no flicker of the image on the mirror, no sign of past stories trying to haunt her.

She unlocked the bathroom door, and Reyna was waiting.

"You look beautiful!" Reyna exclaimed, like she was surprised.

It was true. Ella had made her a dress out of dreams.

The dress was a simple white that fitted her form and opened up below her hips in a full skirt of chiffon. The sleeves were made of the lightest and sheerest chiffon too, and the last layer of the thin tulle had been embroidered with dark red and silver crystals in crisscrossed patterns, red crystals hanging like drops of blood over the white. When she moved, the crystals looked like snowflakes. She saw her reflection again in Reyna's mirror in the living room, and in that moment, Yuki knew the truth that Penelope had so easily pointed out: she was the most beautiful girl she'd ever seen.

Reyna kept staring at her, her lips tight. "Sit down, I'll finish up your makeup."

Yuki sat on the couch obediently, the tiny crystals tinkling as she did. Reyna used black mascara, then asked Yuki to close her eyes as she drew a single line of black eyeliner. Reyna was very careful, and her skin never touched Yuki at all.

"You can open your eyes now," Reyna said, and Yuki did.

Reyna was looking at her, and there were tears at the corners of her eyes.

"You're crying?" Yuki said, panicking.

"It's nothing," Reyna said, shaking her head, blinking fast. "It just dawned on me that this is the last year in school. You grew up too fast."

Yuki moved her hand to reach out to Reyna, on impulse, but Reyna stepped away.

"Promise me you'll enjoy tonight," Reyna said. Her face looked younger than usual when she was trying not to cry. "You're so young. You won't be forever."

The words felt especially ominous, and Yuki didn't want to be reminded of the curse.

"Take your time," Reyna said, blinking again, and Yuki felt something twist within her heart, and she didn't know if Reyna meant the ball or just growing up. Reyna knew a lot of things about her, but Yuki never felt they were close. At this moment, though, Reyna felt like something Yuki had never known.

Reyna felt like a mother.

"Thank you," Yuki said, blinking quickly too, getting herself under control. She picked up her mask, a white silk embroidered with mirrored crystals.

"Oh," Reyna said, and then picked something out of her makeup bag. Yuki puckered her lips as Reyna added a finishing touch. "There you go."

When she looked in the mirror again, her lips were as red as blood.

Yuki went toward the door, moving carefully in her dress. It was comfortable enough that she didn't feel restrained.

"Yuki," Reyna called out.

Yuki looked over her shoulder at her stepmother. "What?"

Reyna wet her lips, then shook her head. "Nothing. Have a good night."

Yuki made her way to the ballroom, her heart a turmoil. Reyna's words had gotten to her, their mix of sorrow and heartbreak and maybe something else that Yuki couldn't quite place, as her own restlessness grew. The more composed on the outside she was, the worse she felt inside, a disarray of feelings as Penelope's question played over and over again in her mind.

What did she want?

Yuki didn't know. Yuki hadn't known for a long time, because she'd only looked at the others, only mirrored their desires, their personalities, and she'd spent her adolescence trying to become something perfect until she couldn't recognize any bit of herself, and all the things that could have steered her away from that path she'd locked away, deep within her heart, where they grew dark roots through her limbs and her body, ensnaring her until all that was left was the perfect exterior.

If Yuki got cut open, all that desire, all that darkness would come spilling out.

Because she wanted things; she didn't know what and how or why, but she wanted them, and she wanted *everything*.

She was hungry for the taste of the world, to run free, to break free from the bonds she'd been caged in and all the things that people expected when they looked at her.

Yuki was none of those things.

She was not gentle. She was *hungry*.

And if her hunger cleaved her open, she'd let the world break in two.

When she got to the ballroom, she searched the room for Penelope. Penelope was wearing an emerald dress that hugged her body, feathers wrapped around the bottom of the skirt, green lace covering her eyes.

"Are you all right?" she asked. "You look like you ran all the way."

Yuki calmed her trembling. "I wanted to talk to you."

"The music is too loud here."

"It's about Ariane's death." Yuki didn't know what she was doing.

Penelope frowned. "What? Now?"

"You asked me about the magic, you said Ariane talked about fairy tales. There's something else I haven't told you."

Penelope's eyes flashed. "All right."

Yuki took a deep breath. "There's a reason I got those weird powers," Yuki said. "You talked about a ritual, and we did one. There was a book, a book Ariane left behind."

Penelope cocked her head. "What are you saying?"

"It's connected to what's been happening in the school," Yuki said. "With the deaths, with everything else. It kind of...predicts how it's going to go. We're all connected to it. And during the ritual, I think I ended up getting some of its powers."

Penelope grabbed her hand, pulling her out of the ballroom, away from the loud music, away from everything.

"I don't understand," Penelope said.

"I'll show you," Yuki said. "I don't know what to think anymore, but it's all in there, in the book. Will you help me?"

Penelope's gaze softened. "Of course I will."

Yuki took a deep breath. "Okay. Good. But I can't show it to you here. I have to get the book."

"Then go get the book," Penelope said. "We'll sort this out. I'm with you."

"We'll meet near the lake. Back entrance of the castle is close enough."

Yuki didn't want to think about the promises she was breaking by showing it to Penelope. She didn't want any of the other girls to know what she was doing.

Penelope turned to go, and Yuki took a deep breath, finally glad she'd been able to tell it like it was. She ran to the library, up the stairs, and found the place she'd hidden it.

The book wasn't there.

Someone had stolen it. Removed it from where they'd kept it safe.

Through the window of the library, Yuki saw two figures headed toward the lake.

The first was Penelope, walking to their meeting place.

Right behind her was Ella.

CHAPTER FIFTY-SEVEN

NANI

Nani didn't know how she could move that fast wearing a dress, but she still managed it.

Rory told her they wouldn't be able to get into the ballroom without the proper attire—if Alethea saw them, it'd be off with their heads. Nani said she didn't have a dress for the ball.

"Of course you do," Rory said, adjusting her own shimmering rose gold jacket. "It's in the box."

Ella had sewed a dress for her too. The dress was a structured, yet voluminous thing, made of a dark yellow taffeta. The upper part molded perfectly to her breasts and waist, leaving a small dip for her cleavage, off-shoulder sleeves, and then it expanded into a huge, full round skirt, with a slit running through the right side. The rich yellow had been embroidered in a dark gold thread, and when Nani looked, she saw that the flowers, which she'd mistaken for baroque patterns, were actually plumerias.

Nani was afraid it wouldn't fit, but it did, and when she looked in the mirror, she barely recognized herself. She kept her glasses on, her curls hanging softly over her shoulders, and only nodded toward Rory.

And then they ran. Rory led the way to Penelope's room through a series of corridors, Nani gathering her skirts in her fists. She almost stumbled a couple of times, but kept her head high, the soles of her sneakers thumping on the floor.

"It's here," Rory said, stopping in front of a door. She tried on the doorknob, and the door didn't bulge. "Here we go."

Rory slammed her shoulder against the door, putting all her weight into it, and the door burst open. She grinned at Nani, and they both ran inside.

Nani didn't know what she expected to find. It was a normal room, for a normal teenage girl. There were clothes on the bed, shoes out of the way. One of the beds was empty. Micaeli's bed.

"I'm not sure what we are looking for," Nani said as she started to go through Penelope's wardrobe. "Micaeli mentioned seeing a book like ours. That's the only clue I have."

"If I'd only looked in the bag sooner," Rory said, upturning things, opening the wardrobe.

"You couldn't have known earlier anyway."

Known that Penelope was a murderer.

She'd killed Ariane. She'd killed Molly and Ian, and even maybe Annmarie, and she killed Micaeli, because she'd known too much.

Nani moved to Micaeli's side, and though it was clean,

already emptied of her things, she still opened the wardrobe and went through the drawers, and there, on top of one of her drawers, was a book. Not their book but its twin.

Its cover was white, the linings in gold.

"There's another one," Nani said, showing it to Rory.

Rory let out a low whistle. "I wonder if she knew about the curse."

"She promised Ariane the truth," Nani said. "She must have known something."

She handed it to Rory, who took it carefully with her fingers.

"Come on," Rory said. "We have to find the others. They'll be at the party."

Rory clutched the book harder against her chest, and Nani still had the black book with her, and they made their way quickly to the ballroom, stopping to look over at the crowded space. All the students and teachers at Grimrose were in attendance, and the music roared in Nani's ears. She felt the dizzying sensation of five hundred bodies moving at once in the same overcrowded space, and she tried to peer over the others to find their friends.

"Can you see them?" Nani asked.

Rory craned her neck. "No sign of them. There's a chance they might be outside." Nani and Rory exchanged a look, not wanting to think the worst.

Penelope had already killed four people. One more wouldn't make a difference to her.

"We have to find them," Nani urged, just as she spotted

Svenja. Nani's eyes lingered on the other girl, on the things she'd wanted to say and didn't. Wondering if this would be the perfect time. Rory saw her looking, and their eyes met.

"Go," Rory said. "I'm going to find the others."

Nani hesitated. "Are you sure?"

Rory looked into the ballroom, and in that look, there were a hundred things left unsaid. A look that meant Rory understood, that Rory had been paying attention, that in the end, she knew even without Nani having to say anything.

It's what being a friend meant.

"Go," Rory said again.

Nani didn't waste any time. She gave the original book to Rory, who tucked it close to her chest with the white one, and then she headed toward Svenja.

Svenja wore a white dress and looked radiant in the middle of the crowd. Her body was all angles and the muscles she'd gotten dancing. Nani went to her before losing her courage.

"Svenja," Nani said, calling out over the loud music and the people that danced around them.

Svenja turned, surprise in her brown eyes. Her hair was cascading to one side, and there was a silver feather ornament pinning it in place.

Nani wondered if Svenja would let her talk, let her say what she wanted to say, so she didn't give Svenja an opportunity to even take a breath before she started speaking.

"You were right," Nani told her. "I didn't give you a chance. I didn't give anyone a chance."

Svenja blinked, but she didn't turn away, which Nani took as a good sign.

"I can't tell you what was going on," Nani said, "I saw everyone as my enemy, because the longer I stayed here, the more I forgot why I came and why I had to leave. And you made it so easy for me to not want to leave."

Her voice faltered, and Nani took a deep breath. Words had never failed her before, but this time, they didn't seem like they were going to be enough. This time, she had to act.

Adventure was more than just a promise.

She shortened the distance between them. As soon as her lips touched Svenja's, everything else vanished from her mind.

The kiss was slow, deliberate. Nani leaned in, feeling every inch of Svenja's mouth, brushing her fingers against her face, swiping hair away from her face, and Svenja's hand rested against Nani's cheek. The music was a distant sound in the ballroom as the world around them spun but they didn't, as the magic extended from her heart to their lips.

Nani broke away first, feeling the heat on her cheeks. Svenja reached out a hand to Nani's face and adjusted her glasses, putting them properly back into place after they had bumped in her nose.

"Good enough?" Nani asked.

"Yeah. But we can always practice more."

This time, Nani let herself crash like the waves against the rocks, let herself feel the promise being fulfilled at last. She grabbed Svenja by the waist, holding her tight. She didn't hold back, and neither did Svenja.

"Better," Svenja said with a smile.

"I have to go. Have to do something. But I'll be back," Nani promised, her voice sure. "I'm not leaving this time."

"Good," said Svenja. "I'll be waiting."

Nani left without saying goodbye.

Because it wasn't really goodbye if it was only beginning.

CHAPTER FIFTY-EIGHT

ELLA

The music from the party in the castle still echoed through her brain as Ella trailed after Penelope on the snowy path. Her feet grew colder as they walked through the gardens toward the lake.

Her heart beat hard with every step, and she felt the cold press of the button she'd sewed on the inside of the dress against her skin.

Penelope stopped near the lake. From here, the ballroom was invisible. The party seemed to be taking place in another world. A chill climbed up Ella's spine as she realized that Ariane would have taken the same path on the day she died, walked the same steps, stopping at the edge, just like Penelope.

The lake wasn't that deep, and as winter had come hard and determined this year, its surface was already frozen. Penelope's green silhouette stood out in stark contrast to the winter landscape around her.

"You can come out." Penelope's voice rang clear through the edge of the lake, where there were no more trees, where the garden path was clear. "I could hear your teeth chattering behind me."

Ella swallowed hard. She felt like her body might freeze over, her dress flimsy and useless now that she was out of the castle's protection.

"Hi, Penelope," said Ella, emerging from her hiding place.

Penelope turned slightly to acknowledge her. Her green eyes were ablaze in the muted colors of the night, only the moon shining through in the darkness. She'd taken the mask off, and so did Ella.

"So, I assume you overheard Yuki and I," Penelope said. "Whatever you want to say, you can say it now, unless you want to wait to say in front of her."

Ella frowned. "Maybe she doesn't have to hear this conversation."

Penelope raised one blond eyebrow at her. "You never liked me much, did you, Ella? You always thought I was stealing your friends away."

Ella's throat bobbed. "Yuki can choose her own friends."

Penelope laughed coldly.

Penelope was wearing the ring. Ella could see it now. She'd said she'd gotten it for her fifteenth birthday. But Ella had remembered that the real Penelope had gotten it for her thirteenth. She was wearing it on the picture.

"Actually, this is not about Yuki," Ella said. "This is about something else."

Penelope waited perfectly still. Ella tried to find her voice, tried voicing her theories.

"They found her body," Ella said. "It was in the paper this morning."

Penelope frowned. "What are you talking about?"

"They're going to know the truth," Ella said. "The police. They'll run the DNA tests on Penelope, and they'll know who she really is. You don't have much time."

Something dark flashed in Penelope's face. She was beautiful, but there was a sharp edge to that beauty, something hidden underneath.

"Are you going to accuse me of something?" she asked. "Ella, the high and mighty. Ella, who always offers a way out. Is that what you're trying to do here? You're trying to *forgive* me?"

Penelope moved toward her. Ella didn't let herself fear. Steeled her heart into place. Every cell of her body wanted to run, and still she stood there. But as Penelope got closer and closer to her, Ella realized that maybe this had been a stupid idea, that she should have waited for Rory or Nani or Yuki, that maybe she didn't know what she was doing at all.

"I just want to know the truth," Ella said.

"Do you? Or do you just want to make the accusations?" Penelope asked. "You love the moral high ground. You already know the truth, don't you, Ella? You just want me to say it. To hear you were right for not trusting me all along."

"How did you know about the book? Why do you want it?"

Penelope's eyes narrowed. "You don't understand what you've stumbled upon."

"Why is it so important? I know I'm in it. I know we all are."

"You don't understand," Penelope said, taking a step forward. "It's not about you or me. It's much bigger than us, so much older, and I can't..."

Ella thought about screaming or running away. She wondered if that had been Ari's reaction too, when she'd set out that fateful night. That all she really cared for was the truth, that she didn't even think about the consequences. Ella was so determined to get to the bottom of what was happening at Grimrose that she never stopped to think what might happen to herself.

"Say what you came here to say," Penelope dared.

"You're not her," she said. "You're not Penelope. The real Penelope is dead in an abandoned house near the train station, has been for the past year and a half. You just took her place."

The real Penelope dead, replaced by someone who looked just like her, who would enjoy her life, and no one would be the wiser. The tale ended with the real girl speaking the truth, but of course it wouldn't end the same here, not with the book dooming them to the unhappy endings.

Penelope smiled at her. "Took you long enough," she said, hands on her hips. "What else are you here to accuse me of?"

"You killed Ariane," Ella said simply. "And maybe the others. You were the one who set the trap for me."

Behind them, Ella heard a rustling. Ella turned, and in that moment, Penelope moved, left arm around Ella, right hand with a knife against her throat. She dragged her across the frozen surface of the lake.

Ella struggled, her feet sliding on the ice.

"Don't move," Penelope hissed. "Or you'll drown us both."

The blade dug deeper into her neck, and Ella didn't dare to flinch. *I'm going to die,* she thought, and it didn't bother her the way she thought it would. *The cycle is going to come to an end.*

And I didn't even lose a shoe, she added as an afterthought.

"Don't come any closer!" Penelope shouted. "Don't come, or I swear I'm going to kill her."

From the shadows of the garden, Yuki emerged.

CHAPTER FIFTY-NINE

YUKI

Yuki took a second to register what was happening.

Penelope and Ella were standing on top of the thin ice surface of the lake. Penelope held a sharp, silver blade against Ella's throat. There was a single line of red blood running down Ella's neck and disappearing into her dress, and her hazel eyes looked at Yuki, terrified.

"Don't move," Penelope said again, and her face had changed.

Gone was the charming girl in the uniform, with the easy smile and the sparkling green eyes. In her place stood something else, a more feral version of the girl she thought she knew. The version that didn't hide behind a mask.

Yuki didn't know whether to feel betrayed or relieved.

"What are you doing?" Penelope asked. She had a sharp gleam in her eye, dangerous. "I thought you were going to bring the book."

Ella's eyes widened.

"It wasn't there," Yuki said. "Someone must have stolen it."

The knife pressed harder against Ella's throat.

"Since when have you known?" Penelope asked.

"I didn't," Yuki replied, her voice clear, though now that she looked back on it, she couldn't even be shocked. All of Penelope's small touches, all the ways she'd nudged them in the wrong direction.

She had been after the book all this time.

It was her fault Ariane was dead.

And Yuki was filled with relief.

Relief that it hadn't been her fault. Relief that there was an explanation. Relief that it was all coming to an end.

The knife, however, didn't leave Ella's throat. Yuki watched as Ella grew paler. For the first time that year, Yuki was completely back in control of herself.

"You bring me the book," Penelope said, "and maybe I let Ella go. Maybe."

"Why do you want it?" Yuki asked. She was approaching the edge of the lake, a few inches at a time.

"I thought you'd figured it all out," Penelope snapped. "Isn't that what you said? That you have magic because of it?"

Penelope pressed the knife harder, and Ella let out the smallest whimper. Penelope was taller than Ella, and she had a weapon. Yuki wanted to say something reassuring, but as she got closer, she finally understood what she was feeling.

White, blinding rage.

Rage like she'd never known before, a passionate anger that burned deep, running through her limbs, filling her like coals.

Someone had put a knife to her best friend's throat. Ella, who Yuki loved. Ella, who Yuki envied and wanted to be. Ella, who still believed in her, even after everything Yuki had done.

Penelope had wanted to know who Yuki was.

Penelope had let Yuki out of her own cage.

Now she would deal with the consequences.

"Let Ella go," Yuki said calmly. "You can still run. Disappear."

"Didn't you hear what Ella said? It's too late for me now. They'll know the truth in a couple of days." Penelope laughed. "You're not going anywhere, Ella. You see, you're the most annoying of them all. It was fun setting you up to find the siblings. It's a pity the trap didn't work."

"You killed them all," Ella said, tears blurring her eyes. "Why?"

"Oh, not all of them," Penelope said with a shrug. "Annmarie was a real accident. You read the book, you know the curse. In the end, they would all have died either way. I didn't kill them. I just sped their fate along a little."

Yuki inched forward, her white dress trailing in the snow, waiting for the right moment, her body still like a predator's.

"Why?" Ella cried.

"If you get your happy ending, I don't get mine," Penelope said. "It's how it works. Some girls get their happily ever after, while I get to be ripped apart as the villain. So I decided to embrace it." She looked up, grinning at Yuki. "You know the feeling. I can see right through you, Yuki."

Yuki felt her rage growing inside her as all of it fell into place. She'd killed the others to get the book. It had all been done to stop them from finding out the truth.

Penelope had already gotten what she wanted.

"You don't know what's happening either," Yuki said. "You tell us what you know, we'll tell you what we know."

Penelope snorted. "You don't know anything."

"We had the book."

"You had *one* book," Penelope corrected her. "How do you think I knew what Ariane had, if I didn't have its twin? How do you think I knew what Ariane was messing around with, if I didn't know it before she did? How do you think I was ahead of all of you, all this time? You only had to hand it over. Drop it somewhere, and it was all going to be forgotten. Well, not for you. You'd die soon enough."

"So the curse is real," Ella said, her voice small.

"Of course it's real," Penelope snarled. "Does that make you feel better? Ariane knew too, and she figured out who I was. She was never meant to find the book, but well, I wasn't either. Still, it bought me a way out. I knew the truth, and as long as I made sure the curse was working, the deaths were happening, my secret was safe. I could be happy here."

"She isn't the real Penelope," Ella managed to choke out, the blade still pressed, ever-threatening.

Yuki looked at Penelope again.

"The goose girl," Ella said, and Yuki suddenly understood.

Penelope was the replacement. The story already over, the villain triumphant.

"I lied," Penelope said. "I've been lying from the moment

I got here. I came here with nothing. I sat across from this girl in the train, and all I did was listen to her talk and talk and talk about how much she hated her parents, that they were sending her to this boarding school in Switzerland as a punishment. She'd have access to the best education in the world, she had everything, and all she could do was complain, while I was sitting in front of her, starving."

Her words tumbled one over the other at the end, her voice trembling, but her hands never faltering.

"I was so hungry," Penelope said. "And all I could think was how this girl had everything, and I had nothing. When we got off the train, I killed her, and I took her place. I became a better version of her than she could ever be. She didn't get her happy ending, but I got mine. It was the only way."

"It's not the only way," Ella said. "You can still run. It's not over yet."

"They won't let me," Penelope said.

"Drop the knife, Penelope," Yuki said, her voice calm, analyzing all her options, even if she didn't understand who Penelope was talking about. The curse was bigger than her. Bigger than them. There was more at work. "We can help you."

"You can't, it's too late," Penelope said. "I made a bargain. I got to stay Penelope as long as I kept the curse going. I found the book, but I needed to get Ariane's to stay safe. Now everyone will know who I am. Well, who I'm *not*."

She took a step back, and Yuki felt sick as they headed toward the middle of the lake, Penelope dragging Ella over the ever-thinning ice.

"It doesn't make a difference," Penelope said. "I told this to Ariane. She was going to tell everyone, and I couldn't have that. I'd just gotten what I wanted, and she was going to ruin it. You have to understand, my story was already over. You don't stand a chance with them."

"Who are you talking about?" Yuki pressed. "What else do you know about the curse?"

Penelope shook her head again. "It's too late," Penelope muttered. "All these deaths in vain. If I could keep the books, then no one else would find out who I was. They wouldn't tell anyone as long as I helped, and I did. I killed to keep my secret, to keep my life. As long as you get your happy ending, I don't get mine. And I *got* mine already."

"If we all die, what difference does it make?" Yuki asked.

Penelope laughed, and she didn't look reckless. She knew exactly what she was doing. Penelope did what she did because she knew who she was.

"I told you, Yuki," she said, grinning. "We are more alike than you think."

Penelope had been right about her all along, about who she was, about who she was trying to be. Yuki had to let the mask fall.

She felt her power coursing through her veins, that tingling sensation that wanted to be let out, whatever the cost, and for the first time, Yuki didn't fight it.

Because it made her who she was. Her magic, unleashed, was herself. She only had to let go, and her lack of control would be her weapon.

Her eyes met Ella's across the lake, and Yuki calculated what she had to do. Ella nodded ever so slightly. Penelope would not get away with hurting Ella, not while Yuki was standing there.

Yuki moved fast so fast that Penelope didn't see her coming. She was sure of her body, sure of her hands, sure of her power. When she stepped onto the frozen lake, she pushed her hands and her power against the layer of ice where the two girls were standing, and the ice below cracked.

It all happened at once.

Penelope gave a yelp, and Ella pushed her arm away, spinning, and the knife fell. The ice beneath them cracked, opening up a hole that grew wider every second. Penelope shoved Ella away as the ice cracked further, trying to get away. Ella tripped, and she disappeared into the hole, engulfed by the water.

Yuki watched as Ella disappeared, cold shock and horror gripping her bones. Penelope stepped away from the hole, but Yuki slammed right into her, not giving her time to react.

Yuki grabbed the knife that Penelope had dropped and plunged it deep into Penelope's heart.

Penelope choked, blood coming out of her mouth, and Yuki's hand stayed on the knife, her white dress stained the same color of her lips with the blood running through her hands. Yuki caught Penelope as she faltered.

Penelope looked at her, eyes wide, and only managed to say one word. "Why?"

Yuki took a deep breath, and answered in a whisper only Penelope could hear.

"You told me to want things," Yuki said. "I wanted you dead."

Penelope smiled, and then her body went limp.

CHAPTER SIXTY

RORY

Rory saw it all unfolding as she ran down to the lake, holding both books. Penelope with a knife to Ella's throat, Yuki calmly talking to her, not even daring to move. And then it all happened so quickly.

Yuki's flash of magic on the ice, breaking the surface, and Ella falling into the cold water, while Penelope seemed to fall into Yuki's arms.

"Ella!" Rory screamed.

A knife plunged into Penelope's chest. Yuki, hands and dress covered in blood.

Ella beneath them in the lake.

As if being recalled from a dream, Yuki's gaze snapped up. Before Rory could stop her, Yuki dove into the watery hole her magic had created.

Rory held her breath as her friend disappeared. She stepped onto the edge of the lake, her feet careful as she sought stability, trying to find something to pull them out. Ella hadn't been under for long, but the water was cold enough to give her a shock. Rory spotted a low branch on a tree and snapped it in half. She skidded across the surface, trying not to cause any further cracks and also trying to avoid looking at the splash of green that was Penelope's lifeless body.

They couldn't stay down there.

Not like Ariane. Rory was not going to lose someone else to the damned lake; she was not going to lose someone else at the school, and that was it. She refused to.

She slid to a stop as close to the hole as she dared. "Come on," she roared, looking down into dark water, still as death beneath her. "Come on!"

Long moments passed, and Rory was about to lose all hope, when the surface of the water rippled. A small disturbance at first, then more. With a big gasp, Yuki burst through, holding a limp body in a blue dress.

"Help me," Yuki said, still gasping for air, trembling.

Rory reached out the branch, and Yuki grabbed it, but she couldn't pull it out herself. She was half cradling Ella's limp body, the clothes making them even heavier.

"Grab it," Rory ordered.

"I am," Yuki said, shouting. "I can't—"

Rory pulled, but her hands let go, cramping at that moment. No. No. Not now. Not when so much depended on her. Not when her two remaining best friends were in the lake, fighting for their lives, and Rory had to get them out.

Tears welled in her eyes, and she grabbed the branch again.

Yuki was trying to stay afloat, coughing and sputtering, but holding on with one hand, her other arm tightly around Ella.

Rory breathed deep, settled herself. She knew her own pain. She knew her body. She knew how it worked, even when she felt like it was betraying her, trying to make her weaker. Rory wasn't weak because of her pain, because of what her body was going through.

She had survived it. Each sleepless night, each morning where she got up and she thought she wouldn't manage to walk, each day where she thought she'd reached the limit.

She always surpassed the limit.

Even when her body tried betraying her, Rory was still strong. She was strong in spite of it, maybe because of it, because she was going to survive it.

This body was hers.

"Hold on!" she shouted, and then she pulled, as hard as she could.

Yuki slid out of the water, gasping and dragging an unconscious Ella with her. Rory felt her arms protesting as she pulled more, desperate to put as much distance between them and the hole as possible.

Ella looked pale, her lips blue, and Rory's whole body shook in fear.

"Let's get her off the ice," Rory said, and Yuki only nodded, her face paler than usual, their fancy gowns dripping with the water. Yuki's dress had already changed colors. The red had deepened over her heart, as if her own chest had been ripped open.

Rory lay Ella down into the bank where there was less snow, just as someone else came running down the path. Golden dress, curls flying behind her. Nani stopped the moment she saw Ella out cold on the ground. Rory grabbed Ella's wrist, searching for a pulse, but there was nothing.

"Come on," Yuki whispered besides them, kneeling down. "Come on, Ella."

Nani knelt down beside them, her skirt billowing out around her. Yuki's grip on Ella was stronger on the other side, and she laid a bloody hand against Ella's chest.

"Your story is not done yet," Yuki said. "You don't get to go like this."

Nani's hand slipped through Rory's, and Rory squeezed it tight, reaching out for Yuki's hand. Yuki held on, and Rory had never felt something so strong before, and then Nani was the one to push her hand against Ella's chest, at exactly the right spot.

The effect was immediate.

Ella's body jolted like a shock, and Rory wasn't sure if it was medicine or magic. Ella's body shook awake, coughing water, vomiting until she could breathe again, her body shaking from the cold.

Rory took off her pink blazer and wrapped it around the shivering Ella.

Ella looked around at each of them. "You pulled me out?" Ella asked.

"Yeah," Rory said, grinning in relief. "Of course I did."

"And you've done something terrible to your hair."

Rory's grin disappeared. "Oh, all right, you can go fuck off and die again, then."

Ella started laughing, and then coughing, and then suddenly, all of them were doing the same thing, Rory slapping Ella's back so she finished snorting out the water, still laughing, and even Nani was smiling, relieved.

They'd survived this part.

Their laughter died down, and the quiet of the night settled over them like a warm blanket.

Yuki sniffed, then whispered, so low that Rory almost didn't catch it, "Don't leave me."

"I won't," Ella replied quietly.

Rory looked out over the lake, at the dead body on top of the ice. They'd survived for now, but this was far from over.

She was going to be strong enough for what came next. She had to be.

CHAPTER SIXTY-ONE

ELLA

Ella dreamed it more than once. Sinking down, just like Ariane. It'd taken her a moment to realize it wasn't a dream this time. It was real.

But Yuki had come for her. A vision in white, diving into the water, and she'd grabbed her, and she wasn't hurt at all, hadn't swallowed water. She looked whole, if not for the blood on her clothes.

But not all of them were whole. She could see Penelope's dead body across the icy surface of the lake, a knife stuck on her chest.

"What the hell happened?" Rory asked, sitting back on the cold ground.

"I..." Ella started, without knowing how to continue.

But it was Yuki who spoke, her voice even. "Penelope was lying about who she was. She was an impostor. She was one of us."

One of the tales.

"And?" Nani said.

"She threatened Ella," Yuki said simply.

She'd threatened Ella, and Yuki had killed her for it.

Ella shivered, taking a deep breath, snuggling harder inside Rory's jacket.

"She killed Ari," Rory said, her voice croaked. "Remember Ari's new bag? Penelope claimed she didn't arrive at school until after Ari was dead. But she knew about the bag. Ari must have brought it with her when she met her the first day of school. Penelope must have gotten into our room and put it back, and we never noticed."

"And she had another book," Nani said.

"She told us," Ella said, her voice thick. "She killed Micaeli. Molly and Ian too."

Nani shook her head, rolling her tongue inside her mouth. Ella looked again at the body, at the golden hair in the middle of the frozen lake.

"Did she say anything else?"

Yuki's eyes met Ella, and she shook her head; they would tell the others about her connection to the curse in the morning.

"God," Nani said with a sigh. "And we didn't even break the curse."

"Yet," Ella said.

They all looked at each other, solemn, and the only thing filling Ella was determination.

There would be no more dead bodies.

Penelope, or whoever she was, would be the last.

"What do we do?" Rory's question echoed through their silence, her voice rising in panic now. "How do we even explain this?"

"No one will know."

Rory and Yuki snapped their attention to her, as if she was suggesting something impossible. She wasn't, though. No one could see them from the castle, and the night was freezing. There would no evidence, if Ella got rid of it.

"They'll identify Penelope's real body," Ella said. "And then the news will be out. They'll just think this one vanished so she wouldn't get caught."

The perfect way out.

"No one will know," Ella repeated, looking at Yuki, reassuring again.

Yuki was the image of placid calm, but her eyes were stormy, dark.

"They ruled the deaths in school as accidents," Nani said, catching on fast. "They won't suspect anything."

"We're the only ones who'll know the truth," finished Ella. She shivered within her wet dress, but it seemed irrelevant to be freezing now. "Are we agreed?" She looked at the other girls.

Yuki did not give an answer, only kept looking at her hands. The hands that had stabbed Penelope, put a dagger through her heart without a moment's thought.

"Yes," Rory said.

"You have my word," Nani replied.

"Good," Ella said. "Now we get to work. I need new clothes. I'm shivering, and I have to get rid of Yuki's dress. You two go upstairs again, make sure you spin a tale about Yuki vomiting in the bathroom or something, and bring out pajamas for us both."

Rory looked sideways at the lake, and then back at Ella. "You sure that's all you need?"

"You have to get inside Penelope's room, pack a bag, and bring it back here. She'd have taken things if she had made a run for it."

Nani and Rory vanished back up to the path of the garden.

"I'll rip the dress," Ella said. "There's enough fabric here for us to wrap the body."

"Okay," Yuki replied, as if it was the most normal thing in the world.

Ella ripped off the chiffon she had so carefully crafted. When all of Yuki's skirts were gone, she picked them up, and they both moved toward the frozen lake.

Ella took out the knife first, sliding it out of the place between Penelope's ribs. Penelope's green eyes were marble and staring at the sky, a faint smile on her lips. Ella washed the knife in the cold lake water, then set it carefully aside. She took the pieces of chiffon and started wrapping Penelope in white, picking up stones from the lakeshore and putting them on top of her body, wrapping them all together so she'd sink to the bottom. Yuki watched, trembling, as Ella worked, as she finished wrapping Penelope's entire body in the chiffon, as her features disappeared behind a white shroud. The ice was still thin, but Yuki's hands emanated cold, strengthening the barrier between them and the water.

When Ella was done, there was nothing left.

She did what she did, because that was all she could do.

Penelope had threatened her, and Yuki had killed to protect Ella.

And now Penelope was dead, and it threatened Yuki, so Ella did what she had to do to protect her in turn.

"Come on," Ella said. "Help me push it."

Yuki did, and they both rolled the body toward the hole Ella had fallen through. She did not think of the darkness below the lake. She did not think of what Ariane must have felt as Penelope held her down there, until her lungs had filled with water.

Ella thought of nothing but Yuki.

"Won't people wonder about my dress?" Yuki asked, as they both stood over the hole.

"I'll fix it," Ella said, because it's the only thing she could concentrate on, or else it would make this surreal. She could fix all of it. "I'll wash away the blood. I'll make a new trail skirt so it looks like we haven't ripped this one."

The lake would eventually wear away the fabric, and it wouldn't fix it forever. Penelope's body might resurface still when the lake melted in the spring, but that would buy them time to fix the rest. The plan had flaws, but she did the best she could with it. Her mind worked at solving one problem at a time. If she stopped, her mind would catch up with her body. With her trembling fingers, with the splotches of blood she had just cleaned from the ice, wearing it down with the rest of Yuki's dress.

She buried Yuki's sin like she buried her father, except this time, she didn't regret any part of it.

Rory and Nani came back with new clothes, and they took off theirs, dressing again. Ella kept Yuki's bloodied dress, putting it in a bag to bring home. She kept Penelope's bag and the knife, and she'd toss them both far away where no one would find this evidence.

The four of them looked at the water, no body to be seen. No blood on anyone's hands, all washed off, the only evidence still on the dress.

"They'll see the hole in the lake," Nani pointed out.

Without saying a word, Yuki crouched on the ground and touched the ice. The layer spread thicker this time, ice covering the hole and the cracks until the lake was smooth once again.

Ella turned around, keeping her head even, her breath calm.

"What's in the other book?" she asked. "They're twins, right?"

Nani nodded, taking it out to show Ella. The book had the same cover as the other one.

One white book. One black book.

When Ella opened it, she expected to find the tales with the happy endings. Something that balanced it out. The four girls stood in a circle, heads bent toward the open pages, and at the end of each tale, there was a portrait of a girl, and ones they recognized.

Ella.

Yuki.

Rory.

Nani.

The four of them, inked on the page. Ella skipped ahead, and she saw more of the familiar faces from school. Micaeli. Molly and her brother. Annmarie. Rhiannon. Alethea. The real Penelope.

When she got to "The Little Mermaid," Ariane's face was there.

She was fading already, the ink not as black and vivid as their own portraits. Ella traced a hand over her friend's portrait.

"That's how Penelope knew," Nani said. "She knew who we were from the beginning."

Yuki looked at her hands, trembling still, but clean now. Ella took them and squeezed. Yuki leaned into the touch, and Ella didn't let her heart falter. She couldn't fail now.

"So what do we do?" Rory said. "We still have to break the curse."

"Yeah," Nani agreed. "And find out how we can do it before our own bad endings come true."

Yuki wet her lips, and her voice came out more certain. "So how do we save us?"

Ella looked at the book, at the tragic stories of so many that came before her. Of faces she recognized, of faces she didn't. Of pictures faded, of pictures fresh on the page like they had just been inked.

"We're not going to save just one girl," Ella said. "We are going to save them all."

ACKNOWLEDGMENTS

It's strange publishing a book about grieving a friend when you're still grieving a friend. Itamar, I wish you were here so you could recommend awful YouTube videos and share Cokes during the weekdays when we weren't supposed to be drinking any. Your memory remains a blessing.

To everyone who lost someone in the past year—friends, family, loved ones: You're allowed to grieve. You're allowed to shake the world for it.

To Sarah LaPolla, who took my hand in the beginning of this publishing journey and stayed until I could walk on my feet. To Kari Sutherland—I'm unbelievably glad to have found you. Finding one good agent is lucky; finding a second feels like I've won a million in the lottery. Thank you for your patience, your hard work, and your encouragement.

To my team at Sourcebooks, who have embraced the Grimrose Girls with such enthusiasm. Annie Berger, my editor, for your notes. Zeina Elhanbaly, for always being so kind and attentive to my emails. Nicole Hower and Ray Shappell, for the cover that perfectly captures the essence of the book. Dominique Raccah, Todd Stocke, Cassie Gutman, and Beth Oleniczak, for making this book happen.

Solaine Chioro, I owe you everything. You picked this book up when it was only an idea, and you told me "This is what you're meant to be doing" about writing in a language that wasn't my own. Thank you for believing in these girls, and for reading what probably felt like three hundred thousand words of library scenes.

Franklin Teixeira, thank you for all seventy-six pages of color-coded notes on this book. Your enthusiasm about Nani kept me going.

To my family, who always encouraged me to pursue my dreams. My sister, especially, for all the unending princess stories. My parents, who made everything possible and helped me move into my own place—I know you only wanted to get rid of all the books I left at your house, but I'm grateful all the same. Paz, for still asking about the book even when all my replies consisted of loud and incoherent groans.

Samia, Rafael, Emily—anything I say here won't feel like enough. Bárbara, I've never been one to believe in destiny, but sometimes meeting you feels like there's real magic in the universe. Iris and Mareska, I love you both to death.

Sense 5 (for surviving years of school with me and beyond), AFB (I love our book club who never reads), New Year Studio (for the best complaining space ever invented), sisterhood of quarantined evil gays (for the berets), Save Ben Solo (for two years of trauma and counting); Mayra, Lucas, Gih, Luisa, and every other friend who's not in a huge group but is so important to me.

Spell Check, you've made my Monday nights the very

reason I look forward to Mondays, which is no meager feat. You guys are the best. Linsey, thank you for all the screams. Dana and Deeba, you're the truest. I'm still waiting for the day we all get to share bookshelves. To every other author I met on this journey, who blurbed this book, who chatted and did video panels and exchanged memes with me, thank you.

Vina, you're not half as bad as Mephistopheles (I think). I would not bet on him in a fight against you, however.

Sofia, words are ????? For a writer, you'd think I'd have figured them out already. Thank you for buying me pizza, listening to me for five straight hours while I worked through the plot of this book and encouraging me to make Penelope the absolute worst. Thank you for providing me a space where I can feel loved and where being queer is the best thing I can be.

And to the readers, old and new. Thanks for picking up this book. You're the reason I get to live this dream. This tale may be old as time, but that doesn't mean it can't be told anew. I hope you like this story with some gay and unhinged fairytale heroines, and I promise to get you safely to the happily ever after. This is only the beginning.

ABOUT THE AUTHOR

© Clara Luisa Fotografias

Laura Pohl is a Brazilian YA writer who lives in São Paulo. Her debut novel, *The Last 8*, won the International Latino Book Awards and is followed by *The First 7*. She likes writing messages in caps lock, never using autocorrect, and obsessing about *Star Wars*. When not taking pictures of her dog, she can be found curled up with a fantasy or science-fiction book or replaying *Dragon Age*. Her favorite Disney princess is Cinderella, and her favorite Disney prince is Kylo Ren. You can learn more about her on her website at onlybylaura.com.

Don't miss Laura Pohl's sci-fi duology about the Last Teenagers on Earth.

THE END OF THE WORLD JUST GOT INTERESTING.